THE
DARK SIDE
OF HEAVEN

THE
DARK SIDE
OF HEAVEN

TAMAR MYERS

THE DARK SIDE OF HEAVEN
ISBN 1-933523-01-8

First Printing: May 2006

Library of Congress Control Number: 2005934403

Printed in the United States of America on acid-free paper.

Book design by Bella Rosa Books

BellaRosaBooks and logo are trademarks of Bella Rosa Books

10 9 8 7 6 5 4 3 2 1

In loving memory of the real Anna Hostetler

THE
DARK SIDE
OF HEAVEN

BOOK ONE

CHAPTER

1

I discover the dark side of Heaven the day Bishop Yoder pronounces me dead. He pokes my shoulder with his index finger, which is as thick and soft as a cow's teat. Such behavior is not the Amish way, but I have provoked the elderly man beyond human endurance.

"Anna Hostetler," he says, "you leave me with no choice."

"*You* leave me with no choice," I say. I have been crying all morning and my throat is as rough as feed sacks. It hurts even to swallow.

"The Elders agree with me, Anna. I must impose the Meidung. Do you understand this?"

I nod, hoping this will keep the bishop from giving me a long explanation. The Meidung means that I am now excommunicated, banned from any sort of meaningful contact with my family, completely cut off from my people. Until I confess my sin—something I cannot do—it will be as if I am dead.

Unfortunately, a bob of the head is not going to stop Bishop Yoder. "Even your parents may not speak to you now. If you remain at home, they will make you eat by yourself, at one end of the table, on a special cloth. If you are stubborn about this, and come to the Sunday service—"

I turn my back on Bishop Yoder and walk toward the Trailways bus station. It is just a stop really, the waiting room nothing more than a row of blue plastic chairs in Miller's Laundromat. My legs are as unsteady as those of a foal taking her first steps, and I long to lie down on the warm asphalt of the parking lot and nap. But I will not show any further weakness, and I will not turn around. If I am dead to the others, am I not dead to the bishop as well? What good does it do to have a dead woman stay and listen? Besides, what else can Bishop Yoder and the Elders do to me? Burn me at the stake? That is what the Catholics did to our ancestors in Switzerland, and it is one of the reasons we are so committed to being a people apart.

The slap-slap of leather tells me that the bishop is following me. Perhaps he thinks he has a right. After all, it is he who has insisted on bringing me here in his summer buggy, for all the world to see. It is just as well that he did so. Mamm and Daat were too heartbroken to deliver their youngest child permanently into the hands of the English. But I have to pay a price for the ride; a lecture that will not end, and tears. Not just my tears either, but those of Bishop Yoder. He is truly pained by what I am forcing him to do. Of that I have no doubt.

"Remember, Anna Hostetler, that God always welcomes a repentant sinner. This shunning is only so that you will find your way back to us again."

I stop walking. "Remember Bishop," I say, without turning, "that God is also the Creator. He gave me this gift. It would be a sin for me not to use it."

"This gift—it involves pride, yah?"

I take my time to think about that. "Not so much pride, as satisfaction. When I paint, I am helping God to create."

"Ach, Anna, that is blasphemy."

I close my eyes, thankful that we are speaking in dialect, known to most of the English as Pennsylvania Dutch. My mother tongue has nothing to do with Holland, but was derived from Swiss German.

"Why else would God give me this talent? And I do

have talent—everyone says so."

"The English say so."

"Yah, and they buy my paintings. They would not buy them if they were not good."

"But you compare yourself to God—"

I look at the Bishop. "I did *not* compare myself to God." Even a year ago, I would not have dared to interrupt the bishop. "What I meant to say, Bishop, is that by using my talent for painting, I am honoring God."

"Yah, a good quilt—"

"My talent is not for quilting. It is for painting!"

"Then paint barns, Anna Hostetler."

Amish culture is based on something called *Gelassenheit*—submission. The individual must submit his or herself to the community and ultimately to God. The ability to yield oneself comes more easily for some than it does for others. For me it has always been next to impossible.

The bishop and I are both silent for a moment. Perhaps he is waiting for me to have a change of heart. I certainly am hoping the same for him.

Finally, he speaks. "You will go to your brother then?"

"What good will that do? You just said he is not allowed to talk to me, even if he wanted—which he does not, by the way."

"Ach, not your married brother, Elam. The brother in Pittsburgh."

I turn. "What brother in Pittsburgh?"

Bishop Yoder leans back. It is as if my words have slapped him.

"You have never heard?"

"Heard what?"

"Your brother, the oldest one—what he did?"

"Elam is my oldest brother," I shout. Shouting at a bishop is surely a sin in itself. It is not just my art that has been a stumbling block. There are a thousand other things for which I deserve to be banished.

Bishop Yoder shakes his head. "I cannot believe no one has told you this." He shakes his head again. "Surely there were rumors."

"If there were, I missed them."

Neither the bishop nor I wear watches, but we have battery-operated clocks in our homes, and we have agreed to arrive at the bus stop early. Besides, like many other Amish sects, we set our clocks a half hour early. Fast time, we call it. It is yet another way we choose to separate ourselves from the world. At any rate, by my reckoning we have another half hour to wait for the bus.

"Come." Bishop Yoder pokes me again, even more gently this time. "It is against the *Ordnung*," he says, referring to the church's rules of behavior, "for us to have this air-conditioning in our homes, but in the English place of washing clothes, it is permitted for us to sit."

Carrying only a sack made from one of Mamm's old quilts and a cardboard tube, I follow the bishop into the Laundromat, into a new world of sights and sounds. Clothes swishing in water, because the English are too lazy, or too much in a hurry to wash them the old way. Clothes spinning in hot machines because the English no longer value the scent of sunshine. And the television. I have seen television, flickering through windows of shops, but never close up. I cannot remember ever hearing one. This television has a black woman in it. She stands on a platform and addresses a large gathering of people. Behind the standing woman sits a man in a comfortable English chair. The crowd is clapping.

There is only one other person in the Laundromat, an English woman in a sleeveless blouse and pants like a man's, only short. She is folding clothes at a table that wobbles, and when we enter, she looks up briefly before continuing her task. No doubt she has seen many of our kind before about town. Our town is very small, I hear, compared to others, and there are many other plain folk living in the area.

The bishop and I sit on the blue plastic chairs. His chair is cracked; mine has a wad of gum in one corner. I put the cloth sack on the floor, but the cardboard tube I balance on my knees. Even though the bishop is old enough to be my Grossdawdi, we are careful to keep a chair between us. Grossdawdi Hostetler is fat, with a neck burned red by the sun, and when he was younger, he had the blackest hair I had ever seen on an Amish man. Bishop Yoder has white curls peeking from beneath his black felt hat, and except for his prominent Yoder nose, he has the face of a sheep. Even his teeth are long and yellow.

I am calmer now, and the bishop seems to sense this. I am sitting with my body straight ahead, facing the television. The bishop is sitting in the same position, but from the corner of my left eye I see his torso turn so that now he is looking at me. The sheep eyes, like all sheep eyes, appear baffled.

"No one has ever spoken to you about Joseph?"

The black woman in the television has just asked the man in the chair a more interesting question. She calls him Dr. Phil, but the question she asks is not about health. How long *is* too long for a man to live at home with his parents, she wants to know. Dr. Phil says something I cannot understand, but it makes the crowd laugh. The English woman folding clothes on the wobbly table laughs along with the crowd.

"Ach, Anna, you cannot pretend you do not remember Joseph."

"I do not." At least I do not want to.

"But you remember the fire, yah?"

"Yah," I whisper.

Fire shaped the history of my people, my family in particular, beginning with the pillar of fire that led the ancient Israelites through the desert. Through Christ we are spiritual descendants of those people, are we not? Then there were the fires of persecution in sixteenth-century Switzerland, although there were many ways in which both church and state persecuted my people. We, the followers of Jakob Ammann, were Anabaptists. We did not believe in infant baptism, and rebaptized—hence our name. We were hunted like rabbits in the field, and had to worship in secret, sometimes in caves. When they caught us they burned us, drowned us, and even pulled us limb from limb on stretching devices. These persecutions are written down in the *Martyrs Mirror*, a book that is found in every Amish home, and we do not forget them. We sing about them in our hymns, we tell them to our children as bedtime stories. They are seared into our memories like the brand on a calf.

In the late seventh century William Penn offered us sanctuary in the New World. There were fires in Pennsylvania as well, but not sparked by religious persecution. On the night of September 19, 1757, a band of Delaware Indians attacked the Hochstetlers— as my family was known then—in Northkill, Pennsylvania. We Amish are pacifists, so although my ancestors possessed a gun, they would not turn it on another human being. The Delaware set the cabin on fire and it burned to the ground. There was, however, a storage cellar under the cabin, and as it was apple harvest season, and cider had just been made, the family wet the ceiling. They were spared the fire, but the next morning my female ancestor, whose first name is not known, was stabbed in the back, and scalped, as she tried to exit the cellar through a small side door.

My great-great-great-great grandfather, Jacob Hochstetler, and two of his sons, Joseph and Christian, were captured alive by the Delaware, and remained their prisoners for many years. From this one ancestor, Jacob, virtually every Hochstetler and Hostetler descend. This is also a story we tell the children. Do not forget our history, we tell them.

Remember that we are a people opposed to violence.

But the fire that occurred on my third birthday is one that I have tried hard to forget. It is, in fact, my first memory. In it I sit by the window that faces the barn and watch men shout encouragement to each other as they try in vain to put out the flames. There are women helping too, passing buckets of water down a line that leads from the pump by the kitchen door, but there are no children. I am the only child, and I am safe inside. Where are the others?

There is another pump closer to the barn, the one Daat uses to fill the water troughs, but no one is using it. Even here, I can feel the heat from the barn through the glass. The frost on the pane has melted and there are rivulets of water running down onto the sill.

I trace the barn in the condensation. I trace the flames leaping from the roof. I trace the men and women in the bucket line. That is my first memory of drawing. Suddenly the barn collapses, sending sparks all the way into the sky, burning the feet of angels. A few of the women scream, a man shouts louder, and then everyone is inside. But still no children. This memory starts to fade, when a woman, whose face I can not remember, snatches me away from the window and carries me upstairs to bed.

"How well do you remember the fire?" the bishop asks.

"Very well. It was Daat's barn that burned, yah?"

"Yah." The bishop sounds so sad I want to reach across the plastic chair between us and touch him, maybe put my hand on his. Of course that is impossible. Only a misfit like myself would think of such a thing.

Neither of us says anything for a moment. In the meantime the lady with no sleeves stops folding to watch the black woman in the television. The black woman is waving her arms and saying that if anyone

ever did *that* to her, well, she'd never invite them into
her home again. The man in the chair agrees and the
crowd claps.

"That is the day I started drawing," I say. How
stupid of me. I only say this because I know the
bishop is trying hard not to watch the television.

Bishop Yoder winces. "Anna, soon the bus will
come, but first there are things I must tell you."

I nod to signify that I am listening.

He sucks in his breath, like he is slurping hot soup.
Before he can speak, the woman without sleeves shuts
down the television and approaches. She stops when
she is so close that I can see that her legs are entirely
without hair.

"Youse two waiting for the bus?" she asks in a
voice as high and sharp as a bluejay's.

"Yah, me," I say. "I go to Pittsburgh."

"Got a ticket?"

"No. I can buy one on the bus, yah?"

"Used to be," she chirps. "But now ya gotta buy it
from me. I'm the local agent. Ya wanna leave Heaven,
ya gotta do it by me." She laughs. Heaven is the name
of the town. I am told it is the only Heaven in
Pennsylvania. English tourists love this name, and our
sign is many times stolen.

"How much?" I have lots of money. In fact, in the
quilt sack at my feet I have almost a thousand
dollars—exactly nine hundred eighty—that I got for
one of my paintings to an English tourist. It was the
painting I called *The Wedding*. In it all the women
wear black, including the bride, but she wears a white
apron as well. Everyone is smiling, except for the
bride.

Faces. Painting faces was on my list of sins. A
picture with a face is like a statue, which in turn is
like an idol. Even our dolls do not have faces.

"Pittsburgh is fifty-nine dollars plus tax."

"So much?' The bishop asks. He looks alarmed.

"Ya can fly from Harrisburg," she says. "But it

won't be any cheaper. Youse allowed to fly?"

Bishop Yoder rises to his feet. "It is better to take the bus."

Amish people are allowed to fly, but only under special circumstances, usually health related. It is the last choice. Although my people are not allowed to own cars, it is permissible to accept rides from Mennonites, our worldly cousins. Sometimes we even hire them to take us places that are too far to reach by a buggy in a day's drive. Of course now that I am dead, what difference does it make how I leave Heaven? Although I know there are those who think I have already fallen from Heaven, like Lucifer. Catherine Beiler, our neighbor, is one of those.

"Than ya better fork it over," the bird woman says, "because I hear the bus coming now."

I jump to my feet. Bishop Yoder has yet to tell me about this Joseph, the one who is supposed to be my brother. The bus stops in Heaven every day but Sunday, and today is Wednesday. There is a small hotel just down the street. Surely I have enough money to stay there one night.

"Well, ya going, or not?"

"I am going," I say. But I have never been so frightened. Excited too. I have never ridden in a bus. I have never ridden in a Mennonite car. In fact, I have never ridden in anything that was not pulled by a horse.

"It won't wait, ya know."

I grab my quilt sack from the floor and open it, looking for the money. Before I can find it, the bus pulls beside the Laundromat. I have seen buses before, but none so large. This one also makes the most noise, more noise even than the generator Jonathan Berkey bought for his dairy, and which the bishop made him return.

"Ya better hurry," the agent says. "He only stops for a minute. If there aren't any passengers, I'm to wave him on."

I find the money and give her three twenty dollar bills.

"The tax."

I give her another twenty. She searches in the pockets of her man's shorts for the change.

In the meantime the bus door opens and three people get off. Two of them are men, and they immediately light cigarettes. They light them as they climb down the steps. The third person to get off is a young woman about my age. She heads straight inside.

"Where's the john?" she yells. She acts like she is talking to no one in particular, but I know she has seen us. Her eyes are as big as buggy wheels.

"That way," the agent grunts, and using the back of her head, points to a corner.

The young woman runs to the rear of the Laundromat. I am still putting my change into the quilt sack when she runs past us again. She is out of breath, but she can speak.

"When you gotta go, you gotta go, and I ain't peeing on no damn bus, that's for sure." The words trail behind her like smoke from a chimney.

Bishop Yoder's pale face turns deep pink. "Anna," he says, "you can—"

The bus honks so loud I drop the quilt sack, but not the cardboard tube.

"Go," the bishop says.

This time I obey.

CHAPTER

2

I climb the steps clutching my quilt sack and the tube. There are three steps; each one takes me higher, yet farther, from Heaven. I turn to see Bishop Yoder and the Laundromat woman watching me through dirty glass. The bishop nods.

"Hurry it up," the driver says. "Got me a schedule to keep." He is a big man, with a belly like Grossdawdi Miller's. His hair is the color of paprika. There is paprika sprinkled across his face too, especially his nose, which is much too small for his face.

I take the first seat, slightly behind and across from the driver. Immediately the bus begins to move. I close my eyes and grip the bar in front of me. It is more terrifying than the time Levi Stoltzfus took me courting in an open summer buggy and made the horse gallop down Hershberger Hill.

"Your ticket," I hear the driver say. I do not realize that he is speaking to me, until the third time.

I dare to open my eyes. The buildings of Heaven streak by, making me dizzy. I feel like I am on the push merry-go-round at Wanamaker Park. Even the bus driver's face is a blur.

"I paid the woman in the Laundromat," I say, "but she forgot to give me the ticket." Then I correct myself, for it is a sin to accuse someone unjustly. "No, it was I who forgot to ask for the ticket."

"I don't give a damn whose fault it is. You either buy another ticket, or you're getting off the bus. One thing's for sure, you're not riding to Harrisburg for free."

"The ticket was for Pittsburgh."

"I don't give a damn if it was for Timbuktu."

Perhaps I am on the wrong bus. "Is Timbuktu on the way to Pittsburgh?"

The tiny nose turns white under the paprika. "You trying to piss me off, lady?"

"I do not understand."

The bus stops so suddenly that I am thrown against the bar. My quilt sack falls to the floor, and the coins the Laundromat lady gave me roll at my feet.

"Aye-mish or not," the driver says, "either you buy another ticket, or you're getting off here."

"Give her a break!" It is the girl from the Laundromat. She has moved from the back of the bus and sits now just behind me.

"Rules are rules," the driver says.

"Pay him," the girl says.

"But I have paid the lady."

"Hey, you wanna get to Pittsburgh, right?"

"Listen to her," the driver says. He makes the bus door open with a hiss.

I pick up the sack and find a one hundred dollar bill. I hand the money to the driver, but he refuses to take it.

"I need exact change."

But I have only these bills."

"The fare is twenty-eight bucks," the driver says, and drops of spit land on my sleeve. "How the hell do you expect me to make change for that?"

"Twenty-eight dollars?" Perhaps I have heard wrong.

"Goddam religious fanatics," he says, shaking his head. "Come on lady, you're making me late. Either pay, or get the hell off."

The girl from the laundromat stands and approaches

the driver. "Here," she says, and shoves a handful of money at him. He grunts as he counts it. The doors hiss again and we move.

The girl makes a silly face at the bus driver before turning to me. "You can pay me back in Harrisburg. We have a half-hour layover there."

"Thank you."

She shrugs. "Come on, let's move back a bit, just not too far back. Those two guys give me the creeps."

She moves to the center of the bus, chooses a seat, and waits. We four are the only passengers. It would be rude of me not to sit with her. Besides, she has done me a very large favor. But walking in a moving bus is like standing in Daat's hay wagon while the horses pull it. Twice I almost fall.

"Sit the hell down," the driver shouts.

I do my best. When I reach the girl, she pats the seat and slides over. I sit and put the quilted sack between us. There is no room to put the tube between my knees and the seat in front of me, so I must hold it between my legs. I am glad the bishop is not here to see this.

The girl smiles. "Name's Brandy—just like the liquor."

"Excuse me?"

"Ya know, like Sherry is some kinda wine. Just glad they didn't name me Whiskey—or Vodka." She laughs as if she has just told a very funny joke.

I say nothing because I do not understand.

"Oh, that's right, ya probably don't know about stuff like that." She tilts her head to think. "It's something to drink, like milk, only stronger." This makes her laugh again.

"My name is Anna," I say.

"Anna? Well, that's easy enough. I thought ya'd have some weird name from the Bible. Maybe something I couldn't pronounce."

"Anna is from the Bible, yah?" Maybe it is only the German Bible that has my name.

"Beats me. So, tell me about yourself, Anna."

"Well, I come from Heaven. I mean, we live near—"

"Whatcha got in that funky tube?"

"My sins," I say. It is the truth, although there is more in the tube than just my sins. But for now I do not feel comfortable sharing.

She nods. "Ya something like a nun, right?"

I am embarrassed for Brandy, how little she knows. Also, the way she dresses. This is how I imagine the Whore of Babylon. She wears black pants that are very tight, and too short—even for a man. They come only half way between the knee and the foot. Her blouse is too short as well, and I can see her stomach. In the belly button she wears a ring, like one Daat would put in a bull's nose, but smaller. In each ear she wears eight more rings, and there is even a ring in her left eyebrow. Her black sandals are on platforms, so that she can step safely in puddles. Everything about her is black; her hair, which she wears like twin horsetails, her toenails, her fingernails, even her lip paint. Only her skin is white, as white as the bus driver's nose when he is angry.

"I am Amish," I say, "not a Catholic. We do not have nuns."

"Then what's with the getup?"

Her slang is too much for my schoolhouse English, but I know what she means. "These clothes set us apart from the world."

"Huh?"

"They are to remind us, and you, that we are different."

"Ain't that the truth! But why do ya want to be that? Different, I mean?"

How do I explain four hundred years of history in one sentence? Or even two?

"It is in the Bible," I say. I am right, only in that the Bible tells believers to be in the world, but not a part of it. The Bible, however, says nothing about our ethnic dress. That is the Ordnung, the rules of our community. There are many other Amish communities, each with their own Ordnung, their own variation of the dress code. It is possible that, to the world, we all look alike.

Today is Wednesday and I look nothing like any other woman in the vicinity of Heaven. I choose to leave my past wearing my Sunday clothes. My dress is black, has long sleeves, and comes well below the knee. I wear black stockings and black tie shoes. My hair is parted in the middle and combed back into a bun, but you can see very little of it, because over it I wear a black bonnet, one that has ruffles to cover the neck. I would be all in black, like Brandy, except for the Sunday apron I wear around my waist, and the V-shaped cape I wear over my shoulders. They are both white.

Again, it is I who choose to leave Heaven in Amish clothes. Mamm, the Bishop, and especially my neighbor Catherine Beiler, want that I should dress in English clothes, so that I do not bring shame on my people. Perhaps they fear that I will climb up on a drinking bar and dance like Salome. King Herod gave Salome the head of John the Baptist because her dance pleased him. Whose head shall I ask for? Catherine's?

Everyone, even Catherine, offers to buy me English clothes from the thrift shop on Main Street. Even fancy new clothes from the new Wal-Mart on the edge of Heaven. But my first clothes were Amish clothes, and I want to leave in Amish clothes. *Ashes to ashes* the Bibles says. Black clothes to black clothes.

Surely there is a Wal-Mart in Pittsburgh. When I arrive, then I will become English.

At any rate, my answer satisfies Brandy. "So, Anna, why are ya going to Pittsburgh?"

"To visit my brother." It could be the truth. Bishop Yoder does not lie. If he says I have a brother in

Pittsburgh . . . unless, of course, the bishop is mistaken.

"Where in Pittsburgh does he live?"

My face burns. "I do not know."

Brandy laughs. "Whatcha mean ya don't know? How can ya visit him if ya don't know where he lives?"

"Well, I will look for him."

"What if it takes weeks? Pittsburgh is a big place, ya know?"

So I have heard. Catherine Beiler says it is the Sodom and Gomorrah of Pennsylvania. Philadelphia too, but especially Pittsburgh. It is a wonder the Almighty has spared it so long. Any day I can expect fire and brimstone.

"I will get a job," I tell Brandy. "And I will find a place to live."

"What kinda job?"

"I am an artist," I say, and the *Hochmut*, the deadly pride, creeps into my voice. "Maybe I will get a job in a restaurant, and I will sell my paintings."

"Ya any good?"

I shrug. That in itself is a lie. I am very good. This I always know.

Brandy sits in silence while we watch Heaven turn into countryside. Then the driver guides the bus onto the turnpike. I have heard of this road, which passes just two miles from my house, but I have never seen it. When the bus is safely on the turnpike the driver reaches a speed I would not have thought possible. The cars on the highways around Heaven never go this fast. I grab the bar again and my knuckles turn white.

The girl laughs yet again. "This is your first time, isn't it?"

"Yah."

"Wow! Like that's really hard to believe. Hey, ya wanna sit by the window?"

"Yah," I say, although I am more frightened than I have ever been. But I will only leave Heaven once, and only once will I see the world for the first time. I do not want to miss anything.

"How old are ya, Anna?"

"Twenty-three."

"No kidding? Me too!"

This surprises me so much I let go of the bar. Brandy looks like a teenager to me. Perhaps it is the round face, or maybe just the clothes of rebellion. Suddenly there are questions I want to ask her.

"Do you live in Pittsburgh, Brandy?"

"Verona."

"Where is that?"

"Think of it as a suburb. It's on the northeast side."

I think she has answered "yes" to my question, so I try another, "Do you live with your parents?"

"Hell no. That's who I was just visiting—well, my mom. My dad is dead. Anyway, I couldn't live with Mom in a million years. I live with the couple I work for—hey, I just thought of something. You're looking for a job, right? And a place to stay?"

"Yah." I try to imagine living with a woman who has pierced her body in so many places, and who wears shoes like platforms so that she never needs to worry about stepping in puddles. If only Catherine Beiler could see me now, sitting next to Brandy. That would fix her buggy.

"Cool," Brandy says, "'cause I kinda owe this couple, see, but I got me a new job. In fact, I need to start it tonight—tomorrow at the latest. Which means I'm gonna be moving out. Soyanara baby!" She giggles. "I think that's Chinese. My boyfriend taught me that."

"Oh." I hope my voice does not show the disappointment my heart feels.

"But don't ya worry, 'cause you can have my old job, see?"

"What is this job?"

"Ya like old people?"

I nod. I love Grossmutter Miller and Grossdawdi

Hostetler. They are my grandparents, so of course I love them, especially Grossdawdi Hostetler. I would love Grossdawdi Hostetler even if he were English. I love Lizzie Augsberger too, and she is not even a relative, just a church member. I do not love Bishop Yoder, but I feel sorry for him, which is a step in the right direction, is it not? Then there is Catherine Beiler. Love your neighbor as yourself, Jesus himself said, but he did not live next door to Catherine Beiler. If Jesus had known Catherine Beiler, the Bible would be much different, I am telling you.

Brandy pats me on the back. "Great! Then it's all settled. You'll move into my old room. All ya have to do is take care of the old lady, see?"

"Is she the mother?"

"One of them's. I never can get that straight."

"Will I have time to paint?"

"Heck yeah, you'll have lots of time for that."

"Thank you."

"Nah, it ain't nothing." Brandy is silent for a while, and although she no longer sits by the window, the shadow of a cloud passes over her face. "It ain't that bad, not really."

"Excuse me?"

"I was just talking to myself."

She digs in her black purse and finds a file. It is a miniature version of the one the blacksmith uses to trim our horses' hooves. Brandy rubs the file along the edges of her black nails. Most of the dust she makes falls into her lap, but some of it floats in my direction and lands on the white apron I wear over my dress. I want to tell her to stop, or that I will move to another seat, but I lack the courage. It has always been this way. I am afraid of small things, but not of big things. No, this is not exactly true—I *am* afraid of the big things, but there are some I must do anyway. But to complain about dust from nails, this is not a big thing.

I turn and look out the window. The farther we get

from Heaven, the faster the world rushes past. The rich farmland of the valley is behind us. Now I see only woods, or maybe a house all by itself. No family, no neighbors, those people are very lonely I think.

Although our bus moves very fast, there are many cars that go faster. Most of the people in these cars look straight ahead, some are even asleep. But every now and then a face turns to look at the bus. The eyes grow wide, and sometimes the person smiles. One woman waves. Another, a little girl, too young even to wear the white apron, sticks out her tongue. My heart feels like there is a millstone sitting on it, but I smile and wave at these people—all except the little girl. I show her my tongue. Then she smiles and waves, and I do the same.

I am thinking that perhaps the world is not such a dangerous place after all, not if little girls who stick out their tongues can be made to smile. Catherine Beiler, you are wrong, I say to myself. And Mamm, your heart is breaking as well, but surely you know that the daughter you raised can take care of herself, even in the English world. There is no need to worry.

Here, my sin is my strength. I am proud, there is no denying it, but it is my pride that allows me to see that I have talent. Because of my pride I can admit that I am intelligent, and even—although this is still very hard for me to say—physically attractive. These are qualities a good Amish girl would not dare to think about. To surrender ourselves, to God and to the rule of the community, that is what we must always have on our minds.

But I am not truly Amish anymore, am I? The bishop has pronounced me dead by the excommunication. He has not used the word dead, but what else is a woman who is cut off from her family? I will never marry an Amish man, I will never bear Amish children. I will never be a Grossmutter, living in a little house attached to the family house, with only light chores to do, and the giving of love to grandchildren to keep her busy.

I am thinking these things when a pair of hands reaches between Brandy and me and grabs the quilt sack.

CHAPTER

3

I stand and turn, and the tube falls to the floor. I pick it up at once. Brandy is also standing, her hands on her hips.

One of the smokers is holding the sack. He has the shaggy hair and the long teeth of a dog. His eyes are small and far apart, almost on the sides of his head. He is two seats back from us where we cannot easily reach, and he grins at us.

"Hey, give that back to her," Brandy says.

"Make me."

"Ya see what I mean? I told ya they give me the creeps."

"Please, sir," I say and extend a hand.

"Not so fast, Amish girl. You might be hiding something special in here. Something me and my buddy want."

"There is nothing special," I say. Only my new life. The sack contains every dollar I own. There will be none coming from home. The sooner I get hungry, really hungry, the sooner I will come to my senses. Then, like the prodigal son, I will return to the farm and beg forgiveness. I will especially beg forgiveness of the elders and the bishop. Then everything will be forgiven, only not forgotten. I will join the church, marry a believer, and settle down to raise a family. When I am very old, then maybe the young people will not remember the Anna Hostetler whose pride forced her out into the world. That is the plan—but it is not my plan.

The man pulls at the sack. It opens easily, for there are only snaps.

"Ah, jackpot!" he cries.

I call to the bus driver. "Sir! This man—"

The bus swerves as the driver turns his head. "Shut up and sit down! All of youse!"

I will not sit. How can I sit when the Dog Boy—he looks more like a boy than a man to me—still holds my life in his hands? Neither does Brandy sit. She has the fire in her of an unbroken colt.

"Ya give that bag back to her," she shouts, "or I'll come back there and beat the crap out of you."

He laughs. "Oh, yeah?"

Brandy leaves our seat. She has formed her hands into fists. I have never seen someone do this in anger, although I have heard that the English do it often. But surely not a woman.

"I said, give that back!"

"Woo, woo, like I'm really scared."

In the very back seat the other smoker laughs loudly, then starts to cough.

"I'm warning youse," the bus driver shouts, but I hear laughter in his voice as well. It is only me who upsets him.

Brandy fears no one. She swings her fists at Dog Boy. He climbs over the seat, but she grabs his leg and bites his ankle. I am horrified. For five hundred years my people have refused to raise their fists, even to save their lives. But now, I am less than an hour's ride by bus from Heaven, and already there is an English girl doing violence for my sake. And what is my sake? Less than a thousand dollars!

"Stop," I cry. "Let him be!" I will bring the matter up with the bus driver again. This time I will speak softly, face to face. If he does not help, then I will speak to the ticket agent in Harrisburg.

Meanwhile the second smoker laughs so hard that

he must lie on the seat to catch his breath. Then Brandy laughs, and so does the Dog Boy. Now everyone is laughing except for me. I do not understand this English humor, but I smile.

"Ya still gotta give her back the bag," Brandy says. She snaps her teeth.

"Bitch!" The Dog Boy throws the sack at me. I try to catch it, but it hits me in the face. A corner of the sack brushes against my right eye, which is open.

Brandy returns to our seat. "Ya see? Ya gotta show them that you're tough. Otherwise creeps will walk right over ya."

I hug the sack. My eye stings. "Thank you, Brandy."

"It wasn't nothing," Brandy says, then smiles. Biting the Dog Boy's leg has made her happy.

I look inside the sack. My money is still in there. So is the German Bible that belonged to Grossmutter Hostetler. There are some personal things as well—I am terrified of having to buy English underclothes—and my three favorite paint brushes. They are made of the finest sable hairs and very expensive, and I have been hiding them from Mamm and Daat. I bought these brushes with my own money, money I got from selling my first oil painting. *The Barnraising* it is called. I sold it to an English woman who stopped to buy one of Mamm's quilts.

Satisfied that everything is still there, I turn my attention back to the scenery that rushes past the window. We are in the mountains, and there are no more houses, only trees. Beside me Brandy is singing. It is a song about bottles of beer on a wall. Why someone puts these bottles on the wall is unclear, but whoever did it, has done a poor job. The bottles keep falling. Soon both smokers join in the silly song.

I allow my thoughts to drift back to the day I sold my first drawing. It was the day after my sixth birthday.

It had been a very cold winter. Our houses do not have
central heating, only the cook stove in the kitchen,
and in cases in which the congregation is very liberal,
another wood-burning stove in the biggest sitting
room. There are congregations so liberal that they
allow gas stoves, but ours is not one of them. We had
only the cast iron stove and kerosene lamps. The heat
must rise through the ceiling to warm the upstairs,
which it never truly does. Ever since I can remember,
ever since the fire, I scratched forbidden drawings in
the frost on the inside of my bedroom window.

Mamm is thin, and she spent that cold winter
keeping her fingers warm by quilting. Busy fingers
not only keep the devil away, but they can bring in
extra money in the tourist season. That winter Mamm
made seven quilts, each one finer than the next.

When spring came the fence out front bloomed with
quilts. Mamm sold four the first day. She would have
sold five, but the tourist insisted that Mamm pose with
the quilt, a Dresdin plate in blue, pink, and white with
a black border and stitched with black thread. It was
my favorite of the bunch, because the blue came from
one of my weekday dresses that I had outgrown, but
the worldly pink came from the Thrift Shop over in
Heaven. It is possible even that the pink was donated
by a Presbyterian.

Mamm refused to pose for the tourist because a
photograph is the same thing as a graven image, which
the Bible forbids. There is also the matter of
Hochmut—pride. Look at the English when they have
their pictures taken, they gaze at themselves in their
mirrors, fix their hair, and paint fresh the lips. Then
they smile to show their teeth. Since the wages of sin
are death, Mamm preferred to lose the sale.

Just one picture, the tourist lady said, for her book
of photos. Again, Mamm said no. By then it was a
battle of wills—God's will, and the tourist's. The

tourist pulled her car up the road, under the shade of a silver maple, and sat there, eating her lunch and waiting for Mamm to change her mind. The sight of an English woman parked on our grass, just waiting for her to sin, was too much for Mamm. Rather than let angry thoughts build up in her head, Mamm asked me to mind the quilts while she went inside to fix lunch for Daat and me. That is when I got the idea.

I took one of the sheets of brown paper Mamm kept under her table in front of the fence to wrap the quilts in. I found the little piece of pencil she used to mark in a ledger the details of each quilt: what the pattern was, when she made it, when she sold it, and for how much. I spread a sheet of paper on the table and drew a picture of Mamm from memory, and then walked over to the tourist. She was eating a chicken leg, which looked, and smelled, delicious. Especially since I had yet to have my lunch.

"Please lady," I said. "Here is a picture of my Mamm. Now will you buy the quilt?"

The tourist smiled when I spoke, but she did not understand a word I said, because I was speaking dialect. At that time, having not yet started school, I did not know a single word of English.

I held the picture against my chest with my arm, and the paper reached almost to the ground. I pointed at Mamm's portrait with my free hand.

"I can do better," I said, "but there was not much time. Please auntie, you must not tell Mamm."

The tourist's eyes followed my finger. They widened, and she opened her mouth slightly, as if to show me the chicken.

She said many things to me in English which, of course, I did not understand. Not that it mattered. By then I was not so much interested in selling a quilt for Mamm, but in the English lady just inches away. Her hair was blond, like mine, but dark in the middle. As dark as Daat's. Her lips were as red as the tulips Mamm grows in the sunny spot between the house and the fence. There were rings in her ears, and rings on her fingers, one with a very large shiny stone, like the piece of gravel I split with Daat's hammer on the cement floor of the barn that very summer.

The English lady gave up trying to get through to the Dummkopf who spoke only dialect. She took the paper with Mamm's face on it, and in exchange handed me a much smaller paper with a man's face. I had watched Mamm do business enough to know that this was not a fair trade. I reached to take Mamm's picture back, but the tourist laughed and threw another bill at me before driving away. The second bill had a different face on it—an Amish man's face.

As soon as the car was gone, Mamm came back outside. I handed her the bills.

"Ach!" she said. Then spun around to count her quilts. They were still there, including the Dresdin plate with the Presbyterian pink. "Anna, how do you come by this money?"

I did not dare tell Mamm about the drawing. "The English gave it to me. She said for me to buy sweets, Mamm. At the Wal-Mart."

Mamm frowned and counted the quilts again just to be sure. Then she looked at the money again. She held it between her thumb and first finger, like she did the tail of the dead squirrel she removed from the downspout by the kitchen door.

"See, Mamm, this one has an Amish man's face on it. Look at the beard. It is worth more than the other, yah?"

"This is not the face of *unser Satt Leit*," Mamm said. "Our sort of people wear always the hat. This is the face of an English man named Lincoln. You will learn about him in school."

"And the other man?"

"Washington," Mamm said, and tucked the bills behind the band of her black weekday apron.

There were to be no sweets from Wal-Mart, but

then, I never expected there to be. Mamm was always tight with the money. It was Daat who bought us treats, and permitted us to ride the plastic horse outside the hissing doors, even though we had four real horses at home.

CHAPTER

4

Brandy and the smokers are still singing about the beer on the wall. The number of bottles goes from ninety-nine down to one, and just when I think this terrible song is over, the singers start again. Now they add bottles to the wall.

The bus driver is too busy to sing. We are out of the mountains and there are many more cars on the turnpike. We pass many houses, and then towns as big as Heaven. The towns get closer together, and so do the houses. Then the driver guides us off the turnpike and onto a road so crowded that the cars do not even move.

"What is the problem?" I ask Brandy.

"Rush hour traffic," she says.

"But we do not even move."

She stops singing and stares at me. For the first time I see that one of her eyes is much smaller than the other. Perhaps it is the metal ring in the eyebrow that causes such a difference.

"Ain't ya ever been to a real city before?"

"I have been to Heaven—"

"Heaven ain't no city! It ain't even a town. Hey guys," Brandy calls to the singers, "this here is Anna's first time in a city."

"Woo, woo," the Dog Boy howls. He stands and shakes his hips at me, like a real dog when it finds a mate that is in season.

The second smoker laughs so hard that again he must lie on the seat. He has black hair like Daat, but he is just a silly boy. It is obvious that Dog Boy is the leader.

"Anna," Brandy says, "ya ain't actually gonna walk around Pittsburgh like that, are ya?"

I shake my head. "I will buy new clothes—English clothes. Pittsburgh has a Wal-Mart, yah?"

"Yah? You're a hoot Anna, ya know that?"

"There is no Wal-Mart in Pittsburgh?" This I find very hard to believe.

"Yeah, Pittsburgh has a Wal-Mart, but whatcha gonna do about Harrisburg?"

"But we will not be long in Harrisburg, will we?"

"Long enough." Brandy grins. "Leave it to me, Anna. I'll have ya looking regular in no time."

"Excuse me?"

"Like normal people," she says.

"Harrisburg," the driver says. "Dinner break, forty-five minutes."

I clutch the sack and the cardboard tube as I follow Brandy to the public toilet. This is a real bus station and there are many people, but only a few bother to stare. I see a family of Amish seated on a wooden bench. They glance at me, I glance at them. Nothing more. They are *unser Satt Leit*, but not of my congregation. The woman wears only a white organdy cap, not the black travel bonnet, and although her apron is black, her dress is blue. Catherine Beiler would say they are one step away from becoming Mennonite. Two steps away from dancing with the devil. The Amish church of Heaven—Mamm and Catharine Beiler agree on this—is one of the most conservative in the state. They are not proud of this, mind you. It is only a fact.

This is my first time ever in a public "restroom." Why it is called that, I do not know, but there is a short bench near the door. I also do not know what to expect. So many sinks, but no place to sit. And so many ladies, waiting patiently in a line. It reminds me of the Sunday dinner all the members of our congregation attend. For a minute my heart aches.

"Where are the toilets?" I ask.

Brandy laughs and points to a row of little doors, so short there is room for a child to pass under. "In there."

I wait in line until it is my turn. Behind each door is a little room, like a milking stall, but it is fancy, with a hook on the door, and a metal shelf on which I can put the sack. I open the sack so that I can balance the tube in it. It wants to fall, but finally I am getting it to stay.

There is also a metal box, about the size of a large book, and it hangs on the wall. I do not open it because, except for the Bible, I have no books with me. I am happy to see that there are two kinds of paper to choose from, the regular, which we use at home, and another kind which is shaped like the yoke of a plow horse. When I use the toilet, I have a terrible experience. I shift my weight slightly and the toilet flushes by itself. I cannot help that I gasp. Outside Brandy shouts with laughter.

Later, when I try to wash my hands, I find that there are no handles on the faucet. There is no bar of soap, and no towel. Brandy must show me everything, and everything to her is funny. By the time I am finished there are many other people laughing, and my face burns with shame.

"Now," Brandy says so that everyone can hear, "we do something about your clothes."

I am afraid that she will somehow produce for me clothes like the ones she wears, but she has other ideas. "Anybody got a scissors?"

A lady with a purse as big as the quilt sack, hands Brandy a scissors. "I have a bus to catch in twenty minutes," she says.

"It won't take that long," Brandy says. She turns to me. "Give me your dress."

"I do not understand."

"Take it off. I got me some work to do."

I will not take my dress off. Not in the public area. But Brandy insists, so I wait again in the line to use a stall. The lady with the scissors is impatient, but Brandy says it will only take a minute or two. I remove my apron and hang it on the hook. Then I hand my dress to Brandy over the stall door.

She is right; it only takes a minute to ruin a dress. I cannot believe my eyes, for Brandy has removed both sleeves. *Completely.*

"Brandy! What have you done?"

"Put it on. We still gotta get ourselves something to eat."

"I need the sleeves, Brandy."

"Too late, I already threw them in the garbage. This is your new look."

My new English look is supposed to be a dress from Wal-Mart. I am thinking something with flowers on it, small flowers, of course. But it will have sleeves, and lots of colors.

"Ya gonna make us miss the bus," Brandy yells.

I put the dress on, but only because I have no choice. I cannot put the apron on over it, because that feels like even more of a sin. And I cannot wear the bonnet now either, so I think to put it in the book box on the wall. But someone else has already put a personal item in the metal box. It is disgusting, what they have put in there. Only a pig would do such a thing. Now I am judging the English, which is surely a sin, even for those who are excommunicated. I pray that God will forgive me, and hang the bonnet on the hook behind the stall door.

I feel like I am hanging Mamm on the hook as well. There are hundreds of stitches in the bonnet, which has many pleats, and which Mamm made by hand. With my head bare, I may as well be all over naked. I think also of our ancestors, Jacob Hochstetler and his sons, Christian and Joseph. Of course my forefathers did not wear bonnets, but the Delaware Indians plucked the hair from these white captives' scalps with clam shells. When they were bald, each with only a thin strip of hair from forehead to neck, my ancestors were no longer Swiss, but Delaware.

"Whatcha doing in there?" Brandy shouts. "Dying of old age?" When I open the stall, she hoots like an owl and claps her hands. "Ya look almost normal!"

I raise my arms. "But the sleeves—"

"Shaggy Aggie."

"Anna," I remind her.

"Your pits," she says, "don't you ever shave?"

I know now what she means, and I am even more embarrassed. This is one thing I did not think about. I had heard that English women shave many parts of their body, and I have seen the bare armpits and legs, but always I have blocked that from my mind.

I do not understand this strange English custom and, until this minute, have no desire to remove the hair God has given me. But with the hair, I am like the calf with the extra leg that was born on the Stoltzfus farm last spring. I cannot be normal as long as it is there.

"I do not feel so good."

Brandy does not hear so well. "Don'tcha worry. You'll look a lot better soon as I do something with that hair." She speaks now of the hair on my head.

Without asking me, Brandy pulls the hairpins out of my bun. My hair has never been cut, for the Bible tells us that it is the woman's *crowning glory*. Brandy gasps when my glory falls below my knees.

"What are you girls up to?" a lady asks. She is English, of course, but not the scissors lady, who has already left to catch her bus.

"Mind your own beeswax," Brandy says.

The lady looks at me with a mother's concern, before leaving quietly. Brandy leads me to the mirror, which is big and covers most of one wall. In front of it stand other women, combing their hair and doing private things.

"Ya see? You're gorgeous! Guys are gonna pee all over themselves when they see ya." She pauses, waiting for me to say something. "So, whatcha think?"

I do not recognize what I see in the mirror. There are some among the Amish who have mirrors, but not in our congregation. To look in a mirror is to be vain. I have seen myself in the windows of shops, and in the shiny sides of pots and pans. Once, when I was eight years old, I peeked in a mirror at Wal-Mart. Mamm saw me do it and when we got home, she hit my hand with the leather strap that hangs by the kitchen door.

The woman in this mirror looks nothing like the girl at Wal-Mart. Now I see an abomination. Everything Catherine Beiler has predicted has come true. I look worse than a Presbyterian; I look like a heathen.

"So?" Brandy demands.

I try to say something, but there are no words. Surely the tears rolling down my cheeks are enough of an answer.

"Ya like it that much? Well, just you wait!" Brandy carries a black purse, no bigger than one of Mamm's ham sandwiches. She finds a thing of lip paint. A tube, she calls it. Before I can protest—no, I do not want to protest—Brandy has painted my lips. "There, what do ya see?"

Again I have no words. I try to say something, anything, and the bright painted lips move to mock me.

"Well," Brandy says, "like I said before, you're gorgeous. Just don't get me wrong; 'cause I ain't no lesbian. But them eyes, that hair. Hell, I wished I looked like that."

Like what? My eyes are gray, not blue like Mamm's eyes, or brown like Daat's. My hair is pale, almost white, like paper left too long in the sun. My face is

even, balanced, I think you call it. Not lopsided like
Ellie Bontragor's. My skin is smooth enough, but
there are freckles on my nose. The bright red lips—
well, they are not mine.

"Brandy," I say, "I cannot—"

A tall woman at the next sink is washing her hands.
She reaches in front of me for a paper square from the
metal box on the wall.

"Pardon me," she says. She dries her hands, starts
to leave, and then turns. "I couldn't help but admire
your hair. How long did it take to grow?"

"All my life," I say. The lips in the mirror move
with each word.

"Well, it's beautiful, just beautiful."

"Yeah," Brandy says, "but she's got split ends."

"You're very lucky," the woman says to me.

When the tall woman leaves, Brandy sticks out her
tongue. I notice for the first time that there are three
little metal balls inside Brandy's mouth. I look from
Brandy to the reflection of myself in the mirror.

Then a strange thing happens. The woman in the
mirror, the one whose gray eyes I share, looks out at
me from the mirror. I no longer see an abomination,
but an English woman. I am the woman Mamm warned
me about. I am the woman Daat would not even look
in the eye. I am the woman Catherine Beiler said
would surely go to hell. I am who I was meant to be.

We have only enough time to "grab a hot dog,"
Brandy says, before the bus leaves. We must walk
through the main room of the bus station. I look only
at my feet. I do not want to see the Amish family,
even to know if they are still there.

They are not, Brandy tells me, so I look up. A man
reading a newspaper stops and smiles at me. Another
man, one with a young wife beside him, and a baby,
nods his head. His wife does not see this, and I feel
guilty.

We grab our hot dogs, which cost much more than the ones at Wal-Mart, yet taste no better. On the way back to the bus, a third man whistles at me.

"See, what did I tell ya?" Brandy says, but she does not sound happy. "You're hot stuff."

The bus driver does not recognize me and asks for my ticket again. When I tell him it is me, he hits the steering wheel with the palm of his hand.

"Well, I'll be damned," he says.

I feel my face turn red because of his reaction, and because of the swearing. "This ticket is still good, yah?"

"Babe, I'd punch your ticket anytime."

"Gross," Brandy says and pulls me away.

Now there are many more people on the bus. Brandy and I take the last empty seat, the one directly in front of the smokers. At first they do not seem to recognize me. Then they look at me with wide eyes.

When the bus has gone only a little ways, Dog Boy taps me on the shoulder. He taps me on the part that is now bare. I cannot help that I jump, but I do not turn and look.

"Lenny," he says.

"What the hell?" Brandy says.

"That's my name."

"Like who cares?"

"I wasn't talking to you," Lenny says. Even I can tell that he speaks the English better than Brandy.

"Yeah? Well, I was talking to ya."

"Bitch."

Brandy turns and shows Lenny her fist. This I see from the corner of my eye.

"Woo, woo, like I'm really scared."

"Ya oughta be, 'cause I can pound the shit outta ya."

This is already too much for me. The Amish, those in every congregation, want only *Gelassenheit*. We desire only calm and quiet conversation. We—but I am no longer one of the people, am I? Is this part of

the price I must pay to honor the talent God has given
me?

"Please," I say, "can we not make peace?"

"Speak for yourself," Brandy says. "This guy's
irritating the—"

"Justin." The other smoker, the one with the dark
hair, puts his hand between Brandy and me. He desires
me to shake it.

I do not want to shake his hand because I am afraid
that it is a trick. Or perhaps he will see it as an
agreement, one I do not wish to make. It is easier to
do nothing.

"At least pull his finger," Lenny says.

Both smokers find this very funny. Even Brandy
laughs, although she covers her mouth, thinking I
cannot see. This angers me, although I cannot say for
sure why it is so.

"I am not in the spirit for games," I say, and lean
my head in the corner, where the seat and window
come together.

"Spirit?" Lenny says. "This chick might be hot, but
she's plenty weird."

"I like weird," Justin says.

"Shut up, both of ya!" Brandy shouts.

Everyone on the bus is looking at us now. I close
my eyes to escape theirs, and think of the games
Bridgett Monroe taught me; the games that led me to
the dark side of Heaven.

CHAPTER

5

The tourist lady returned the following summer. All
the English seemed alike to me, with their bright
clothes and loud voices, and I had forgotten the face
of the woman who bought Mamm's picture. Our fence
was blooming with Mamm's quilts again, and Mamm
was inside making supper, when the long black car
stopped, and the lady with blond hair stepped out.

"Hi there. I was hoping I'd find you here!
Remember me?"

I shook my head, but not in answer to her question.
Behind me now was one year of school, but my
teacher was herself Amish. Miss Lehman's English did
not sound like this, and even my friend Elizabeth
Schrock who, Daat said, talks faster than a horse can
gallop, could not make words come out with such
speed. Sometimes I could not understand Elizabeth,
even when she spoke dialect.

"I was here last summer and—never mind, you
don't understand a word I'm saying, do you?"

I shrugged.

"Do you speak English, dear?" The tourist says the
words loud and slow.

"Yah, English," I say.

"Good. Well, that's a relief." She glanced around.
"Where's your mother?"

I pointed to the house.

She smiled. "I was hoping for that too. Don't get

me wrong, dear." She walked over to the nearest quilt, a nice star pattern, and felt the material.

"Do you want to buy?" I asked.

"Yes, but not a quilt. This time I want to buy another one of your pictures."

It took a moment for her words to get through my Dummkopf. "Ach," I cried.

"Oh, I see that I've upset you. Please, allow me to introduce myself. My name is Bridgett Monroe." She stuck out her hand. Her *English* hand.

What was I to do? If either Mamm or Daat saw me shaking hands with the tourist, it would be the strap at the kitchen door for me. At least that's what Levi Schumacher's parents did to him when he allowed the English to take his picture. But it was a sin to be rude, even to *anner Satt Leit*, the other sort of people.

I did nothing.

The tourist took back her hand. "What is your name?"

"Anna," I said. I would not tell her the family name, even if she tied me to the stretching machine and pulled me into tiny pieces.

Suddenly the English looked sad. "Anna is a lovely name. It's from the Bible, isn't it?"

I nodded.

"I have a silly name. My parents named me Bridgett after a French movie star. Actually, it was a compromise. Mother wanted to name me Marilyn, but—oh, dear, you're not getting any of this, are you?"

I nodded, and then shook my head. That should answer her question.

Bridgett Monroe bent so that her face was no higher than mine. "I had a little girl. Her name was Amanda."

I searched for the right words. "How old is Amanda?"

She smiled again, but her face was still sad. "Amanda is in heaven."

"Daat took me to Heaven yesterday. We bought

sugar and many other things." I had yet to learn the words for what we bought at Pat's IGA on Harper Road.

The sadness left her face. "So, Anna, do you have a picture to sell me today?"

I looked down at my bare feet.

"No? Well, I have a present for you."

I looked up. That was also a word I did not know. Perhaps it meant candy.

"Stay right here," Bridgette Monroe said. "And close your eyes."

I stood as still as a Catholic statue while Bridgette went to her car. She was gone only a few minutes, I am sure, but it seemed like another year had passed.

"Now open them," she finally said. What she held in her hands was more valuable than any amount of candy.

I awake to find a pain in my neck. The bus is dark, but outside there are the lights of more houses than I have ever seen. More lights even than the stars, and there are many stars in Heaven,

"'Bout time, sleepy-head."

My stomach feels sick. I do not want to hear this voice. I want now nothing more than to be in my own bed, with Daat snoring in the next room. He sometimes does not remember that I am grownup, and checks still to see if I am breathing. Oh God in Heaven, I pray, please let this be a dream.

This prayer, like many others, does not come true. I remain on the bus, seated next to Brandy. With each turn of the wheels I see more lights. Although it is night, there are people walking outside, or standing in little groups talking, as if they have no place to go, no homes waiting for them. Most of the people are white, but there are black ones too. I press my nose to the glass. These are the first black people I have ever seen, besides the woman in the box.

"Where are we?" I ask.

"Pittsburgh. Ya slept right through the stop in Breezewood. Didn't wanna wake ya up, 'cause it was only gonna be a short stop. Didn't know if ya wanted me to get ya anything to eat, but I got ya this anyway." Brandy shoves what looks like a giant cookie under my nose.

I thank her and put the cookie in my sack. Then I look out the window again. I see signs with moving lights, signs with flashing lights, and signs with the outlines of women on them. The women are English and wear very tight clothes—or—this I can not believe! Is it possible they are naked, like Eve in the Garden of Eden? *Adult Entertainment*, some of the signs say. *XXX. Hot Chicks. Black Diamond Escort Service.*

"Makes ya mad, doesn't it?" Brandy says. "Women acting like whores. Where's their self respect?"

"Woo, woo, woo." The smokers, Lenny and Justin, see the signs too.

"Shut up," Brandy says. She pats my arm, which is now as bare as Eve's. "Don't let them bug ya. We'll lose those buttheads soon as we hit the station." I shiver and Brandy feels it through her hand. "Hey, you're scared, ain't ya?"

"You see?" Justin says. His voice is very loud so that I will hear. "I told you, Len, to lay off that shit."

"Hey man, it was your idea."

"Shut up, the both of ya!"

I think to myself there is no reason to be afraid. I am no longer Amish, but I still have God. And I have Brandy.

The Pittsburgh bus station is bigger than the one in Harrisburg, but Brandy knows her way around. She pulls me by one arm like I am her child, but I do not mind. This is the bus to Verona, she says, but it goes the long way, through Wilkinsburg. We will have to wait a half-hour more if we want the express. Which do I want?

I tell her I do not care. In that case Brandy wants to wait. I find a quiet place to sit and eat the cookie Brandy gave me. While I eat, I guard Brandy's luggage; three pieces that came from the belly of the bus.

Meanwhile Brandy makes many calls on the telephone. They are not the little telephones without wires, that I have seen tourists put in their pockets, but telephones attached to the wall. I cannot hear from where I sit, but I see her arms moving up and down, as if she is trying to scare starlings away from the tomato garden. Brandy must always be moving, just like the creek on my farm, although sometimes the creek must move under a shell of ice.

Lenny and Justin are at the far end of the room. They have tried to follow us, but Brandy would not allow it. I watch Lenny and Justin disappear into the crowd and I give thanks. They are bad news, as Brandy says. Especially Lenny.

When there are five minutes left to catch the bus Brandy gets off the phone. "Hey," she says, "ya ready for your new adventure?"

"I am ready for sleep," I say.

"Jeez! Ya slept half the way here." But she is in a good mood, and again she pulls me like a child.

Brandy surprises me by paying the driver. She tells me I can pay her back by helping with the luggage. This I am glad to do, even to lift the bags over my head and throw them on a rack. I put my sack up there too, but the tube I hold in one hand.

The second bus is smaller, and there are soft benches, not individual seats. But all the space has been taken, so that Brandy and I must stand. The lights remain on and it is hard to see out the windows. Except for Brandy, I tell myself, nobody knows I started the day Amish.

Then the bus makes many turns, and I must hang on

to the bar above my head. "Shaggy Aggie," Brandy says again. This time she whispers, but my face burns.

After many stops, there is finally a seat. "Ya take it Aggie," Brandy says.

I take the seat which is by the window. The glass has grease on it, but when I look close, I see that we are following a river. On the other side the dark hills are covered with lights, and the sky above them is pale as dawn, although the night is not over. On my side of the river the hills are steep, and the houses cling to them like wasp nests. The English, as Mamm would say, are a queer people.

More stops, and now only Brandy and I remain on the bus. "Hey, how far younz going?" the driver calls.

"Verona!" Brandy shouts. "The most beautiful little town in the whole U.S.A."

"Give me a break," the driver says.

"Yeah, like you know anything," Brandy says. She sticks out her tongue with the metal balls at the driver. If he sees, he does not say.

When we stop he does not offer to help with Brandy's bags. But Brandy does not help either. She gets off the bus and looks in the window of a store that sells toys. It is I who must carry Brandy's bags down from the bus. While I do this the bus driver watches me with the eyes of a tomcat.

"You French?" he says.

"No, American."

"You sure?"

"Yah."

"Ah, German. I like German girls too."

I am disappointed, thinking that somehow he knows I am Amish. Then I realize he is thinking I am from Germany. This bothers me too. I want to sound like a regular American, but this will take time.

"I am from Heaven, Pennsylvania," I say.

"Heaven? Never heard of it."

"It is very small."

He shrugs. "Hey, how about giving me your

number?"

"Twenty-three."

"Not your age, your phone number."

My face burns again. Twenty-three is the number of my bus seat, but it is also my age.

"I have no telephone," I say.

"What about her? She got a phone I can reach you at?"

"I do not know."

"Is that so? Well, get off the bus. I got me a schedule to keep."

I must make three trips to get Brandy's bags off the bus. I almost forget my sack and the cardboard tube. When I remember them I give thanks to God, although it is possible he no longer hears my prayers, especially now that my head is bare.

The bus leaves and I am alone with Brandy in Verona. We are on a street with shops, but they are all closed. A few cars pass us, but there are no people on the sidewalks. No signs advertising XXX. Behind us is the river, and in front of us a hill so steep, Noah Miller's crazy children would not dare to sled down it.

"Up there," Brandy says, and points to a street. She begins to walk.

"Brandy, your bags."

"Ya carry them."

I can carry only two of the bags, and my quilt sack and the tube. "Brandy, I can not carry them all."

Brandy wobbles back on the shoes that are too high. She reaches for my sack and the tube, but these I will not give up.

"Jeesh," she says and grabs the smallest bag. "Some thanks I get for landing you this job *and* paying your fare."

I say nothing. Yah, I am grateful, but even a horse does not carry this weight. There are hills near Heaven, but the roads there wind, like the zigzag pattern on some of Mamm's quilts. In Verona, the streets go straight up. Soon I am very hot, and the breathing comes hard. Even with her shoes to slow her down, Brandy is far ahead of me.

"Hurry up," she yells. "We're almost there."

But there is much more to climb. The steep street is crossed by another that is level, and I stop to catch my breath. Brandy does not stop. I rest only a moment, then climb again. Another level street, another stop, but always Brandy is ahead. The houses are crowded together, but only a few of them have lights. In her black clothes Brandy is hard to see, and then suddenly I cannot see her at all.

I put down Brandy's bags and call her name softly, so that I do not wake the people who sleep. She does not answer, so I call again, this time louder. A dog barks and a porch light comes on. A man pokes his head out the door.

"Hey," he says, "what's with the noise out there? People are trying to sleep."

I hope maybe he is Brandy's father. "I am looking for Brandy," I say.

"Damn drunks," he says and slams the door. Then he pokes his head out again. "Just so you know, I'm calling the cops." The door slams and the light goes off.

I do not know what to do. Should I wait for the Cops, or should I look for Brandy? Perhaps the Cops are the friends of Brandy I will be working for. It is also possible the Cops are Brandy's parents. She has not told me her last name, but Brandy Cops is a pretty name.

Yet the man who slams doors is not happy, that much I know. The dog, which still barks, could that be Cops? If that is the case, I feel the sudden urge to kick Brandy's bags down the hill. The girl has betrayed me. She has abandoned me high on a hill in this Verona. But why?

Somebody grabs my elbow and I scream.

CHAPTER

6

"Shhhh!" It is only Brandy. "That's Mr. Goldschmidt's house. Ya don't wanna mess with old Otto."

"He said he was calling the Cops. What does this mean?"

"Shit! It means we gotta vamoose." She digs her black fingernails into my arm and pulls. I see that she no longer has the third bag.

"Where is the bag, Brandy?"

"I already been ta the house. Ya were supposed ta keep up, ya know? I thought ya Amish girls was strong—even stronger than the guys, and that ya had your babies out in the field, and then went right back ta work."

This I have never heard. Elizabeth Zug is stronger than her twin brother Thomas, but only because he was born with arms and legs which stay always skinny, like the tail of a cat. But Amish women always give birth at home, with the midwives, unless there is some great complication. Then, since Heaven has no hospital, only a doctor, we ask our Mennonite neighbors to drive us to a town where there is a hospital. I myself have never been in one.

"Brandy," I say, as I try to keep my voice calm, "I am not a horse."

"Giddyap," she says and spanks my buttocks, but she does not help me with the bags.

We are almost at the very top of the hill when
Brandy pushes me off the sidewalk. I run into a metal
fence, the kind the English use to lock up their dogs.

Brandy does not notice. "That's it," she says
pointing to a house. "That's gonna be your new home.
Home, sweet home."

It is a brick house, two levels high, and there are
dark bushes all around the bottom. I see only one light
inside and it is blue.

"Come on," Brandy says. She unlocks the gate and
pulls me up the private walkway. When we get to the
door she unlocks that too, and grabs from me one of
the bags. "Here she is!"

At first I see no one, only the man in the television.
Then I realize that Brandy is saying I am here. When
my eyes adjust to the darkness I see a woman standing
in a doorway. She looks at me with narrow eyes and
smokes a cigarette.

"You sure she's the one?"

Brandy laughs. "She's Aye-mish."

"Doesn't look Aye-mish to me."

"I told ya. I gave her a makeover."

"Shhh," the woman in the doorway says. She and
Brandy listen very closely to the man in the
television. He has a gap between his teeth like my
brother Elam, and sits behind a large desk. The
television man reads a list of ten things that many
people find funny. Except for Brandy and the woman
with the cigarette, I cannot see the people who laugh
so loud at things I do not understand.

When the man in the television is done reading, the
woman in the doorway points a small black box at him
and he disappears. Now the room is very black except
for the burning end of the cigarette.

"What's your name?" the woman asks.

"She means ya," Brandy says and pokes me in the
ribs.

"Anna Hostetler," I say.

"I call her Aggie," Brandy says and laughs.

"You really Aye-mish, Aggie?"

"My name is Anna."

"Whatever. Answer my question."

"No, I am not Amish."

She makes the room all at once light. I have heard that this can be done, but have never seen it. I gasp, but it does not matter, because no one hears.

"What the hell," the woman says. She marches over to Brandy and slaps her. "You better explain this, missy."

There is a red mark on Brandy's cheek, but she moves only to glare at me. "Tell her ya are really Aye-mish, Aggie. Tell her!"

I see now that it is my fault. "I was Amish," I say quickly, "until this morning."

The woman snorts like a horse that does not want to be hitched. "Then what? The Tooth Fairy waved her magic wand?"

She asks a riddle I cannot answer. "The bishop has excommunicated me," I say.

The woman stares. "What kind of bullshit is this? You want me to believe Aye-mish are really Catholics."

"Not Catholics!"

"What she means," Brandy says, although her lips do not move, "is that she did something really awful and they threw her out."

"Who asked you?" The woman turns to me. "That true?"

"Yah, it is true."

She laughs. "Welcome to the real word. So what did you do that was so awful?"

"I did not obey." I do not want to tell this woman more than that.

"That's all?"

"I was given many chances."

"Yeah? Well, if you're going to stay here with me, you're going to have to start following orders. Do I make myself clear?"

I nod my head foolishly. If only I can turn back the clock. Maybe not all the way back to Heaven, but to the Pittsburgh bus station. On the way to the Laundromat, Bishop Yoder told me he had once heard of something called the YWCA, where Christian girls could get a bed for the night. He was not sure if the place still did business, but it would have been worth the try. Even sleeping in the bus station could not be as bad as this.

The woman with the cigarette gives me her hand to shake. It is like a bunch of dry sticks. I think that the hand will catch fire any second.

"Just don't double cross me," she says. "By the way, name's Gloria. My husband is Jim. You'll meet him tomorrow."

Brandy pokes me then. I know this is a signal, but for what? I poke her back.

"Later," she whispers.

Gloria has the ears of a fox. "What's that?"

"She wants ta use the bathroom. I told her, 'later.'"

Gloria steps closer. She looks at me, from my hair down to my shoes, like Daat examines the horses when there is an auction. She misses only my teeth.

"The last thing I need around here is trouble. You're not going to be trouble, are you?"

"I want no trouble."

"Okay, then," she says to Brandy. "Show her the ropes."

Brandy leaves all the bags by the door and tells me to follow.

The ropes and my new job are the same thing, Brandy explains. She flips a tiny knob on the wall, and a long hall is flooded with light. Again I am amazed, but this time I make no sound. I am not as simple as Mamm's cousins from Somerset County who believe that airplanes are less than the size of your smallest finger.

I follow Brandy to a room at the end of the hall. She makes another lamp light with just the flip of a knob and points to something. There is a terrible smell in the room; one of sickness, and also the toilet.

"There's the ropes," she whispers.

I see an old lady, small and bent like Grossmutter Hostetler the year before she died. This woman lies naked on a bed, without sheets or quilts to cover her. Her hands are tied to the bedposts with bandages.

I am not able to speak for a long time.

"Whattsa matter," Brandy says, "ain't ya ever seen a naked woman before?"

"What has she done? Why is she tied like this?" I have other questions too, like why does no one clean the mess, and why is she naked?

"She has old-timers disease," Brandy says.

"Old-timers? I have not heard of this disease."

"Maybe you Aye-mish don't get it then, but I hear about it all the time. Anyway, your job is ta look after her. Ya know, clean that shit off the bed. Feed her when it's time. That kinda thing. Oh, and give her her medicine. She takes tons of pills, and it ain't easy getting her to swallow them. Sometimes she spits them right back up in your face." Brandy laughs. "So, ya think ya can handle it?"

I look at the woman lying on the bed. Her head is almost bald, her stomach round. She reminds me of a baby robin that has fallen from the nest. How can I not agree to help her?

"Who is she?"

"Mrs. Scott, Gloria's mom."

"Why is there no cover?"

"She'll just get it dirty, that's why."

"Does she not get cold?"

Brandy shrugs. "She can't talk. I don't think she feels anything. Yah know, like an animal or something."

This I know is wrong, but there is no point in saying this to Brandy. "Where is there a blanket to put over her? I do not mind washing it."

Brandy yawns. "Forget about it for tonight. She's sleeping fine, can't ya see? Come on, let's go to bed."

"You go. I cannot leave her like this."

"Ya better. Jim will be pissed if you wake him up."

"Who is Jim?"

"Gloria's husband. Ya ain't met him yet, and believe me, ya don't want ta be anywhere near him when he's pissed."

"Brandy, just one blanket, a sheet even—"

"Ya don't get it, Aggie, do ya? It ain't your job ta be a hero." She pinches my arm to make me follow.

She pulls me back to a room next door. This time I watch how she makes the light. It is very simple—just flip the knob. I do not think it matters which direction.

"Welcome to the Ritz," Brandy whispers, and laughs.

Perhaps there are crackers in the room, but I do not see them. I see one small bed, a dresser, and clothes piled everywhere. On the floor even. And there are many pairs of shoes. Back home I have only five pegs on the wall. From one peg hangs my Sunday dress, from two pegs hang my four weekday dresses, two on each, from one peg hang my aprons, and the fifth peg is only for bonnets. I have two pairs of shoes, and the ones that are not on my feet are under the bed. I too have a small dresser, but it holds only stockings and the personal garments for under my skirt.

Brandy pulls me inside and closes the door. "So what do ya think?"

"It is *strubbly*."

"What the hell does that mean?"

"It is messy."

"Ya, so what? I'm a working girl. I gotta attend to the important things in life." Brandy shoves a pile of clothes and shoes from the bed to the floor. "Well, let's hit the sack." Brandy has already removed her black top, the one with no sleeves, and now she takes off the black pants. Then she removes the undergarments, like there is nobody in the room but her and God. Although one should not be so bold even in front of God if you ask me. I try not to look in her direction, but to look only everywhere else is too obvious. Therefore, I cannot help but see that there is no place Brandy has not pierced with the rings.

"Whatcha standing there for?" she says.

"I will not be naked."

"So, sleep in your bra and panties."

This I cannot do either. The garment for under my skirt is homemade, but I am not ashamed of that. What stops me is that I do not wear the English brassiere. Mennonites wear this, and I have heard that some Amish do, but the women in my church do not. This clothing, which is designed to raise and make the breasts more visible, leads to *Hochmut*. Pride.

"I will sleep in my dress," I say.

"Don't be silly. Hey, you're embarrassed, ain't ya?" Brandy pulls a shirt from a pile on the floor and throws it at me. It is what the English call a T-shirt. This one is long and comes almost to the knees. "There! But don't think for a minute that ya turn me on, 'cause ya don't. I don't swing that way."

Even though I do not understand exactly what Brandy says, I understand enough to know what she means. I do not "swing" that way either. Two years ago Benjamin Stucky and Jacob Rensberger were caught swinging in the loft of the Stucky barn. Jacob repented of his sin, but Benjamin would not. Today, it is said, Benjamin swings in San Francisco, and that he is an Episcopalian.

I put on Brandy's T-shirt and crawl into the bed. It smells of perfume and stale food. Maybe cheese. Brandy crawls in as well. Since she does not swing, I do not worry. Soon her breath tells me that she is asleep. I wait until she is snoring like Daat when he has had too much to eat, and then I get very quietly from the bed.

There now comes moonlight through the windows

and I do not even have to turn the knob in Mrs. Scott's room. I have with me many clothes from Brandy's floor. I clean the old woman and the bed as best as I can. There is much smell, and I want to vomit, but I do not have a choice. Although I must turn her over, and pull the clothes on over her head, she does not wake.

Yet even with the clothes Mrs. Scott shakes, so I lie on the bed next to her and put my arms around her, like a mother might do to a child. Like Mamm held me the night of the fire.

When I fall asleep I do not dream of the fire, or even of Mamm. I dream of Bridgett Monroe. She was holding in her hand a large tablet of paper and a box of colored pencils. The tablet had a pink cover and a border of flowers. The pencils were in a bright yellow box.

"They're for you," she said.

I shook my head. I knew it was wrong to accept things from strangers, especially English tourists. But my eyes, I am sure, were as big and round as the mill wheel on Crowder's Creek.

"Go ahead, they won't bite you."

"No, thank you."

"You can hide them in the barn, Anna. Maybe in the hayloft. Nobody needs to know."

I shook my head harder. "No, thank you."

"Very well." Bridgett turned and started toward her car.

"Please!"

Bridgett Monroe turned again and her eyes were smiling. "It's not a sin, Anna, I promise."

Where was the harm? I was not yet baptized; I had not yet promised to obey the Ordnung. Besides, as the English woman said, no one needed to know.

I grabbed the tablet and the pencils. I held them close to my chest and smelled the sweet scent of paper and wood. I felt the possibilities.

"Next time I stop by, I want to see some pictures. Draw me some pretty pictures."

"What shall I draw?"

"Whatever you see. Whatever calls to your heart."

I nodded. When the English woman drove away I sneaked into the barn, and in the hayloft, in the very spot where the barn cat had kittens that spring, I hid the tablet and pencils. When Bridgett Monroe returned, I would have a surprise for her.

CHAPTER

7

I wake before the first light, as is my custom. Mrs. Scott no longer shivers. Her breath is sour, like that of a pig, but it is soft and regular. I look up and see there is someone standing in the doorway.

"Ach!" I sit and stretch Brandy's T-shirt so that it covers my bare legs.

It is a man, not so old as Daat, but older than my brother Elam. He is also a half-naked man, wearing only the sweatpants the English like so much. Why the English must always show flesh, is a riddle to which only God and the Devil know the answer.

"Well now, this is very interesting," the man says. "Who are you?"

"Anna Hostetler. Who are you?"

"Jim."

"So you are the grandson?"

"Son."

"Then the other woman, Gloria, is your—"

"My wife. Okay, Anna Horsetetler, now that I know your name—"

"It is Hostetler, not Horsetetler."

It is still too dark for me to see the color of his eyes, but they shine like a cat's. "Now tell me what the hell you're doing in my mother's bed."

"I keep her warm."

He watches me, and I say no more. I feel like a mouse, or a bird, and that he will jump on me if I move.

"Where is Brandy?" he asks after many minutes.

"She sleeps in her own bed."

"Figures." He shakes his head. "So, your name is Anna Hostetler, and you're keeping my mother warm, but what the hell are you doing in my house in the first place?"

"She is my ropes."

Again he watches me, but says nothing.

"It is my job to take care of her," I explain. The man who is half naked and has bright eyes, is not right in the head like Isaac Redenbacker.

"You're for real, aren't you?" he finally says.

It is best to ignore such a man. It is enough that God loves them; we don't need to understand.

"You're a foreigner, aren't you? German?"

"Yah, German." It is more true that I am Swiss. Swiss-German. Although my people have been in this country three hundred years, we use German in our church, and speak the dialect, which is like German, at home.

"You been in this country long?"

"Yah, three-hundred years."

"Funny, but you don't look that old."

Always I must explain to this man. "I am twenty-three. It is my descendants who are here that long."

"That would be your ancestors."

I repeat the word to myself. I have been to eight grades of school, but there is much to learn about this English.

He comes into the room. I look to see that there is a window behind me. Perhaps it is locked—I have heard that the English do such things. But I am a fast runner, and if he comes far enough from the door, I can surely get around him.

"Well," he says, "if you're going to do your ropes, you need to give her a bath."

"A bath?"

"You do bathe in Germany, don't you?"

"Yah, we bathe." In Heaven we bathe every Saturday night. It is my job to heat the water in the kettles on the stove and pour them in the cast-iron tub that was Great Grossmutter Ellie Hostetler's wedding present from her parents Jonathan and Lydia Mast. Four kettles of hot water, three of cold. Daat bathes first, then Mamm. When it is my turn I add another kettle of hot water. But I have used the toilet in the Scott house and have seen another kind of tub, and there is no stove upon which to heat the water.

"Good," he says. "You go start the water, and I'll carry her in there."

"You start the water, please, and I will carry."

He smiles. "Sure you're up to it?"

"Yah," I say, but it is only a guess. The English speak always in riddles. If it is my strength he wants to know, then I have answered correctly. Mamm drives the hay wagon, Daat throws the bales up to me, but is my job—my ropes—to stack the bales. Sometimes I must stack them as high as Daat must throw them. I have no fear that I cannot carry Mrs. Scott. Even Mamm, who is thin like Gloria, could do the same.

"I'll holler when it's ready," he says.

Even Isaac Redenbacher is more right in the head.

Mrs. Scott does not wake when I pick her up. She weighs less than a bale of hay I think. Her sour breath is soft on my arm.

I forget I am wearing just the T-shirt that comes to the knees. I remember only when I see the man with no shirt. He bends over the tub and turns a knob.

"This should be the right temperature."

"And the other knob?"

He smiles. "The cold water. And this," he touches a third, "is for the shower."

"Shower?"

"Don't tell me that you Germans don't have showers."

I shrug. It is my best answer.

Bright eyes shows me what this shower is. He

shows me how to "flush" the toilet, and I am
embarrassed that in the night I used it, but did not
flush. How was I to know? The toilet at the bus
station does not need this flush.

"You're not really from Germany, are you?"

"I am from Heaven."

He stares again. I am thinking this is very rude, but
then he smiles.

"You certainly look like an angel."

"Heaven, Pennsylvania. I am—I was—Amish."

"You're serious?"

"I do not pretend."

The eyes grow more bright. "No, I can see that you
don't. Well, if you have any more questions, just
holler."

Already I have a question. "What is this holler?"

He laughs. I see that his teeth are very straight and
white. I look away from his face, to his chest, and
then his arms. There is less flesh on this man than on
one of Mamm's scarecrows. He could not do the work
of even a very small Amish boy, I think.

"Just ask," he says. "That's what it means."

I nod. I will remember this word holler. My pride is
great, but I cannot help but know that I have a quick
mind.

"Well," he says, "if you think you've got it under
control, I'll let you do your job."

He leaves the room and I put Mrs. Scott slowly into
the water. I lean her against one end of the tub, so
that only her head is above the water. I balance her so
that she does not slide under. There comes now a
smile to her face, and suddenly her eyes open wide.

I jump back, and hit my arm against the toilet.
"Mrs. Scott! You are awake."

She does not answer. The open eyes look, but they
do not see. They are the eyes of an animal that
appears to be as intelligent as a human, but is not.
They are the eyes of a goat.

"Mrs. Scott, do you hear me?"

She has no words. The goat eyes say nothing.

"Mrs. Scott, I am giving you a bath, so that you feel clean, yah?" Like a mother talking to a baby, that is how I am.

I tell her everything as I do it. "Now I wash your arms," I say. "Now your face." I must close her eyes with my hand when it is time to wash the hair. Through all this she makes no complaint.

I am washing Mrs. Scott's hair when Brandy comes into the bathing room without knocking. She wears only a T-shirt, one that does not even cover her most private area. I think at first she does not see me, because she goes straight to the toilet and does her business.

While she is still on the toilet she speaks to me. "I woulda done that, ya know, if ya woulda waked me."

"I do not mind."

"Just because you're taking over my job, doesn't mean ya gotta try and make me look bad."

"Brandy, this I do not try to do."

"Duh. I keep forgetting you're Aye-mish. You're like perfect, right?"

"No!" Only God is perfect.

"And who said ya could use my clothes on her?" She points with her chin to Mrs. Scott. "Somebody's gotta wash them things now, and it ain't gonna be me."

"I will wash them, Brandy." I pray that I do not have to wash them at a laundromat.

"Well, just so ya know, it sure as hell ain't gonna do ya any good to put the moves on Jim."

"Jim?"

"Yeah, first of all, he ain't interested. And second, Gloria will smack the shit out of ya. And third, ya just better leave him alone." Brandy sounds like she too wants to hit me.

"Brandy, perhaps I am not right for this job." It causes my heart pain to say this. I have the address of Bridgett Monroe, but she has not answered my letters for two years. I do not have her telephone number. If I leave this house I will have to go to this WYCA. Yesterday, I was willing to do this. Even eager. Today it brings me comfort to bathe Mrs. Scott. And the man with the bright eyes—ach, he brings me comfort too.

Brandy makes the flush and jumps up. "No, ya can't back out on me now, Anna. Ya gotta stay."

"But you are angry, Brandy."

"I swear I'm not. Sometimes I just overact. And don't ya worry about Gloria. Which isn't ta say ya should mess around with her husband. Comprendé?"

"Always the riddles," I say.

"It's Mexican I think. It means, do ya understand?"

"Yah. You do not want me to go."

"That's right, 'cause otherwise I gotta stay, and that's the last thing I wanna do."

"I will stay," I say quickly. I am much relieved.

"Good. Hey, Aggie. I was thinking. After ya get done with that, and feeding her, ya might want to take a shower yourself. Then, if ya want, I can borrow Gloria's car and we can run over to Waterworks and get ya some new clothes."

"Waterworks?"

"It's like a shopping center on the other side of the river. Or we can run all the way down to Monroeville Mall, if ya wanna."

This, I think is also a store, but I do not want to ask. I want very much to buy some clothes, English clothes, even the brassiere, but I am afraid for Brandy's new job.

"Do you not have to work today, Brandy?"

"Yeah, but I called in already. They said one day wasn't gonna make any difference. But I gotta start tomorrow. So, ya up to it?"

"But who will care for Mrs. Scott?"

"Who do ya think did when I was gone? Gloria, that's who. The old lady's her mom. Besides—"

"Jim said she was his mother."

She glares at me. "He was yanking your chain,

Aggie."

I try to think of the right thing to say, but no words will come, except for Dummkopf.

"Geez, Aggie, don't ya understand anything? He was jerking ya around. Ya know, joking or something. Or maybe ya just plain didn't understand. Ya ain't the brightest bulb in the chandelier, ya know?"

"Yah, perhaps I do not understand."

She nods. "Now where was I, before ya so rudely interrupted me?"

"Clothes—"

"Yeah, ya can't be running around here with no clothes on, can ya?"

It is settled then. After I am done with my chores, and have bathed, Brandy will take me shopping. She will turn me into an English woman.

I take the shower. It is my first. The warm water runs down my body like summer rain, but now my body is bare, not just my hands and face. It is like sin, which is not sin. I want to stay in the shower until the water is gone, until the well runs dry. But then Gloria will be angry, and this is something I do not want on my first day.

Soon I will be dressed like an English woman, like Bridgett Monroe, although the pants I will not wear. I think of Bridgett. What will she say when she sees me? Perhaps she will be as surprised as that day I showed her the tablet full of pictures.

It was a day I thought would never come. I had spent many hours in the hayloft, which was also my hiding place, drawing on the tablet. Some of the pictures pleased me greatly, some did not. I was anxious to see what the tourist in the fancy car thought. I certainly didn't expect it would take Bridgette Monroe an entire year to return.

Mamm had much work to do in the vegetable garden, and with helping Daat in the fields. Now that I was eight, the quilt fence was my job. I was still not to speak to the English about anything other than the quilts, unless they asked honest questions about our faith. We did not try to make converts like the Baptists, or even the Mennonites, so the conversation was only for the sake of politeness.

It was a sin for me to pray that Bridgette Monroe's fancy car would drive down Hershberger Road like Elijah's chariot, but I was a girl of many sins. What difference did one more make? I prayed hard for it to happen, and it did. This I could hardly believe, especially since most of my other prayers, good prayers, were never answered.

"You look like you're seeing a ghost," Bridgette Monroe said. She was driving a different car, so at first I did not recognize her.

"Bridgett Monroe?" I asked, still not quite sure this was the same woman.

She laughed. "The one and only. Good for you, Anna Hostetler. You haven't forgotten my name. Do you remember our secret?"

I nodded.

"Will you show it to me?"

I turned to look for Mamm. She was behind the house in the vegetable garden, and would not see me if I made a wide circle to the barn. Daat was on the other side of Heaven attending a horse auction, and we did not expect him home until supper.

I nodded again. Then I remembered the quilts. What was to stop Bridgette Monroe from putting all of Mamm's quilts in her fancy car and driving off? This I dared not ask, but Bridgett knew what I was thinking.

"Don't worry, I'm not going anywhere with your quilts, and I'll make sure nobody else does either."

I ran to the barn, and back again. My heart was pounding, but not from the running. I had never known such excitement. I was afraid too. The English woman might be angry if she thought I had wasted the beautiful white pages with my silly pictures. I held the tablet tightly in my hands.

"Don't be shy," Bridgett said and took the book before I could change my mind.

She looked at every page carefully. Some pages she looked at twice. When she was through, she frowned.

"Anna, did anyone help you with these pictures?"

I shook my head.

"Are you sure?"

I nodded.

Bridgett Monroe put the book in the back seat of her car. Then she took my hand in hers. Her fingers were as soft as kitten fur and smelled of rose petals.

"Anna, please go get your mother. There is something very important I must tell her."

CHAPTER

8

I think Brandy is a terrible driver. There are many hills in the area and the road curves like a horse's belly. Brandy does not make slow at the curves, and she does not stop at the signs that say we must. The lights that hang above the streets have three colors, and for the red one, Brandy does stop. The green one, she says, means "go." The yellow one, "step on it."

She takes me to Monroeville Mall. We must get on something called the Parkway, which is like the Turnpike, she says, but there are no tolls to pay. We pass a strange and wonderful white building which Brandy calls the Ice-cream Palace. Is it really made of ice-cream, I ask? Brandy laughs and says it is some kind of temple. Hindu, she thinks. This I think she makes up, because even I know that Hindus live in Africa, where the Mennonites have many missionaries.

I am thinking Monroeville Mall is a street of shops, but it is a city, bigger even than Heaven. The air inside is cool and there is music all around. The shops have strange names and contain many curious things, but the people I find even more interesting. Some have spikes for hair and dress like Brandy, but there are many fashions to be seen. I wear my Amish dress, the one with no sleeves, but no one, not even the children, looks my way.

Brandy grabs my hand and pulls me into a store called the Gap. I must buy jeans, she says, and tank tops. She leads me to a table where there are piles of jeans in many sizes.

"Here," she says, and holds up a pair she thinks will fit.

"But Brandy, it is dirty." I do not tell her that I have already decided I will not wear even clean jeans.

Brandy laughs. "It ain't dirty, Aggie. It's supposed to look like that."

"I do not like them."

"Then try these. They're cut extra low. I wouldn't mind getting a pair of these myself."

"Brandy, it is the skirts I want to wear, yah?"

"No problemo." She takes me to a bar from which hang many skirts.

I hold one against my legs, and even this embarrasses me. "They are much too short."

"Geez, Aggie, ya want old lady clothes, don't ya?"

We visit many more stores of Brandy's choosing, but I find what I want only at Penney's. The clothes do not cost pennies, but many dollars, even more than the clothes at Wal-Mart. I take two dresses, two skirts, and three blouses to the lady who sells. I have with me two night dresses—one for me, one for Mrs. Scott—three brassieres and five of the undergarments Brandy calls panties. I will not try on the brassieres even though Brandy insists I must. She and I look to be almost exactly the same size, and I am sure my numbers will be the same as hers.

"Will that be cash or charge?" the selling lady asks.

"I will pay with money," I say.

Brandy laughs. "She don't have a credit card."

The selling lady gives Brandy a hard look, but smiles at me. "Would you like to open a charge account with us? Takes only a minute."

"Go on," Brandy says.

I shake my head. I have heard much of this English business with the credit cards. Daat says it is a sickness, like gambling, but worse. With the credit card you always lose.

"It will make a real American outta ya, Aggie. Everybody's got one. Hell, I've got so many, I've lost count."

The selling lady still smiles. "You'll get ten percent off just for opening the account."

"I will pay only with money."

"That will be three-twenty-seven, fifty-nine," the selling lady says, but she no longer smiles.

I reach into the quilt sack and remove the brown envelope. The Bible and the cardboard tube I have left at Gloria's house, but the sack I have always with me. I start to count.

"Here is one hundred dollars," I say. "And—" I stop. There are only six large bills in the envelope when there should be nine. I look in the sack but find nothing.

"Miss, there are people waiting."

"Yeah, pay up," Brandy says. "I wanna get me something ta eat at the food court."

I stand with my feet far apart, like a calf does when it wants to nurse, but must be pushed aside for the milking. "Brandy, I have not all the money."

"Ya have enough for these clothes, don'tcha?"

"This is true, but I—"

"Hey, maybe ya dropped it somewhere." Brandy looks quickly at the floor. "I hate ta tell ya this, Aggie, but ya ain't gonna find it if that's the case. Finders keepers, ya know?"

The seller taps her fingers on the counter. "Lady, please pay, or I'm going to have to wait on someone else."

"There was more than nine hundred dollars in the envelope," I say, and give her the money. I do not care if everyone around can hear. I am feeling in my stomach that Brandy has the missing bills.

Brandy stamps her foot. "I don't have ta take this, ya know?"

I look straight ahead at the selling lady. "I did not drop the money."

"Are ya accusing me of stealing?"

"I did not lose it."

"Then the hell with ya," Brandy says. She pushes past the people who are waiting and disappears behind a rack of clothes.

I get my change from the selling lady and my bag of new clothes. I put the quilt sack carefully in with the clothes, and then look for Brandy. She is not to be seen. I look for her all over the store, but with no success. Several times I ask the seller if she has seen my friend, and always the answer is the same.

Then the seller becomes angry and says that if I do not stop making a bother, she will call security. I do not know what to do except leave the shop and go back into the mall. There is a bench near the door. I sit on this and pray. If God answers the prayers of Mennonites, and even Presbyterians, there is a chance he will hear the prayers of a girl who used to be Amish. Even if leaving the church was her own fault.

I pray with my hands folded and my head bowed. I pray in German, which is the language of the Bible, and which, Mamm says, God knows the best.

When I am through praying I open my eyes to see if God has sent Brandy. He has not. But there is a man standing in front of me who is very tall and has the face of an angel.

"Hi," he says. "I was wondering if I could be of some help."

Angels are supposed to have wings, which this man does not. But his shoulders are broad, and if he had wings, they could certainly be large enough for him to fly.

"I have lost my friend," I say. In Heaven I would never have this conversation with an English man who is alone.

"Yes, I know. I was behind the two of you at the sales counter."

"Yah?" I do not remember this man, only the missing money and Brandy's anger.

"I don't normally shop in the women's department, but it's my sister's birthday next week."

I smile and nod because I think this is a nice thing this man is doing. My brother Elam would never buy me a gift, not even from the Wal-Mart.

"You want to see what I bought for her?" He does not wait for my answer but opens the bag. From it he takes a sweater that is the color of Mamm's periwinkles. "I heard her say she needed a new cardigan, and I didn't know if I could find one in July. Fortunately, the retail business keeps getting further and further ahead of itself. This, I think, is next spring's model." He laughs and he puts the sweater back in its bag. "Well, I guess we still haven't solved the problem of your missing friend. Have you tried having her paged?"

"Paged?"

"They announce her name over the store's intercom. If that doesn't work, you could ask the person at information desk out here in the mall to do the same."

I look at him with the eyes of a goat, the eyes of Mrs. Scott, Gloria's mother. The angel with no wings is quick to understand.

"I can see that you're new in town. Where from? Switzerland?"

"Yah!"

"Thought so. My sister dragged me to Europe once on vacation—one of those seven day whirlwind things. You know, if it's Tuesday, it must be Belgium? Anyway, Zurich was one of the stops. Can't remember much except that it was a beautiful city, clean as a whistle, and everything ran like clockwork, but—and I hope you don't mind me saying this—the prices were a bit steep."

Already now, I am feeling guilty. My people are from Canton Bern, but it is three hundred years that they are in this country. To not share this is a lie.

"I am not recently from Switzerland," I say. "I am

from Heaven."

"Yes, I can see that."

"You can?"

"Well," he says, "you look like an angel to me."

I think maybe he has read my mind and I feel my face get hot. "Heaven is in Pennsylvania. I am—I mean I was—an Amish woman."

"You're serious?"

"I do not joke."

This brings a smile to his face. "In that case, I'll help you page your friend Miss—uh—Miss—"

"Hostetler." My name is Anna Hostetler."

"Landon Frasier," he says. "Just think Michael Landon and Brandon Frasier You know, the actors."

These names mean nothing to me. "I do not go to movies, Mr. Frasier."

"Then just think of me as another guy with two first names." He put the bag with the sweater under his arm, and rubbed his hands together. "Now, let's go see if we can page your friend, shall we?"

I do not know why, but I trust this man with two first names, even though the page does us no good. After perhaps an hour of waiting, Landon Frasier rubs his hands together again. It is a habit I am beginning to like.

"I sure hope you weren't counting on her for a ride."

"But I was."

He looks at his watch. "If you give me a minute to make a call, I can give you a lift."

"I do not need a lift, Mr. Frasier. I need a ride."

He smiles again. "I can give you a ride—right now, in fact. Where do you need to go?"

"Verona."

"No sweat. What's the address?"

This I do not know. Only that it is at the top of the hill, and has many large bushes in the yard. I do not even know Jim and Gloria's last name. Only the name Scott, which is that of Gloria's mother. The name of

Otto Goldschmidt, I do remember, because it is German.

"It is the house of Otto Goldschmidt," I say. Each new lie is easier than the last.

"Well then, what are we waiting for?" Landon Frasier picks up my bag. He tries to pick up my sack too, but I will not let him.

"You know this Mr. Goldschmidt?" I ask.

"No." Everything he says is with a smile. "Is that where you're staying?"

"Yah."

"Which street does he live on?"

My face burns more hot. "I do not know."

"No problem," he says. "When I make my call I can find out."

He goes to the wall of telephones and looks in a big book. Then he makes the call. Then another. When he returns he says that it will be no problem to find Otto Goldschmidt's house. His name was in that book.

I do not know if I should trust such a man, but then I have no choice. I follow him to his car. He says that I must let him be a gentleman and open the door. When I sit he says that I must put on the seat belt. That this is the law. This is not something Brandy made me do, and I am not sure if this is so. I do not like this belt, which is tight across my chest, but I do what I am told.

Landon Frasier knows a shortcut to Verona, he says, and I think maybe it does take less time. But I am not sure if it is the right way, because everywhere there are tall hills covered with houses, but I do not the see the ice-cream palace of the Hindus, and I do not see the river.

"Where is the river?"

"Down there, through the trees. We took a back way."

I see a small piece of the river and then we are climbing the steep hill on which Mr. Goldschmidt lives. Just when I begin to relax, we are at the house.

The big telephone book, I am thinking, must tell one
many things.

"Well," Landon Frasier says, "how's that for
curbside service?"

"Thank you." It is what I have planned to say, even
though he asks now a riddle.

He takes a small piece of paper from his money
holder. "Here's my card. That's my home address and
number. If you need a ride again, just holler."

"Yah, I will holler."

I know the way to Jim and Gloria's house is straight
up the hill. But I take only a few steps and the door of
Otto Goldschmidt's house opens.

"You," he shouts, "come here."

I look around. I am the only one in the street.

"Yes, you. Come here a minute."

I remember Brandy's words. He is not a man I want
to mess with. This, I think, means I do not want to
make *strubbly* his yard by throwing papers and
bottles, like the English do on the roads around
Heaven. There is no reason not to be polite, even if
the man spoke harsh to me the night before. I edge up
the short walkway that goes from the street.

Otto Goldschmidt sticks his hand out for me to
shake and begins speaking at once. "Sorry about last
night. I was having another rough one—insomnia. But
you really shouldn't be hanging around with that
crowd up there." He points up the hill at Gloria and
Jim's house.

"That is where I stay."

"You family or something?"

I do not owe this man an explanation—even a
simple country girl like me knows that—but I must
always show respect to the elders. "I take care now of
Mrs. Scott."

Otto Goldschmidt is younger than Grossdawdi
Hostetler, but older than Daat. His head is bald and

smooth, like a giant egg. His lips are bright, and very pink for a man. They remind me of the skin on a turkey's neck. Mr. Goldschmidt's neck I do not see, because even though the day is very warm, he wears around it a scarf, such as a lady would wear.

"How's she doing?" he asks.

"I think not so well." Already I regret saying this, for it is not my place to comment on the business of others.

"That's a shame," he says. "She's the only good apple in that barrel, if you ask me. The rest of them are bad news."

I do not know what to say.

"Hey, where are my manners? Name's Otto Goldschmidt."

"My name is Anna Hostetler." Once more, I do not know why I say what does not need to be said. After all, I will not see this man again.

"Anna, I can't help noticing your accent. Are you an au pair?"

"I belong to no church now," I say, "but I am still a Christian."

I see that he tries not to smile. "You're an exchange student, right?"

"No, I am not a student."

"But you are from overseas."

The Mennonites in Heaven have missionaries overseas, and they are all in Africa. I have heard much talk of this. Does this man with the lady's scarf think I am from Africa? Perhaps he wants to ask why the Amish do not have missionaries, but the Mennonites do. I will have to tell him what Bishop Yoder told me when I asked the same question. It is because we do not wish to force our way upon others.

"I am from Heaven. Heaven, Pennsylvania."

"Heaven? Now that's a new one to me. I've heard of Hernia and Intercourse, but never Heaven. Where abouts is it?"

"East of Harrisburg."

He nods. "Welcome to Verona."

I am thankful that he asks no more questions about my religion. I cannot wait until I sound like Brandy, and no one asks where I am from.

"You are German?" I ask.

He laughs. "No, only my name. My parents were German, but I was born in this house. Used to hate the name Otto, especially during the war, but I like it now. Kind of distinctive, don't you think?"

"Yah," I say. I do not know anyone named Otto, but I know many Goldschmidts.

"Anna, would you like to come inside? For a coffee, or something, I mean."

I am no longer afraid of Otto Goldschmidt, but to be alone with a strange man in a house, even an old man, this I cannot do. Also, I must hurry back to Mrs. Scott. Still, it would be nice to have another friend in Verona besides Brandy.

"I must return to work," I say, but my eyes say to invite me another time.

He nods again. In his eyes there is the look of man who knows much he will not tell.

"Watch your back," he says.

CHAPTER

9

I watched Mamm's back in the garden. I watched it straighten and bend, straighten and bend as she wound the young bean plants around the poles Daat planted in the soft, rich soil. In two months, maybe less, we would have all the string beans we could eat, and Mamm would preserve the rest. It would be my job then to break the beans into bite size pieces, while I waited for customers.

Mamm felt my eyes on her and turned. "Anna, what is it?"

"There is an English woman here to see you."

"What does she want?" There was just a hint of impatience in Mamm's voice. The fence of quilts was my job, and I was supposed to be old enough to take care of it without her help. Ten percent was all I was allowed to give as a discount for those who insisted, and Mamm had written the discounted price for each quilt on a special piece of paper that I kept under the money box.

I shrugged, which was the same as a lie. I did not know exactly what the English woman wanted, but I knew it had something to do with me.

Then Mamm noticed my empty hands. "Where is the money box?"

"On the table."

Mamm was older than most of my friends' mothers. She was thinner too. She had "the nerves" I once heard two of the other mothers say. I didn't know what "the nerves" were, but I suspected they had something to do with the reason Mamm's eyes were always moving, first here and then there, like a fly who knows it's about to be swatted. When Mamm's nerves acted up, she could go from happy to crying in a matter of seconds.

"Come," she said, and grabbed my wrist with fingers that were cold and hard as bands of iron, yet I felt that they would snap if I struggled at all.

I stumbled along behind Mamm, my heart filled with dread and excitement. When she saw it was *this* English woman, the metal bands tightened.

"What have you done, Anna?"

"Nothing, Mamm."

Mamm walked faster. I had to run to keep up.

"Yah," she said to the English woman, "how can I help?" The words were calm, but her hand on my wrist trembled.

Bridgett Monroe smiled. "Mrs. Hostetler, I would like to speak with you about your daughter."

"What is it you have to say?"

"Could we possibly speak alone?"

"Anna must stay."

Bridgett Monroe smiled at me then. "Very well," she said, and took the tablet from the front seat of her car. "Mrs. Hostetler, I'm sure you're aware that your daughter is very talented."

Mamm said nothing.

"Why, just look at this," Bridgett Monroe said, and began to turn the pages slowly. "Her ability to create what her eye sees is incredible. I've never seen such realism from a child this young." Bridgett Monroe paused to tap a drawing of Mamm's clothes line, upon which Monday's wash flapped in the breeze. "Even more remarkable than her ability to reproduce photographically, is her command of perspective. I have fourth-year students who couldn't do this."

Again Mamm said nothing.

"Mrs. Hostetler, you must be very proud of your daughter."

It was the worst thing the English woman could have said. The iron bands released me.

"Go to your room, Anna."

"But Mamm—"

"Go!"

I could tell by Mamm's voice that she was about to suffer again from the nerves. I started for the house, but slowed my steps when Bridgett Monroe spoke once more.

"Mrs. Hostetler, your child is a prodigy. A gift like hers happens only once in a million."

"She will not leave the faith, Mrs. Monroe."

I was so surprised that Mamm remembered our visitor's name, that what had just been said did not sink in right away.

"Nobody said anything about her leaving the faith, Mrs. Hostetler. She could develop her talent right here."

"That is not possible."

"Oh, I'm sure we could work something out. We could have some sort of correspondence arrangement, and I could come by periodically—"

"Please leave, Mrs. Monroe."

"Sure, all right. I understand."

"You will not take this child," Mamm said, her voice rising.

"But I don't want your child. I just want to—"

"Please!" It was too late. Mamm was having the nerves. Her voice rose until it resembled one of our Swiss yodels. Then it rose so high I could no longer hear her. Her mouth opened and shut like a baby robin begging its mother to be fed, but there was no sound. I turned to watch what happened next.

Bridgett Monroe looked at Mamm, then she looked at me. She looked at Mamm one last time, and quickly got into her big shiny car and drove away. It wasn't until much later that day that I realized Bridgett

Monroe had taken the tablet of my drawings with her.

Gloria shouts the moment she sees me. "Where the hell have you been?"

"Brandy took me to buy new clothes."

Gloria puts the cigarette she is smoking her in mouth, grabs the bags from Penney's with both hands, and dumps the clothes on the kitchen table. She must see everything, and how much each piece costs. Finally she grunts like one of Daat's brood sows.

"Why two nightgowns?"

"The white one is for me, the pink one is for Mrs. Scott."

"What the hell is that about? You think I can't provide for my own mother?"

"It is gift from me. That is all."

"Yeah, well it better not have been Brandy's money you spent."

"It was my own."

"Where is Brandy?"

"I do not know. She left me at the mall."

"Yeah? Well, the old lady needs you again. That was a hell of an idea you had dressing her up in Brandy's clothes. Now who's going to wash them?"

"I will."

Gloria knocks the ashes from her cigarette and some of them fall on my clothes. "If they don't come clean, you owe Brandy some of these."

It is not right that I should have to give Brandy my clothes because Gloria does not keep her mother properly covered. But that is another problem. Although I am afraid what Gloria might say, I have no choice but to tell her what must be done.

"Mrs. Scott needs diapers." I say this quietly, and with great respect. I do not want Gloria to get the nerves.

"Oh yeah? You know how much disposable diapers cost in adult sizes?"

"We can make cloth."

She knocks more ashes onto my clothes. "Outta what?"

"Old sheets, old towels. That is what we did for my Grossmutter."

Now she laughs. "Your what?"

"My father's mother."

"Why didn't you say so in the first place? Brandy was right, Aggie. You are a little on the strange side. I don't know if you're the right person to look after my ma, or not."

I say nothing, but neither do I look away.

"Okay," she says, "I think there's some old beach towels on the top shelf of the hallway closet. Last time we used them was a trip to Cedar Point—like that will ever happen again. Go ahead, take them. But you're washing them, you hear? And not in my washing machine either, but down at the Laundromat."

"Gloria—"

"Now what? I suppose you want diaper pins too. Well, you're going to have to settle for plain old safety pins. There's some in the sewing kit. That would be the cigar box on the middle shelf."

"Pins, yah. But I was going to say thank you."

"Thank you? For what?"

"For the diapers."

Now Gloria looks like she will have the nerves. She crushes the cigarette in a little bowl, then she pushes my new clothes to the floor.

"Look you little snot, don't you get all self-righteous with me. You haven't the slightest idea what I've been through with that bitch."

"She is your Mamm."

"Ha! Some mother she was! Never gave a damn about any of her kids. Always busy, always thinking of herself, when she wasn't hitting one or the other of us up the side of the head. You know what my fondest memory of her is?" Gloria does not wait for me to answer. "She was a party girl, you see. Stayed out all night drinking and slept with everything in pants, and thank God back then only men wore them. Drove my pap to an early grave. Literally. He dropped dead of a heart attack when he was only sixty-three.

"Pap was the kindest— never mind. I was about to tell you of my one good memory of Ma. My *only* good memory of Ma. She was getting ready for this really hot date. And it wasn't with Pap. Ma was all gussied up in this red dress cut so low you could practically see her navel, and she was wearing black fishnet hose. A whore outfit, Pap called it. And he was right. She even had this red feather boa to go with it. Anyway, Ma was being picked up by some of her girlfriends— she didn't dare invite the men she slept with back to the house—and she couldn't find her matching shoes. She sent me into the back of the closet to look for them. And if you think Brandy's room is a mess, well, you haven't seen a real one yet.

"Of course I had trouble finding them. The shoes, I mean. I thought Ma would be mad—the bitch had a temper shorter than a sparkler fuse—but for some reason she was in a good mood that day. She actually climbed into the closet with me. Either her girlfriends were late, or she was early getting dressed, because she told stories and we giggled. I had the best time I could remember, sitting there with Ma in the dark closest. Then when her friends did show up, she let me answer the door wearing the red high heels and feather boa."

Gloria picks up the crushed cigarette and then puts it back. For a long time she says nothing, just stares at the cigarette bowl.

I think she will not speak again, so I reach quietly for my clothes. But I am wrong. Gloria grabs my arm with fingers as cold as Mamm's.

"That ain't your run-of-the-mill sweet little old lady in there, you know, and what goes around, comes around. I just described the best day of my life. The *best*. Someday, when I think you can handle it, I'll tell you the worst." Then she lets go of my wrist.

I gather up my new clothes and hurry from the kitchen. Again Mrs. Scott is lying naked in the bed, and her hands are tied to the post. I look for the towels.

Mrs. Scott now wears a diaper. It has on it a picture of a fat naked lady sitting on an alligator. The words say "Crack Kills." I think this is the best place for this towel. And anyway, when I put the pink night dress on her, the diaper does not show.

I sit by the bed on a plastic chair and watch the old lady sleep. She does not look like someone who would hit her children up the side of the head, or anywhere else. This, I know, means nothing. Mose Miller was the biggest, strongest Amish man in Heaven, but one day his wife caught him wearing women's clothes. Because Mose was so big, and his wife small, they were not even her clothes, but clothes he had stolen from Alice Keims's clothesline. But unlike me, Mose repented of his sin, and remains one of the people. This incident is now of the past, and no one mentions it, except for Isaac Redenbacher, who is foolish in the head and cannot help himself.

To pass the time I tell Mrs. Scott stories of my family, the Hostetlers. I tell her about the day of the massacre, what happened after the cabin burned down and most of the family escaped through the trap door in the cellar floor. Perhaps it is wrong to tell such a woman this, how my five times great Grossmutter was stabbed in the heart and then scalped, because the Delaware did not like her and would not give her the honor of a tomahawk death. I do not know if Great Grossmutter hit her children up the side of the head, but I do know that she too suffered from the nerves, and once, long before the massacre, when the Indians had passed through asking for water, Great Grossmutter ran them off with a broom. There are those who say this is why the Indians attacked.

There is much more to tell, but Brandy comes now into the room. Always she is like a thunderstorm.

"Where the hell did ya disappear ta?" she asks.

I cannot believe this is the same Brandy. Now her hair is blue and in spikes. Her eyes are striped like a cat, or maybe a fish, except that these stripes are yellow and purple.

"Brandy, how can this be?"

"What? Ya didn't think I could get a ride."

"Your eyes."

"Oh, them's just contacts."

I know of this thing, contacts. Unser Satt Leit are not supposed to wear them because they are vain. Instead, if there is need, we wear glasses. In Heaven there are many from the outside who wear contacts, but none are striped. Verona holds many wonders.

"So," Brandy says, "ya ain't answered my question yet. Where'd ya go?"

"I went nowhere, Brandy, but to look for you."

"Yeah, well ya really pissed me off, accusing me like that. Besides, if ya really wanted ta find me, ya should have tried The Clip Joint, at the opposite end from the food court."

"I'm sorry, Brandy." This I say to the girl who I think has my money. It is not because I am such a good Christian, but because I want no more trouble.

"So how'd ya get home?"

"A man drove me."

"What? Ya let a stranger pick ya up?"

"He was very nice."

"Did he try ta put the moves on ya?"

Always the riddles. I can only shrug.

"The make! Did he grope ya? Stick his tongue in your mouth, that kinda thing?"

I shake my head. I know now what she means. In Heaven there were many boys, Amish boys, who tried to put the move on me. When Daniel Weaver turned sixteen and got his first buggy, he drove me all the way to the top of Hertzler Mountain. He said that in order for our courtship to continue, we must get to know each other better. By this he meant that I should show him my breasts. Of course I would not, so instead Daniel showed me something that belonged to him. This, I did not ask to see. At first I thought it was a chicken neck, but then it grew, and a chicken neck, once it is removed, does not grow.

"Ach!" I cried, and turned away.

But Daniel said he would not take me home unless I touched it. It was in December when this happened, and very cold, and I did not want to walk all the way down Hertzler Mountain. I had no choice then but to touch it, but I touched it only for a second. Daniel begged me to touch it some more, but I refused. He would not listen to me, so I got out of the buggy and walked all the way to the bottom of Hertlzer Mountain anyway. All the way down Daniel followed in his buggy and begged me to touch it again. Half way down the mountain it started to snow, and my church shoes, which were also my courting shoes, got very wet and shrank when I finally dried them near the stove. Mamm had a case of the nerves when that happened, but I never told her why I walked home that night.

"Well," Brandy says, "better luck next time."

"What?"

"Ya still a virgin, ain't ya, Aggie?"

"I am not married, Brandy."

"Ya are! Youse is a virgin."

"Leave the kid alone."

I see Gloria's husband, Jim, standing in the doorway.

CHAPTER

10

"This ain't none of your business," Brandy says.

"The hell it isn't."

I do not like this talk. I am not used to such words, but it is the anger in their voices that bothers me more. This place, with Brandy, Gloria and Jim, and even Mrs. Scott who hit her children, is not good for my soul. I must leave. Even returning to Heaven would be better than to stay here. But I do not have to return to Heaven, because I have another plan.

"Excuse me," I say, and try to walk from the room.

Brandy gets in my way. "Aggie, ya ain't going anywhere, 'cause we ain't done talking."

"I said, leave her alone, damn it."

Jim is as white as a pot of farmer's cheese and is shaking all over. He steps into the room, but then must grab the door to keep from falling.

"All right, all right," Brandy says and pushes past Jim. Then I hear the door to her bedroom slam.

"I'm sorry, Anna."

I look once more at Mrs. Scott. Perhaps Gloria was lying. Maybe the old lady with goat's eyes is as innocent as a baby, but still, she is not my responsibility. My responsibility now is to Anna.

"Yah, I am sorry too, but I must go."

"Please, Anna, you can't."

"I have no choice."

"But you do. If you go, who's going to take care of

my mother-in-law?"

"Ach, you said she was your mother!"

"You must have heard wrong."

"I did not hear wrong."

"Well, in any case, who's going to take care of her?"

"Maybe you should."

"This is not just an excuse, Anna, but I'm sick."

He looks sick, this I cannot deny. "Brandy is not sick," I say, "and neither is Gloria."

"You're absolutely right, Anna, they aren't sick. My wife isn't sick, not physically, but she has me to take care of—and well, as I'm sure you've heard, there is no love lost between her and my mother-in-law. I won't go into it, but this family has its share of problems. More than its share."

"And Brandy?"

His eyes move to the bed. "She's been trying to help, but Brandy is—well, Brandy. I'm afraid my daughter marches to her own beat."

"Your *daughter*?" I point at the bed. "This woman is Brandy's Grossmutter?"

"It's not that Brandy doesn't care." Jim has to hold the door now with both hands in order to stand. "Brandy's been her grandmother's sole caregiver for the last year and a half. It's gotten to be too much, that's all."

What am I to do? I cannot abandon an old woman who needs help, yet I cannot stay.

"What is your sickness?" I ask.

"I have AIDS."

There is nothing I can think to say.

"Do you know what that is, Anna?"

"Yah." Everyone in Heaven has heard about AIDS. First it was a disease of the homosexuals, but now it has spread to many English. I have heard even of an Amish boy in Indiana, one who was born with a blood disease and must have many transfusions, who now has the AIDS. But for most of unser Satt Leit, it is the English Disease.

"Anna, I would take care of her myself, but there are times when I can't even get out of bed."

"Then you must hire someone else."

"I wish that were an option. Gloria won't stand for it."

"Why?"

He sighs, or maybe it is pain, because now he must sit on the bed with Mrs. Scott. "Anna, please, just a few more days—until we can find somebody else. I'll speak to Brandy, tell her to back off a bit. And don't worry about Gloria. Her bark is worse than her bite."

The Bible tells of the Good Samaritan who helps a stranger, one of the anner Satt Leit, who is in need. I think maybe the Good Samaritan would not be so quick to help if he was in this house.

"Three days," I say, but it does not sound like my voice.

It is my second day in Verona and I must visit the grocery store. Gloria has given me twenty-five dollars, and with it I must buy bread, milk and cigarettes. Brandy has taken the car to her new job, Gloria says, so I must walk. The grocery store is called Giant Eagle, and it is at the bottom of the hill, and then I must turn right. Ten minutes is all it should take.

If it is only ten minutes, I think, then why does Gloria not walk there herself? I do not say this, because I am happy to be outside. In Heaven I am outside every day, and I can smell horses and hay, and the flowers in Mamm's garden. In Verona, except for my trip to the mall, I have been only in the house that smells of sickness and pain.

I wear my new English clothes to the store. My skirt is white, and my shoes, which are called sneakers, are also white. For the first time I wear a blouse that is pink, the color of harlots and vain women. It is also the color of the scarf Mr.

Goldschmidt wears today.

He is in the yard when I pass, and comes over to the street. "Hi, how's it going up there?"

I look at my new sneakers. The laces are pink too. Mine are the feet of a harlot as well.

Mr. Goldschmidt laughs. "That bad, eh?"

"I will leave the day after tomorrow."

"Oh? Then where will you go?"

"I have a friend in Pittsburgh." I am thinking of Bridgett Monroe, whose address I have memorized, although I have not received a letter from her in two years.

"That's nice. Which neighborhood?"

I am not sure what this neighborhood means. "It is Wentworth Lane."

"Ah, that's in Shadyside."

"Yah, Shadyside," I say. It is nice to know.

"Well, if it doesn't work out—I mean, if she's out of town or something—I could always rent you a room here."

"That is very nice, Mr. Goldschmidt, but that will not be necessary." This I will keep in my brain too.

"Please Anna, call me Otto. Can I give you a lift?"

I smile, since I know now what this lift means. "No thank you, Otto. I will walk. I go only to the Giant Eagle."

"Whew! That's a long way."

It has already taken me a few minutes to reach Ottos's house. "It is only ten minutes, yah?"

"If you're a galloping horse, which, you're obviously not. You sure I can't give you a ride?"

"I am sure." It is not because I think Otto Goldschmidt will try to make me touch him like Daniel Weaver, but because I truly want to walk. Otto, I am beginning to think, is more like Jacob Stoltzfus, my friend Sarah's husband. It has been said many times around the quilting frame that Jacob's eyes look first to the men, and then to the women. Sarah is now in her second year of marriage, and still there is no sign of a baby.

"Well, good luck," Otto says, "and be careful crossing Allegheny Boulevard."

I say goodbye to Otto Goldschmidt and walk down the hill. When I reach the boulevard I remember to turn right. I pass only two shops when I see there is a place that cuts hair. "Walk-ins Welcome," a cardboard sign says and I think maybe that means me. Since I have with me the cloth sack, I stop to ask. Fortunately there are no other customers.

A lady in a blue apron, a smock, I think it is called, tells me to take a seat. "So, what are you after? Just a trim, to get rid of those dead ends?"

"Please, cut off this much." I put my hands to my shoulders.

"You've got to be kidding."

"No."

"How long did it take you to grow that, if you don't mind me asking."

"It has never been cut."

She shakes her head. "I don't know if I can do it."

I pat the quilted bag which is in my lap. "I will pay."

"It's not the money, dear. Somehow it just doesn't seem right."

"But your hair is short."

"Yeah, but it's always been that way. Look, why don't you think about it for a few minutes? You know, have a seat by the window. There's plenty of magazines over on that table, and I could get you some coffee. It isn't the best in the world, I'll grant you that, but if you stir enough of that fake cream in, and plenty of sugar, it's drinkable."

"I would like only to have my hair cut."

She sighs. "Well, it's your hair I guess. But mind if I make a suggestion?"

"What do you suggest?"

"I could start slowly, say maybe three inches at a time. Give you a chance to change your mind before we've gone too far."

"Please, up to here." I pat my shoulders again.

"All right. But just one more suggestion."

"Yah?" My patience is no longer thick.

"You might consider donating the hair we cut off to Locks of Love. They make wigs out of it for cancer victims who've lost their hair."

"This I can do?" It pleases me to think that my hair, which has never been cut because it is my "crowning glory," but which in Heaven must always be covered, will be worn by another woman. An English woman who does not mind that her crowning glory is admired by all.

"Honey, this hair," she pulls it through her fingers, "heck, I wouldn't mind having it myself. It's natural, isn't it?"

"It is my own." There is no end to the silly questions the English ask.

"I mean the color."

"Yah."

"Such a beautiful shade of pale gold," she says and makes the first cut.

I close my eyes. When the act is done I look in the mirror for the first time. I am no longer Anna Hostetler from Heaven; now I am Anne of Verona.

"What do you think?" the cutter asks. "Do you like it?"

"Yah, it is good." What I think is that the cutting of my hair is like a second baptism. Once I was Amish, now I am English.

She tells me how much to pay. I think it is a lot of money, but I do not argue. Still, she does not seem satisfied.

"Too broke for a tip?" she says. It is the voice of someone who tries to make a joke, but is not happy."

"Tip?"

"Of course that's up to you. But two dollars is what I generally get on haircuts."

I give her three dollars.

Then she smiles. "So, who gets to see the new

hairdo first? Your boyfriend, I bet. Am I right?"

"I have no boyfriend. I go now only to the Giant
Eagle. It is that way, yah?" I point to the right.

"Yes, if you want to go all the way into Oakmont.
The Giant Eagle in Verona is much closer."

"It is to the left?"

"Straight down Allegheny River Boulevard. You
can't miss it."

My head feels so light I think I will float. Although it
is vain, I look at my reflection in every shop window I
pass. Then I look quickly away. Who is the girl in the
English clothes with the English hair, but who has
still in her half of an Amish heart?

I cross Allegheny River Boulevard safely where
there is a stoplight. By now I know that one must
cross when the light is red. I keep walking until the
stores end, and then there is a row of trees, and finally
the shopping center with the Giant Eagle. I must walk
very fast now to make up for the time it took to cut
my hair. Even without a haircut, it is not a ten minute
walk from Brandy's house.

A car pulls beside me and a young man puts down
the window to ask me directions He wears glasses to
protect his eyes from the sun, and I see only my face
in them.

"Hey, beautiful. Want a ride?"

"No thank you."

"I'll let you sit on my lap."

I walk faster.

"Hey, that was a joke. I'm only trying to be
friendly."

There is nothing for me to say.

"What's the matter? You think you're too good for
me?"

"I want only to shop. Please, leave me alone."

"Stuck up bitch," he says and drives very fast away,
so that the tires scream.

I have done nothing to make this man angry, so my eyes fill with tears. I stumble into a shopping basket on wheels. It is what the English in Heaven call a buggy, but it is not a real buggy like the ones Amish people ride in. I push the wire buggy in front of me, feeling like an English woman. If the man in the car drives by again, I will push the buggy in his direction.

Gloria says to buy milk and bread, but she does not say what kind. I have been to Pat's IGA in Heaven to buy spices for canning, and things like sugar and flour, but never to buy milk and bread. Daat has thirty dairy cows, and Mamm and I make our own bread. Now I see for the first time that there are fifteen, maybe twenty, different kinds of bread. There is even a bakery right inside the store. And the milk—no percent, one percent, two percent—there are enough choices to make my head spin, although I do not think there is a cow inside the store. For such shopping, I think, the English must train their children very early. That is why many small children ride in the wire buggies.

After much worry I choose a loaf of bread from the bakery. It is called pumpernickel and almost black, so I think it will have much flavor. I choose also the no percent milk because it has a pretty blue color I think Gloria will like.

Gloria says that I must buy Camels brand cigarettes with no filters. This she underlines two times. It does not matter, because I will not buy cigarettes.

Members of my congregation back in Heaven are not allowed to smoke, but I have seen Amish men from other churches do so. I know even that down around Lancaster there are Amish who grow tobacco on their farms. Bishop Yoder says that our bodies are temples of the Lord, and for this reason we must not smoke, or drink alcohol. This is not the reason I refuse to buy the cigarettes. I think they stink.

While I am walking across the parking lot the car comes by again. "Anna?" the driver says.

My people have been pacifists for five hundred years, but now I want to throw the black bread and blue milk against the car. I want to call this young man "bitch" as well. I have been in the world just two days, and already I think like the English.

"Go away," I say instead, but it is not the voice of a Christian.

"Anna, it's me—Landon."

"Ach!" I see now this is a different car. My face burns with shame.

"Anna, I can hardly believe it's you. Damn, but you look like a million bucks. When did this happen?"

"A million bucks?" Someday maybe I will write a book of English riddles.

"Well, not that you didn't look like a million bucks before, but hey, you know what I mean. That haircut really suits you. The clothes too."

I know now he wishes to compliment. "Thank you."

"Hey," Landon says, "you didn't walk all the way down here, did you?"

"Yah. That is how I got the haircut."

"You want a lift back up?"

I am happy to take this lift. The white sneakers rub now against my baby toes and it is painful. If I must walk back up the hill, the blue milk will turn into farmer's cheese before I reach the top.

"Yah, I will take the lift."

"Hop in."

Landon does not stop at Otto Goldschmidt's house. This is my fault because I do not remind him. He is telling me of a baseball game he will see with some pirates. How can this be, I wonder? But to tell the truth, it is also the smell of Landon that makes me forget. He smells of soap and flowers and fresh chopped wood, and I want to tell him he smells like a million bucks. Maybe even two million.

Somehow Landon knows to stop in front of Gloria's

house. Even I do not recognize it at first because there is a fancy car in the driveway. A silver car.

"Here you go," Landon says.

"Ach! This is someone else's house." It is a small lie, one that I can repent of later. It is nothing like the lies I was forced to tell Mamm.

"That's funny, I thought for sure you were staying here." Landon is smiling.

"I did not say that."

"Anna, these people you're staying with are bad news."

Always the riddles! The English I learned in school, the English I spoke at the Giant Eagle in Heaven, and the Wal-Mart too, it is not the English of Pittsburgh and Verona.

"Please," I say, and I cannot help the anger, "explain in words I understand. How is it you know I live here?"

"Anna, I've been keeping an eye out for you, for your sake. I don't mean to sound patronizing, but given your background, life in the big city isn't always what it seems."

I understand enough. "You think I am too stupid to take care of myself?"

"No, that's not what I meant. But see that Jaguar there?"

"I see no such animal. Now who is the stupid one?"

"That car, Anna. Whose do you think it is?"

"Perhaps my friends have visitors."

"Your friends?"

"Yah." I think of Brandy, who gave me a ride to the mall, even if she did take my money. And I think of Jim, who is kind.

"Well, Anna, maybe you need to give your new friends a little thought."

He does not say more, but waits for me to get out of the car. I take the bag of milk and bread and do as he wishes. But then I slam the door. Anne Hostetler is not stupid. Proud like the English, yah, but not a

Dummkopf.

Then I hurry up the driveway, because I too am anxious to see the owner of the silver leopard.

CHAPTER

11

"What the hell are you doing back already?" Gloria
stares at me. "And what the hell have you done to
your hair?"

"It is cut."

"I can see that. It looks like shit."

"Not to me."

"Ach!" I jump when I hear this. There is a young
man in the sitting room with Gloria. He is very
handsome, with dark curly hair and blue eyes. When
he smiles I see that his teeth are very white against
his skin.

"Sorry, didn't mean to scare you. Name's Mickey,
by the way." He offers me his hand to shake. It is
warm, and he squeezes hard.

"My name is Anne."

Gloria is smoking a cigarette and she coughs. "I
thought it was Anna."

"Now I am Anne."

"Well, Miss Anne, trot that milk on into the kitchen
before it sours. But first give me the cigarettes."

"I did not buy them."

"You better be kidding about that, because I'm
down to my last pack. My last five cigs as a matter of
fact."

"No cigarettes. Only bread and milk."

"Now what the hell am I supposed to do?"

"I will put the milk away," I say.

"Wait just one damn minute. You spent my cigarette money on your hair, didn't you?"

Mickey winks at me. "Gloria—"

His help is not needed. "It was my own money I spent."

"Then give me back mine."

I give her the money, but she tosses her head. "Show me the bread and milk."

This I am happy to do.

She takes the bread out of the bag. "What kind of shit is this? Nobody eats this crap except Polacks and Jews."

Mickey winks again. "Pumpernickel is my favorite, and I'm Irish."

This makes Gloria even angrier. She pulls the milk out of the bag. "What the hell is this supposed to mean? Skim milk! You must think I'm fat as a cow."

Gloria is almost as skinny as Mamm. Perhaps that is why they both suffer from the nerves.

"You are not fat as a cow."

"Yeah? Then how fat am I?"

"Hey, Gloria," Mickey says, "how about giving the kid a break?"

Gloria is still angry and throws the jug of milk at me. It is slippery, but I catch it. She throws the bread too. I try to catch it, but I drop the milk. I am very grateful that the plastic jug does not break.

"Put this shit away, and then go clean up my mother."

I walk to the kitchen and am surprised when Mickey follows. There is a door that swings, and when it closes for the last time, he takes the milk from me and puts it in the refrigerator. He looks at the bread and laughs.

"I hate this stuff," he says and squeezes the package so that it is flat in the middle.

Now Gloria will really be angry. I take the bread from him and try to make it again plump.

"Don't worry about her," Mickey says. "I'll make

her lay off you."

"There is no need." I know such a thing will not stop Gloria from feeling angry. She has the nerves.

He puts his hand lightly on my arm. "You're worried about retributions, aren't you?"

I move my arm away. "What is this retribution?"

He smiles, but it is not mocking. "You're foreign, aren't you?"

"I am from Pennsylvania, Mr—"

"Hanahan, but call me Mickey. What I meant was, you're originally from someplace overseas. My guess would be Sweden. Am I right?"

"You are wrong. My people come from Switzerland, but they have lived in this country three hundred years."

"No kidding."

"I do not joke."

He laughs. "You've got moxie, that's for sure."

Moxie? This sounds to me like a good name for a dog. I do not think that even Miss Kurtz, who teaches all of the eight grades in Heaven, would know this word. Again, because I am ignorant, I remain silent.

"And you're coy, too. I like that. Anne, I hope you don't think I'm coming on too strong here, but I'd like to see you sometime."

"What do you mean?" I say. But I know what he means, it is in his eyes. It is the same look that was in Daniel Weaver's eyes the night he asked me to show him my breasts. Now my face burns with shame because I would not mind so much showing Mickey my breasts, and him I have only just met. Bishop Yoder and the ministers have preached many sermons on this. Lust, they call it. They use even the English word so we will make no mistake when we rub sleeves with the world.

"I thought we might go clubbing."

The lust flees from my body. I cannot believe how violent the English are. Always they make war, and even among themselves there is much shooting. When the Delaware attacked on the night of September 20,

1750, my ancestor Jacob refused to let his sons defend
themselves. Now this Mickey Hanahan wants me to go
clubbing? What does he wish to club? Rats? Although
I have not seen any since my arrival, I have heard that
there are many in the big cities.

"Do you dance?" he asks, as if this clubbing is not
bad enough.

"Ach!"

The door to the outside opens and Brandy comes in.
Today both her hair and her clothes are pink. Her
mouth opens wide when she sees me.

"Hey babe," Mickey says to Brandy.

She makes a fist, all except for the middle finger,
and shows it to him. "What the hell is going on here?"

"Anne and I are just getting acquainted," he says.

"I bet ya are."

"It's not what you think."

"Ya don't know what I think, ya bastard. And her
name ain't Anne, it's Aggie."

I step back. I want now only to clean up Mrs. Scott,
and then to leave. This is a house of much sin and
unhappiness. Mamm and Daat were right about the
world, even though they were wrong about the gift
God gave me. I will find a way to live in the world
and not be a part of it.

"Where do ya think you're going?" Brandy is now
angry with me.

"I have work to do."

"Ya got that right, and your first job is to stay the
hell away from my man."

"I'm not your man, Brandy." Mickey speaks softly,
like one must speak to a cow that will not let down
her milk.

"Bitch!" Brandy says to me. "And after every thing
I did for ya."

"Brandy, you have done much for me, and I am
grateful, but I do nothing to hurt you."

"Please Anne," Mickey says, "give us a few
minutes alone."

This I am glad to do. I walk quickly from the room, and although I must pass through the sitting room in which Gloria smokes, I do not look her way. Somehow I will make a plan for myself, and when I do, I will never have to look at Gloria and her family again.

Bridgett Monroe had a plan. She took the tablet with my drawings with her to Pittsburgh. She had what is called a gallery there, a shop in which to hang paintings. And she had many rich friends. Bridgett cut one of my pictures out of the notebook, framed it, and hung it in her shop. That very same day a regular customer came into the shop and bought the drawing. It was only a simple drawing of Mamm pumping water for her garden, but the man—and Bridgett called him a collector—paid three hundred and fifty dollars for it.

The next day Bridgett hung three more drawings and charged four hundred and fifty dollars. Two of those sold the same day and one the next. Imagine paying that much for a picture of Rutchich, our plow horse, Daat's straw hat with the hole in it, and an old fence post with an empty bird's nest inside. A woman from Pittsburgh's newspaper even wrote an article about them. She called them "evocative."

Bridgett sent me a copy of the article along with a short letter. It was I who brought the letter in from the mailbox, but it was Mamm who opened it. She thought at first it was for her, since Anna is also her name. When I saw her face turn white and her hands tremble, I knew the letter was for me.

"Mamm, what does it say?" I asked.

She could not answer, but crumpled the letter and ran crying from the room.

I uncrumpled the letter and smoothed it with my hand. It was the first piece of mail I had ever received. I read it with great care.

Dear Anna,
Everybody loves your work. Just this morning I
sold that sketch of the broken windmill. Thanks
to the enclosed article, we got two thousand
dollars for it. I am keeping it all for you in a
trust fund—minus my commission, of course.

Anna, I can't tell you how proud I am of you.
You're going to be a huge star, you know that?
Keep the faith.

Bridgett.

It was the nerves, Daat explained at supper. It was not
my fault. The two of us ate alone, because Mamm was
in bed. I was a terrible cook, at least by Amish
standards. But now that I have eaten Gloria's cooking,
I think the food of even this seven-year-old Amish
cook was not so bad. Daat had two helpings of my
yumzetti. With Mamm not there to look over my
shoulder, I had put extra slices of Velveeta on the
ground meat and noodles before baking.

I asked Daat to read me the letter, but he too
refused. Even when I begged and cried, he would not
change his mind. But the next morning Bishop Yoder
read it to me. To be accurate, he translated both the
article and the letter into dialect so I wouldn't miss a
single word. The only words the bishop could not
translate correctly were "evocative" and "trust fund."

"Anna," he said, his voice both gentle and filled
with wonder, "there was sex in these pictures?"

I shrugged. In addition to the pictures mentioned in
the article, there was a hayloft with a pitchfork, a
buggy with only three wheels, and Mamm's flower
garden. I did not remember drawing any sex, but then
I did not know what that was.

"Ach, what questions!" Mamm cried. She had
recovered from the nerves enough to come downstairs
when the bishop arrived.

"She does not know what this means," Papa said.

The bishop nodded. "These drawings, Anna, who taught you to make them?"

Again I shrugged. Drawing was something I could always do, like sleep and breathe.

"Where did you get the tablet, Anna?"

Finally a question I could answer. "The English woman, Bridgett Monroe."

"Did she tell you what to draw?"

I nodded.

"Ah," the bishop said, "now we are getting somewhere."

"She told me to draw anything I wanted."

"*Anything?*" Mama asked. She was about to get the nerves again.

Then I remembered Bridgett's words. "Whatever calls to my heart."

"My straw hat with the hole," Daat said gently, "this calls to your heart?"

"Yah. That is the hat you wore when I twisted my ankle and you carried me on your shoulders."

Daat smiled. "You see," he said to the bishop, "it is an innocent child's thing."

"Perhaps," said the bishop, and he sighed heavily, "and perhaps not. Anna, what does this mean, 'keep the faith'?"

I answered with my shoulders.

"Of what faith is this woman? Is she a Mennonite?"

"Ach," Mama said, "I think not a Mennonite. She looked like a Presbyterian. Maybe even a Methodist."

The bishop smiled. "Has she given you money, Anna?"

I shook my head.

"Then she steals," Daat said. "The letter spoke of much money. Anna, should get her share, no?"

The bishop's eyes said Daat was wrong. "Anna, there are to be no more drawings. Do you understand?"

I nodded.

"And why is that, Anna?"

"I have no paper."

The bishop smiled again, and so did Daat. Even Mamm looked like she wanted to smile.

"Anna, you are not to draw these pictures because they lead to pride."

"Sarah Gindlesberger draws pictures," I said.

"Ach," Mamm said, "Sarah cannot draw like you. Those are the pictures of a child."

"Sarah is seven years old, just like me," I said.

Bishop Yoder had kind eyes, but the biggest nose I had ever seen. He rubbed it with the back of his hand.

"What your Mamm means, Anna, is that your pictures are too—uh—uh—"

"Fancy," Mamm said, happy to supply the bishop with an answer.

"Yah, fancy. This is what leads us to pride."

"Then I will draw plain pictures."

The bishop considered this by rubbing his nose again. "But you will not draw animals, or people with faces, yah?"

"Why not animals? And people do have faces, do they not?"

"The Bible says we should not worship idols," the Bishop said, "and our people honor this commandment by not making statues or even drawings that look too much like real people."

Mamm had told me this many times before. That is why my dolls, like all Amish dolls, had no faces. Maybe if a doll had a face somebody might try to worship it, just like the Catholics worshipped the statue of Mary. But who would worship a piece of paper? And nobody worshipped animals, did they? Well, except maybe for geese. I had seen statues of geese in yards of the English.

Brandy comes back to her old room, my new room, and slaps me across the face. I fall upon the bed. My cheek stings.

"I oughta rip your heart out, Aggie."

"I do not understand."

"The hell ya don't. I oughta rip your heart out, 'cause that's just what you're doing to me."

"Brandy, what have I done?"

"Don't ya dare play Little Miss Innocent with me, ya conniving Amish bitch. Mickey's got the hots for ya, and you've been leading him on. Ain't that right?"

I do not need to understand the words to get the meaning. Brandy is jealous. But I have done nothing to deserve her anger. I do not share these hots for Mickey.

"Brandy, I do not desire your boyfriend."

"Oh yeah? Well, that's not what he says."

"What did he say?"

"That you were all over him like white on rice."

This riddle I think I understand. "I did not touch him."

"So, ya calling him a liar?"

"Yah." To make such accusations is not the Amish way, but how many of my ancestors have been accused of being white on rice? I think the old ways will not work in the modern world of the English.

Brandy sits on the bed beside me. "Ya know what? Strange as it sounds, I believe ya. Can't go anywhere with Mickey that he isn't checking out this hootchie or that. 'Put your damn eyeballs back in your head,' I always have to tell him. Or, if that pisses him off, I tell him it's all right to look, but not touch. He didn't touch *you*, did he?"

I shake my head.

"Aggie, I'm sorry I went off on ya like that. Ya ain't mad, are ya?"

Of course I am angry. But the Bible tells me to forgive my brother *seventy times seven*. And Brandy is my sister, according to the Bible.

"It is okay," I say, even though the words come out with difficulty.

Brandy puts her arm around my shoulder. "You're something else, Aggie, ya know that?"

I have nothing to say.

"Hey, I'm outta here. Mickey's taking me to dinner and a club 'cause I made him feel like shit. Ya oughta try it Aggie, it works every time."

CHAPTER

12

I'm outta here, like Brandy says, except that I cannot leave Mrs. Scott in that house with Gloria and the husband who has no backbone. I would not treat a snake the way they treat Mrs. Scott, and snakes I hate very much.

Each morning I clean and feed the old woman, and then I must give her the pills. With her lunch she has pills too, and then again at night. They are, I think, the same pills Mamm takes to control the nerves, but Mrs. Scott does not have the nerves. I think she gets worse every day. Now she is like an old sheep, and when she opens her eyes, they too are like those of a sheep. How can I leave one who needs so much help?

Today I think I will not give her all the pills. Maybe just two with each meal, instead of the three. At first I am afraid. Perhaps Gloria will see me. Or Jim. But I am silly for having this worry. When I am with her mother, Gloria is never there. Jim sleeps most of the time, and as for Brandy, I think now she has started her new job. I have not seen her for five days.

There is no change in Mrs. Scott, so after another day has passed, I give her only one pill at breakfast. The same I do at lunch, and at supper. The next morning when I wake, Mrs. Scott lies beside me on the bed with her eyes open wide. They are not the eyes of a sheep now, but the eyes of a goat, which is more intelligent, yah?

This excites me very much, but it scares me too. Perhaps I have gone too far. Perhaps the pills are not for her health, but to make her sleep. The doctor gave Mamm nerve pills, but she would not take them because they made her sleepy.

"Mrs. Scott," I say, "how are you this morning?"

This I say every morning, but on this morning Mrs. Scott smiles. Now my heart is in my mouth. "Mrs. Scott, do you hear me?"

She blinks. I think there is a desire to say something, but she cannot.

"Mrs. Scott, do you want your breakfast?"

She blinks again.

I give Mrs. Scott her breakfast, but without pills. After breakfast I must walk to the Laundromat to wash her clothes. The lady who owns the Laundromat is very kind and helps me understand the machines. She even helps me fold the clothes, although I tell her this is unnecessary. We have spoken before. Her name is Victoria and she is an Italian. She tells me there are many Italians in Verona, and Irish too. Even Czechoslovakians. In Heaven there are only Swiss-German and English.

It is very difficult to carry the laundry back up the hill, which is much steeper than any hill in Heaven. I think even Hertzler Mountain, where Daniel Weaver tried to see my breasts, is not as high or steep as this Verona hill. I must climb past the elementary school, past a place called the athletic field. By then I am breathing like a horse that has galloped all morning, and there is still much of the hill yet to climb.

When I get back to the house it is already time to give Mrs. Scott her lunch. Gloria does not cook, except to heat the meals she calls TV. There is also the pizza man. Mamm sometimes made pizza, but not like this, which is real Italian pizza because of all the Italians in town. But always we must wait in the driveway for the pizza man. He must never see us open the door.

Jim is the first man I know who can cook, but mostly he stays in his bedroom because he does not feel well. Still, there are things with which to cook, and today I make chicken and dumplings with potatoes and carrots. Gloria, who eats less even than Mamm, smiles when she tastes them. She says they are the best thing to pass through her lips since God created dark chocolate. I do not let this disrespectful talk of God bother me, because Jim also is enjoying the dumplings very much.

"Anna," he says, "this is wonderful. You should open a restaurant."

"Yah?"

Gloria's good mood does not last. "The hell she will. She's got a job right here."

But this is not a job. I do not get paid, only food and a place to sleep. Now that Brandy is gone, I sleep in her room, but I must not touch any of her things. "Touch my stuff and I'll kill ya," she says.

Of course Brandy is only joking; she will not kill me. She will be very angry if I touch her stuff, so I do not. But there is so much stuff. She has even toys! Imagine this, a grown woman with dolls, each one with a face, and all of them are named Barbara. She has many electric toys, the names of which I do not know.

After we three have lunch—and it is I who must do the dishes—I feed Mrs. Scott. I save for her the chicken legs because they have the most flavor, and I cut the meat into very small pieces so she will not choke. I cut even the dumplings and vegetables in small pieces.

I sit Mrs. Scott up in bed, which still smells of the toilet, although I keep it very clean, and speak softly. "I have made a special lunch, Mrs. Scott. It is my mother's recipe."

She opens her eyes, and they are now not even the eyes of a goat. They are the eyes of a woman who knows her own mind.

"Help me," she says.

This surprises me so much that I drop the spoon, and the chicken and gravy fall down her chest.

"Ach! You speak!"

"Of course I speak. I am not an idiot, child."

I do not know what to say. My hands shake and I must put down the bowl.

"So, are you going to help me, or not?"

"I will help," I say, although I still cannot believe we have this conversation.

"Good, I knew I could count on you."

"Please, Mrs. Scott. Explain."

"We haven't much time, dear. My daughter is a dangerous, vindictive woman. Do you understand?"

I do not know this vindictive. Only that Gloria is an angry woman, with only a little bit of kindness in her soul. She would not hesitate, I think, to beat a horse that was not fast enough.

"I think I understand."

"What is your name, dear?"

"Anne."

"Anne, you must get me away from here as soon as possible."

"Where do you wish to go?"

"The police station." Mrs. Scott speaks slowly, and some words are not so clear.

"The *police*?"

"Yes, child. Are you hard of hearing?"

"No." It seems that perhaps Gloria's apple did not fall so far from her mother's tree.

"Do you know where to go?"

I shake my head. "I know only the laundromat, the haircutter, and the Giant Eagle."

"You know enough then, because the police station is right up the street from the Wash 'N' Dry."

"How will we get there?"

"Do you think you can carry me?"

I think not. Mrs. Scott is perhaps not much more

heavy than the laundry, but her I cannot drop.

She reads my mind. "Maybe I can walk."

"Maybe—"

"Shh! Someone's coming."

It is Gloria. I smell first the smoke, then she puts her head in the door.

"What the hell is going on?"

"Nothing." It is a lie, but for a good reason, yah?

"Who were you to talking to? Her? Look Aggie, don't you be wasting time on that, because if you're done feeding her, I've got plenty of other things for you to do." Gloria sees the bowl of dumplings which is still almost full. "Ha! I see she doesn't like your cooking."

Yet you do, I think. Of course I say nothing.

"Well, just don't sit there like a lump on a log. If that's all she's going to eat, then wash that damn dish and report to duty."

I must appear calm. "She was asleep, but now I think she will eat. And then I must take her to the bathroom."

"Whatever. Just don't think you're getting a free ride here." Then she leaves, only her smoke stays behind.

When I am sure Gloria cannot hear, I close the door softly. "You must eat," I tell Mrs. Scott, "so you will have strength."

She eats a little. It is more than she has eaten since I arrive, but it is not enough. When she tries to stand, she cannot, and I must catch her so she does not hit her head. There is still strength for the swearing. From that, more than anything, I can see she is Gloria's mother.

"Do not worry," I say. "I will think of something."

Gloria keeps me very busy. I must wash and wax the kitchen floor. Then I must use something called the vacuum cleanser to clean the rugs. This I hate. The

machine is very loud and will suck into itself anything
in its way. My shoelace is in its way and now I am
glad the vacuum is so noisy, because no one can hear
me scream. But it is only a short scream, because I
gather my wits and turn the machine off. It is not so
easy to pull my shoelace from the mouth of this
hungry machine.

Although I work very hard, and get much done for
Gloria, I must either go to my room, or Mrs. Scott's
room, whenever the doorbell rings. When I am
permitted to come out, Gloria gives me the "all clear"
sign. I am not permitted to ask the reason for this
strange behavior. It is part of my job to obey without
questions.

For supper Jim makes tomato soup and grilled
cheese sandwiches, but Gloria gets angry, because
soup is only for winter she says. I do not mind the
soup, and neither does Mrs. Scott. She eats all her
soup and a sandwich and a half, but still she is too
weak to walk. Do not worry, I tell her. I will think of
something.

But I think of nothing. My mind is still empty when
Gloria tells me what I must do for tomorrow. The big
shopping, she says. Brandy is supposed to come home
to drive me back from the Giant Eagle, but if she does
not, then I must push the buggy up the hill.

I do not mean to laugh.

"What's so damn funny, Aggie?"

"It is Anne."

"I said, what's so damn funny?"

"I cannot push a buggy full of groceries up the hill.
It is too steep."

"Then that's your damn problem, because here is
your list. Make three trips if you have to, I don't care.
Just do it."

After this I go to bed, but I do not sleep. First I
pray that Brandy will do what she has been asked.
God can do anything, but this prayer I think will not
be answered. Then I think of something which is

maybe the answer to a prayer I have not prayed.

When it is very early in the morning, when I am sure everyone is asleep, I get out of bed and dress. It is unfortunate that my clothes are no longer black like those of the Amish. Brandy's room has a window, and I must climb out into a bush that scratches my legs, but it is no matter. Brandy, I know, has done this many times.

It is not so easy to run down a steep hill. There is danger of going too fast. Up at the top, where Gloria lives, there is not even a sidewalk, only a street they call gobble stones. This is more hard on the legs than any bush. It is only when I get down to where there are more houses, that the sidewalk appears. But there the street is even steeper.

I am tired and out of wind when I reach the Giant Eagle parking lot, but I am filled with joy too. Just as I suspect, some of the buggies are still outside. I take one which I find in a ditch between the parking lot and Allegheny River Boulevard. Its absence will not be noticed, and it is not a sin if I return it.

Running down the hill was the play of a child. Now I must run up the hill, pushing the buggy. I must stop to rest twice; once in the schoolyard and once in front of Otto's house. It is funny that a man I did not like at first, now feels like a friend. When I reach the end of the street where there are only gobbles, the cart makes much noise. I understand then why it is called this; because the sound is like that of a turkey. But there is also much barking from dogs, and I am afraid that the people who live along the street will look out their windows.

I do not wish to speak badly of the good people in Verona, but it is a fact that many of them sleep past the hour of five. Many, I have been told, sleep past six, and I speak not just of Brandy and her family.

But Mrs. Scott lies awake when I enter her room.

She sits.

"Where the hell have you been? I thought sure you'd skipped out on me."

This causes me great fear. "You heard?"

"Honey, before that excuse for a daughter doped me up like that, I heard Brandy sneak out a million times."

"And you did not tell?"

We speak softly, but Mrs. Scott's laughter is not so soft. "Wouldn't you sneak out too, if you had a mother like that?"

I say nothing. It is what Brandy calls a historical question, one that requires no answer. Yah, Mamm suffers from the nerves, but they are not the nerves of Gloria. Mamm wants only good for me. I obeyed Mamm and all the rules of the Ordnung, except for one. This one is why I must now take an old woman in secret to the police.

Mrs. Scott, I think, has the nerves too. "Don't be so damn rough," she says when I pull her through the window.

"I am sorry." Does she not realize that I stand in a bush?

"What the hell is that for?" she says when she sees the buggy.

"For you to ride in. It is called a buggy, but it is not like the buggies—"

"I know what the hell it is, but there's no way in hell I'm going to sit in that thing."

"But you want to get away, yah?"

"I expected a car. What do I look like? A sack of potatoes?"

I hope this is another historical question. "I do not drive."

"How old are you?"

"Twenty-three."

"What's the matter? You get your license revoked?"

I reach my limit of patience. "Do you wish to stay?"

"Are you nuts? You know how they've been treating me. Put me in the damn thing, and let's get going."

I put the old woman in the buggy as gently as I can, but still there are many complaints: the wires are too hard, they are too cold, she must sit with her knees under her chin.

When I push the buggy she grunts at each gobble stone, "This is going to kill my kidneys."

I push faster.

"What are you trying to do, kill me?"

"Ach!" I would not do such a thing, but now I have an idea I must force out of my head.

"And don't think I won't sue if you manage to hurt me in any way."

Sometimes the voice of the devil is too sweet to ignore, so I let go of the buggy.

CHAPTER

13

It is my intention to let go only for a few seconds, just long enough to teach Mrs. Scott a lesson. This is not Amish thinking, but I am no longer Amish, yah? But perhaps God has a lesson to teach me.

The buggy bumps down the gobbles and Mrs. Scott screams. This is what I want. I run after the buggy, but it is very fast. I almost catch it when I twist my ankle.

"Ach!"

"Help!" Mrs. Scott screams. "Help! This lunatic is trying to kill me."

My ankle hurts very much, but I have no choice but to run. Yet always the buggy is faster. There is a smooth street that crosses the gobbled one, and when the buggy reaches that it goes so fast I think it is flying.

"*Gott in Himmel!*" I cry. "What have I done?"

"God damn you!" Mrs. Scott screams.

I think I will never catch the buggy. Each gobble twists my ankle more. Only now do I wish I had never met Bridgett Monroe, that God had never given me the gift.

But God is looking out for me. Near the school yard the gobbles line up so that the buggy runs off to the side, then it hits a tree. It tips and Mrs. Scott falls to the ground. It is not far that she falls, but she screams like I dropped her from a cliff. I am sure everyone in

Verona hears this.

"Please, Mrs. Scott, they will catch us."

"I hope they do. I hope the cops lock you up and throw away the key." This she shouts as well.

"The police, yah. But what if it is Gloria and Jim?"

She is quiet for a minute. Somewhere I hear a door slam. A dog barks.

"Well, just don't stand there, you fool. Put me back in the damn buggy."

I put her in and she moans, but she does not scream. Again my heart is in my mouth. I think she is really hurt.

"I am very sorry," I say. I do not want trouble with the police. I do not want that anyone, even Mrs. Scott, should be hurt.

"Don't just stand there, you idiot. Get us the hell out of here."

I have only to guide the buggy down the hill. There is no need to push. Many times I must dig hard with my foot, the one that has not been twisted like a pretzel, to slow the buggy. I am in much pain and wish to climb into the buggy with Mrs. Scott, but of course I cannot. I must finish what I have started.

Already I have brought my family much shame. If I am sent to prison the shame will be too much for Mamm to bear. It will be too much for me as well, I am afraid. Brandy has been to prison. She said the guards searched her most private parts with a flashlight. She said she had a "boyfriend" in prison who was really a woman named Sam. She said that without this boyfriend, who was really a woman, she would have been beaten every night. Maybe even worse things would have happened. Brandy said the only way to get along with anyone in prison, even the guards, was to buy them cigarettes. I do not want to have a boyfriend who is really a woman, or spend my money on cigarettes. I think though that in some ways prison will be better than Gloria's house.

When we get to the bottom of the hill it is much

easier, and I can even rest my foot on a bar across the bottom of the buggy. If I remember to hop. Once I do not remember and I fall flat on my ass. That's what Mrs. Scott calls my buttocks.

Because it is still dark, and most English are still in bed, there is only one car on the street. When it passes a man calls out from the window.

"Get a job, why don't you? Worthless bums!"

"Screw you!" Mrs. Scott screams.

The man does not hear us and drives on.

There is a small light on in the police station. I knock on the door but nobody answers.

"You have to pound on the door, you idiot. It's okay to make noise now," Mrs. Scott says.

I knock louder. A young woman in a police uniform opens the door. Her eyes grow round when she sees Mrs. Scott in the grocery buggy.

"Is this supposed to be some sort of a joke?" she asks.

"No joke," Mrs. Scott shouts. "This moron tried to kill me. I want her arrested."

The young woman tells us to come inside, but we must leave the buggy.

"Then I will have to carry Mrs. Scott," I say. I hope that the police woman will carry her for me.

"Lay a hand on me again, and I'll sue until you don't have a pot to piss in."

The police woman shakes her head. "Younz is for real, aren't you?"

"Yes, we'uns is," Mrs. Scott says. It is clear she has no taste for this woman.

The police woman, whose name is Sergeant Bright, tells me it is all right to bring the buggy in. She says it in such a way that lets me know she has no taste for Mrs. Scott.

I push the buggy into the police station. Mrs. Scott tries to climb out of the buggy, but she cannot. She shakes with anger.

"Arrest this woman!"

Sergeant Bright tries not to smile. "On what grounds?"

"Are you deaf? I said she tried to kill me."

"How?"

"She put me in this damn buggy and gave me a push down South Street. Do you know how steep that is?"

"I'm well aware of how steep it is. Did you consent to get in the buggy?"

"Well, I can see there's no use talking to you. I want to call my lawyer."

Sergeant Bright smiles. "Why? You aren't under arrest."

"But I have a right to a phone call, don't I?"

"Be my guest. There's a payphone right there."

"I don't have any money." Mrs. Scott looks at me, but I shake my head. For what do I need money in the middle of the night?

Sergeant Bright gives her a quarter. I push Mrs. Scott to the phone and wait while she calls her lawyer. When she talks she says only swear words. Then she slaps the phone on the hook.

"Dumb shit is still asleep, won't even talk to me. Got his damn answering machine. You'd think the maid would at least pick up."

I push the buggy back to Sergeant Bright. My ankle pains me even more, and is swollen now.

"You're hurt," the police woman says. She has a kind voice.

"You're worried about *her?*" Mrs. Scott screams. "I'm the one who almost got killed." She turns and points a crooked finger at me. "How come you haven't arrested her yet?"

I speak. "Mrs. Scott, I am very sorry you fell—"

"Don't listen to a damn word," she says to Sergeant Bright. "This foreign girl tried to kill me. Look, I've got bruises to prove it."

There are marks on Mrs. Scott, but they come from

the ropes Gloria used to tie her to the bed. Nothing
else. Sergeant Bright looks at the marks, then she
looks at me. I must respond.

"She was tied to a bed. She was, how do I say this,
like in a coma. Drugs, I think. Pills for the nerves. I
did not do it. It was the daughter."

Sergeant Bright turns to Mrs. Scott. "Is this true?"

"Yes, it's true, but that doesn't change the fact that
this one tried to kill me."

"I help her to escape, yah?"

"Is that part true?"

"So what if it is? That doesn't change what she
did."

"Just a minute," Sergeant Bright says. She goes to
her desk and speaks quietly on the phone. I think she
makes two calls. When she returns she looks more
serious. "Are you willing to press charges against
your daughter?"

The eyes, which first remind me of a sheep, and
then a goat, now remind me of a cat. "How long do I
have?"

"Take as long as you want. But if what you say is
true, I suggest the sooner the better. You don't want
them getting rid of evidence."

"But I have a witness!"

"The same woman who tried to kill you? The same
one you want me to arrest?"

The cat thinks. "Okay, so maybe what she did was
an accident. But I still could have been hurt."

"Are you willing to put that in your statement, that
she didn't mean to hurt you?"

"What the hell. All right." The cat turns her head to
me. "But you better be willing to testify on my
behalf."

"Yah," I say, but I do not know what this testify is.

"You should both be looked at by a doctor,"
Sergeant Bright says.

"Yah." I have heard English doctors cost much
money. Mamm knows what to do. And what Mamm

does not know, the midwife who grows herbs knows.
The Amish in Heaven call this midwife The Healer.

"I could call younz an ambulance, but my shift ends
in fifteen minutes, so I'd be happy to drive. Run you
right over to St. Margaret, it's practically on the way
home. Or," Sergeant Bright looks hard at Mrs. Scott,
"I'd be happy to drive you over to Western
Psychiatric."

"I'm not crazy." Mrs. Scott grabs the sides of the
buggy and tries to shake them, but she is too weak.
"*She's* the psycho."

"Then it's settled. I'll drive."

St. Margaret hospital is across the river. To get to it
we must drive first through the town of Oakmont, and
then across a lavender-colored bridge. It is light now
and I see that below there is an island with houses,
but no bridge to get to it. Only small boats. That is
where I want to live; someplace that is safe from the
world, but close enough for me to visit.

All the way to the hospital Mrs. Scott complains
about her injuries or how she will sue the "ill-fitting"
blouse off my back. Sergeant Bright must remind the
old woman several times that I am her only witness.

At the hospital they make us fill out many papers. I
do not have insurance, so I must speak a long time
with a woman in a gray dress. She calls me indigent,
but I do not mind. She asks if there is anyone in
Verona or Pittsburgh who will be responsible for my
bills. I tell her there is no one, except for myself. She
says she must have the name and an address of
someone. I give her the name of Otto Goldschmidt,
but tell her I do not know his address.

I think Mrs. Scott must answer many questions too.
When we are done they put us in separate little rooms
called emergency cuticles. The walls are not so thick
and I can hear Mrs. Scott. She no longer speaks of
suing me, but of suing the hospital.

"I better leave this freaking place with all ten fingers and all ten toes."

"You'll be just fine, Mrs. Scott. I just want to check your blood pressure," the nurse says.

"It should be through the roof after all I've been through."

The nurse who comes to see me makes a face. "Your friend is—" she bites her tongue.

"She is not my friend."

This makes the nurse smile. She takes also my blood pressure, and my temperature. When she is done I still have all ten fingers and all ten toes. When the nurse touches my foot she is more gentle even than The Healer. The doctor, when he comes, is not so gentle—maybe more like Mamm. He sends me for an x-ray, which does not hurt as bad as it sounds.

"There's no break," he says and holds to the light something which is supposed to be a picture of my foot. I think that if the pictures I drew for Bridgett Monroe looked like this, I would not be sitting here. "But you've got yourself a nasty sprain. Stay off that foot for several days. Doctor's orders. The nurse will give you complete instructions."

When everyone is done I am put in a wheelchair. It is like a buggy, but with two very big wheels. I have no doubt this is my punishment for letting go of the buggy when Mrs. Scott was in it. The nurse pushes me back into the main room, and there is Otto. I do not know why, but the smooth head, pink lips, and lady's scarf bring me great comfort.

He winks at me. "Anna, we've got to stop meeting like this."

"Ach."

He takes the chair from the nurse and pushes it to the door. "Your chariot awaits, Madame."

If I live to be a hundred I will never understand the English. Always they must joke. Otto has only a car, not a chariot. The Prophet Elijah went to Heaven in a chariot. Yah, it was a chariot of fire, but still it did not look like this.

"Lean on me," Otto says. He smells like a woman's perfume, the smell of harlots.

Otto's car is much nicer than Brandy's. I think this is because it is clean. He drives much slower as well.

"So, you've had yourself quite a night, I hear."

I turn. There is a ring in Otto's ear. It is not of the small variety I have seen in some men's ears, but is long and swings, with shiny stones like diamonds. Suddenly I realize that Otto is a man who lies with other men. I have heard that there are many among the English who do so. The Amish do not accept this, so those who admit to this, and do not repent, are banished. Like me. It is only whispered, but I have heard of Amish teenagers who hang themselves in the barn, because they cannot bear to leave the families they love. This I think is more true when said of the boys. Sometimes the girls of this sort can refuse to marry and become aunties, maybe even teachers. But what is in their hearts must never be spoken of.

"From who do you hear this?"

"Sergeant Bright is a friend of mine. Trust me, this won't go any further. But I would have given my eyeteeth to see that old bat flying down the hill in a buggy."

"I only meant to let go for a second."

"Now, now, Anna, don't sell yourself short. Personally, I would have tied rockets to that buggy— might have shot it all the way over the Allegheny River. I don't suppose there was room for the rest of them in there."

"You do not like this family." That was a Dummkopf thing to say, but I could think of nothing else.

"They're trash, the whole bunch of them. I would have felt sorry for the old lady, but I heard she got pretty abusive. Swore like a sailor."

We ride in silence for a few minutes, then I think again I am a Dummkopf. "Mr. Goldschmidt—"

"Uh, uh, uh! Otto, remember?"

"Yah Otto. But where do you take me?"

"To my house, if that's okay. I thought you could stay with me a few days until you figure something out. At least until you get back on your feet." He laughs.

Now I am glad that Otto lies with other men. Perhaps it is wrong to feel this way, but it is one less worry for my mind. Like Otto says, I will need a few days to figure something out.

CHAPTER

14

I figured out how to be a good girl. After the bishop
left, Daat wrote Bridgett Monroe a letter. He said she
must never come to visit again, because this would
lead me into temptation. When Daat was through
writing that letter, he put my letter from Bridgett into
the box by the kitchen door which we keep for trash
that must be burned. It was my job, every Tuesday, to
burn the trash in a barrel behind the chicken house.
Mamm always worried that the barrel was too close to
the chicken house, but Daat said the smoke killed
fleas, even if it made the chickens so upset they did
not lay on trash days.

Anyway, I did not burn Bridgett's letter. I could
not hide it in the hayloft, because now Mamm knew
where to look, so I hid it in the hen house, under the
roof. Nobody looks up in a hen house.

After that, I was good. Mamm taught me how to
quilt, and even took me to quilting bees, where I was
the youngest girl there. I could have become the best
quilter, with the straightest stitches, but now I had
learned. Pride is a worse sin than making bad stitches
on purpose. Although I made good stitches, they were
never as good as those of Catherine Beiler. When
Catherine Beiler is happy, the world is happy, Mamm
once said when her nerves were particularly bad. The
next day she baked an applesauce cake for Catherine
Beiler.

Bridgett Monroe never wrote again. For two years Mamm made me work in the vegetable garden while she sold quilts from the blooming fence. Then I think Mamm trusted me, and it became my job again.

I loved selling quilts to the English. I had heard that they were not content because the world was always on their minds, but the English who came to Heaven seemed as happy as any Amish person I knew. In fact, they laughed much more than we Amish, certainly much more than Catherine Beiler. They were fatter than us too; Daat said that was because they did not know the meaning of hard work.

They asked many questions about how we lived, and I did not mind answering, even when they laughed at the answers. And it was not meanness I heard, but the voices of people who are surprised and do not know how to act. Almost everyone wanted to take my picture, but of course I had to refuse. Only once did I permit it. She was a little girl, maybe just six years old, and her two front teeth were missing. I do not know why I did this; perhaps I saw myself in her eyes.

I did not see myself the same way the English saw me. They told me I was beautiful, and how much more beautiful I would look if I let my hair down from a bun and put on English clothes. One man said he was from Hollywood, California, and did I want to act in movies? I would not even test for the screen. Another, a woman, said she was from New York and had many famous models work for her. I did not know what these models were, and was afraid to ask. Then she said my face could launch not only a thousand ships, but a magazine, so I knew they were models of ships. Such were the riddles the English asked, but no one except for Bridgett Monroe ever asked me to draw. Or to paint. Not until I reached the age of rumschpringe.

When we reach Otto's house he asks me if I have any luggage, then he laughs. "I suppose there wasn't any room in that buggy. Well, no use worrying about it now. What you need to do first is take a nice long nap. If worse comes to worse, I can always take you shopping. Hope you don't mind me saying so, Anna, but you're going to be fun to dress."

"This you cannot do!" I will not allow even a man who lies with other men to see me without clothes.

Otto laughs. "I didn't mean that literally! Believe me, girlfriend, I have no desire to see you naked. It's just that I love to shop."

Suddenly I am very cold. What was I thinking? I have left everything behind at Gloria's. Did I think Gloria would not care that I helped her mother escape? Or perhaps that was too strong a word. The Mrs. Scott in the buggy, was not the same Mrs. Scott in the bed. Perhaps I put my nose in business where it did not belong. But that does not change the fact that my new clothes are in Brandy's room. So is my quilt sack. Most importantly, the cardboard tube.

"I must go back up there," I say.

"Anna, you can barely walk."

"Then drive me please."

"Not until the police sort this out."

"But my clothes—"

"I'll buy you new. I may have been just a teacher, but I always paid myself first. Investments, I mean. I don't mind floating you a loan."

"Thank you, but that will not be necessary." I start to walk up the hill, even though each step is agony.

"Wait up!" He must run to catch me. "Now I've insulted you, haven't I?"

"No Otto, you did not insult."

"Then Anna, why are you going back? The police are probably up there right now."

"I left things that I must have."

"What? Family pictures? Because, Anna, if its just money, I say forget about that too."

"Yah, there is money. And there is my Gross— ah, grandmother's Bible. But there is also a—uh, a cardboard tube."

Otto pants. He stays at my heels, like a dog with no hair.

"Did you say cardboard tube? You mean like a toilet paper tube?"

"Yah, but much bigger." I open my arms to show him how big. Also the thickness with my hands.

"What's in the tube, if you don't mind my asking?"

But I do mind that he asks. Maybe someday I will show him what is in the tube, but not now. Now I want only to get it back. I walk even faster.

"Okay, okay," Otto says, and he must catch his breath. "I'll get the tube for you."

Now I stop. I do not want to see Gloria and Jim again, and I want no further trouble with the police. If I cause too much trouble, they will put me in jail, or even worse, send me back to Heaven.

"How will you get it?"

"As you already know, Sergeant Bright is a personal friend of mine. If I have to, I'll pull strings."

"Otto, do you really think you can get it for me? The sack too?"

He nods. In the early morning sun his head, which is now wet, shines.

"Then pull ropes," I tell him.

Otto shows me to the guest room. It is very clean and neat. The bed has a tent over it, which Otto calls a canopy. On the bed there is a silk pillow shaped like lips.

"Lie down," he says. "Take a long nap. When you wake up Uncle Otto will have your stuff for you."

I need no more urging. I put aside the pair of lips and climb into bed. They are the softest sheets I have ever felt, and there are other, regular, pillows with soft cases. They smell of sunshine, like sheets fresh from a clothesline; not like the smell of Brandy's house.

Otto puts the lip pillow under my ankle. "Sweet dreams, my fair little one."

I fall asleep before Otto leaves the room, because I have no fear. When I awake Otto is back. He sits in a chair in the corner. He is smiling, and in his hand is the cardboard tube.

"Mission successful," he says. "Got the tube, got the quilt bag, and even some of your clothes. Got a whole lot of attitude too, but we won't go into that."

I am embarrassed to get out of the bed, even though I am wearing clothes. This is just another silly part of me I must get over if I am to be truly English.

"Thank you very much, Otto. Very, very, much."

"Sergeant Bright deserves the thanks, not me. Just between you and me, she may have broken a few rules, but I won't tell if you won't." He laughs.

"I will tell no one."

"They're scum. They deserve what they get."

"What will they get?" Jim, I think, is not as bad as Gloria.

"That all depends on whether or not the old lady presses charges." He looks away from me, and I know there is more he wishes to say.

"Please, Otto, what is it?"

"She's obviously confused. Seems to think you were part of the problem."

"But I only helped her escape. She would still be tied to the bed even now, if it were not for me."

"Well, we'll just have to wait and see—hope for the best. In the meantime, how about an omelet? I'm a pretty fair cook, if I say so myself."

I tell Otto I am very hungry, which is true, even though I am very worried about the possibility of these charges. Otto says I should eat anyway, because the food in prison is not so good. He says this as a joke, and I try to laugh.

Otto does not joke about his cooking. Never have I tasted such an omelet. It has potbelly mushrooms and fetal cheese. The coffee has hickory and is strong, but

very good, and I must have second helpings of
everything.

Otto has a machine to wash the dishes, and after
breakfast we sit on what is called the patio and talk. It
is in the back of the house, and no one in Gloria's
family can see us. The yard is very small with an iron
fence around it. There is only grass and a dirty bath
for birds. Otto explains that he likes flowers, but has
a black thumb. By now I am used to English riddles
and say nothing.

"So, Anna," he says, "how about showing me
what's in that tube. You've got me so curious, I can
hardly stand it."

"It is nothing."

"I had my head chewed off this morning for
nothing?"

"It is just some silly paintings," I said.

"Like rolled up canvases?"

"Yah."

Otto frowns. "Anna, those are rightfully yours,
aren't they?"

"I do not steal!"

He laughs and spreads his hands in front of him, as
if to protect himself. They are very small hands, like
those of a young girl.

"Hey, hey, take it easy. It's just that you're so
secretive." He laughs again. "If I let my imagination
run wild, I could see you as a German spy."

"I am Amish."

"No kidding!"

"I *was* Amish. I am no longer."

He stares. "That does explain some things. I mean,
I didn't want to ask, didn't want to be rude, but I
thought you were a woman of mystery."

It is true that I have many secrets, but there is no
need for Otto to know them. Not now.

"Anna, I realize we barely know each other, and
that you have no reason really to trust me, except that
I did live up to my promise and get you that." He nods

at the cardboard tube which holds my paintings.

It is my life rolled up inside this tube. I have traded the contents of the tube for my family, for my faith, for five hundred years of history. One simple cardboard tube with ten paintings, like ten broken commandments.

But I was a good girl after the bishop's visit. That evening the elders came to our house and prayed with me, and on the next meeting Sunday the entire congregation prayed for me. They prayed that God would show me that the ways of the world were false, that I would understand my gift was nothing more then a test set before me by God. A test of my obedience to his will. I prayed in my inner voice, so that no one would hear, that I would understand how something which produced such beauty could be a test for sin.

When my prayer was not answered, I prayed that I would have the strength to endure the restrictions of my faith, so that I, unlike others I knew, would not be separated from my community.

That prayer went unanswered as well. When I turned sixteen, the age of rumschpringe, I did not disappoint my parents. It is the practice of the Amish to give their children much freedom during the late teenage years, so that they get the taste of the world out of their mouths. Then when they are grown, about the age of twenty, they will no longer feel the pull of the forbidden fruit. There are, I think, many Amish youth for whom the forbidden fruit is very tasty.

Levi Gindlesperger bought a used car with his hay-bailing money. It was no secret that he kept the car behind the barn—you could see it from Troyer Road—but even the bishop said nothing. And when Levi, who did not have the driving license, drove past you so fast the horses pulled hard against the reins, lifting their front legs off the ground, Mamm and Daat looked at each other and shook their heads. But they said nothing against Levi.

Some boys, like Elijah Stucky, even cut their hair, put on English clothes and moved to a big city like Philadelphia or New York. Elijah stayed for one year, and when he returned would not say what it was he did to earn his food or a place to stay. Soon after the bishop made an exception and baptized Elijah when he was still only seventeen. From that day on Elijah was no longer considered a child, and for him rumschpringe was over.

Amish girls are not allowed the same freedom as boys, but they too are expected to rebel. Rebecca Mast wore lipstick and face powder for two years, but of course not at church. Elizabeth Mishler wore a brassiere under her Amish clothes—even to church! But that was just one Sunday, because the bishop put a stop to that. Just because Elizabeth was in rumschpringe, did not give her the right to flaunt it in the face of God.

And then there is the bundling. Many congregations do not permit this anymore, but in Heaven it is allowed. Parents look away while couples who are courting lie together in the same bed. Our Ordnung says there must be a bundling board between them so they do not touch, but I know of many cases where such a board was not used. The Ordnung also says that they must keep always their underclothes on, but again, not everyone obeys. Lydia Bontrager has a son who is almost four years old, but she been married only for three years.

But I did not bundle with Daniel Weaver, and I did not ride in Jonathan Miller's car. I did not even paint my face. True, I wanted to do some of these things. What harm could there be in simply riding in a car? But I did not. I knew that Mamm's nerves would not take such behavior, and I truly wanted to be good.

Then one day I rode into town with Daat. We went first to the Giant Eagle because Mamm needed vanilla extract, and then to Armbruster's Hardware. Daat wanted to see if the prices at the new Farmers

Exchange were any cheaper for such things as wire cutters and post-hole diggers.

While Daat looked at the tools and talked with Mr. Armbruster, I looked at those things which interested me. I was in need of new work gloves—not to keep my hands soft, because that involved pride—but to protect them from thorns, so that I could work more. I did all the gardening, both vegetable and flowers, because Mamm did not trust me to deal with the English. This she did not say directly, of course, but a good daughter can read a mother's mind. It was not just the fear that Bridgette Monroe might return that worried Mamm, but now there were many times young English men would honk and sometimes even stop to talk with me. They called me names like Hottie, and Good Looking, so I did not mind so much the work behind the house.

The cotton gloves with the flower print were too fancy, and not allowed, but the plain leather ones, which would last much longer anyway, cost twice as much. There were plain cotton gloves, but these I did not want, as they were for men. Daat is cheap with the money, and I did not want to use mine, that which I got for quilts of my own design. As I thought about this I walked to the end of the aisle, and that's when I saw Mr. Armbruster's new display. That was when my rumschpringe began.

CHAPTER

15

I make Otto move the patio furniture and then wait
inside. Because of my foot I must hop like a bird, but
I manage to spread six of the paintings on the concrete
floor. I roll them the opposite way so that they lie
flat, but for some this does not work and I must
carefully put small stones on the corners. Then I call
Otto.

"Holy shit!" he says. "What did you do, rob the
Louvre?"

"I do not steal!"

"That was a joke, Anna. Of course you don't. But
where did you get these?"

"I painted them."

"Now you're joking, right?"

"I do not joke."

Otto sucks his bottom lip, and then clucks like a
hen for many minutes. "Man, these are really good. I
mean *really* good."

I look at the paintings. They are good. But to feel
this way is pride, even though it is perhaps the same
feeling the Lord felt when he created the world. *And
He saw that it was good,* the Bible says.

"Do you really think so?" I ask.

"Damn straight. Who taught you?"

"I learned from a book. *Water Colors Made Simple.*
I found it in Armbruster's Hardware in Hernia.

"You taught yourself?"

"Ach, it was not so simple. I wasted much paint and many papers. Some things I did are not in the book, but the idea I think is the same."

He nods. His eyes go from one painting to the next. "Did you ever try oils?"

"Yah, I tried them first. But they take too long to dry. And they do not come off easily from the hands. With the oils I could not keep my painting a secret."

"And that was necessary?"

"Yah. Paintings such as these are forbidden by my people." Then I think, *my people!* The Amish are no longer my people. I have no people now.

"So you came here to paint? To Verona, I mean."

"I had no choice."

"The ban," he says. "I heard about that. Thought maybe it was just something Hollywood made up. Never dreamed it was real. So how long does this ban last?"

"Until I repent of my sin."

He points to the nearest painting. "*That* is your sin?"

I say nothing. I do not want even a nice man like Otto to mock the Amish ways.

"You know, Anna, you should have your own show, like in a gallery. Have you thought about that."

"Yah. There is a woman, Bridgett Monroe—"

"I remember. Your friend from Shadyside."

"She has a gallery."

"Does she know you're here? What you have?"

"No, I have not had time to call." It is true, but also I have been afraid. Perhaps Bridgett will not wish to speak with me. Although I have broken the Ordnung many times with my paintings, I have honored my promise to Daat and Mamm to have no more contact with Bridgett. Now it is different, I think, and the promise no longer matters.

"Well," Otto says, and his face is that of a boy with a new sled when the first snow of the season arrives, "why don't you call her now. You have her number?"

"No." That is another reason I have not called.

"I'll try directory assistance," Otto says. But it is no use; there is no Bridgett Monroe in Pittsburgh. "Do you remember the name of her gallery?" he asks.

"No. The letter is hidden in Mamm's hen house. But I think the name had in it wood."

Otto taps the table on which the phone sat. "This kind of wood?"

"Yah."

Otto looks through a thick book called the Yellow Pages. "No galleries with the word wood in them. Can you think of another connection?"

I think hard, but it has been many years since Bishop Yoder read the letter aloud to me. "I cannot."

"Well, I'll tell you what we'll do then. Put those paintings back in the tube and we'll take a spin over to Shadyside. We'll cruise every street if we have to. Don't worry though, we'll find it."

I do not even get as far as the patio when there is pounding on the door.

"What the hell," Otto says, "can't they see the bell?" He moves slow to answer it.

The pounding grows louder. "I know you're in there, ya lousy Kraut."

"Brandy," I say.

"Quick," Otto says. "Get outside and I'll pull the drapes."

My foot hurts, but I do as he says. When Otto opens the door Brandy enters like a storm that has built up all afternoon. "How dare you break into my house and steal?"

"I didn't take anything that was yours."

"Oh yeah? How do ya know?"

"Search the house," he says.

My heart pounds. I want only to put the paintings back into the tube and run away. But I am afraid that Brandy will see me move in the crack between the curtains. Or perhaps she will hear the scrape of my shoes, or a rolling stone.

Brandy says nothing for many long minutes. I think maybe she is searching the house, but then she speaks.

"I don't want to mess with your faggot stuff. Just tell me where Aggie is."

"There isn't anyone named Aggie here."

"Don't give me that shit. Ya know who I mean."

"No, I don't."

There is another long silence, then Brandy speaks. "Well, tell Aggie I'll miss her. And tell her what she did for the old—I mean, my grandma—well, it was kinda neat. I guess I shoulda done something like that a long time ago. Tell her she's really got guts."

"If I see her, I'll tell her."

"Don't give me that shit," Brandy says, and then the door slams.

"Bitch," Otto says, then he opens the curtains, and then the sliding door. "All clear."

But I must see for myself that Brandy is already halfway up the hill before I roll the paintings and return them to the tube.

Otto must change his clothes for Shadyside. He puts on white pants and a blue silk shirt he does not button all the way. His scarf is bright red.

"Very patriotic, don't you think?" he says. He looks in a mirror that hangs above his couch and rubs his head. "Hmm, if I'd known we were going out, I'd have gotten a haircut."

"But you have no hair." I put my hand over my mouth, for I have said too much.

"I meant a shave. But there is hair there, darling, just not enough, unless I want one of those dreadful comb-overs."

This makes me homesick. An Amish man would wear a hat, except in the house, of course, where it does not matter. To be English is a great deal of work.

I do not have clothes to match Otto's, but I put on a navy skirt and a white blouse. I have nothing red, not even lipstick, which I have yet to buy. Otto is pleased anyway.

"Fabulous," he says. "You make one hell of a fine broad, Miss Hostetler."

Ach, again the riddles. But I say nothing. Otto is a careful driver, and now that we go slow, and it is light, I see how pretty it is along the river. The big sycamore trees all lean in one direction, and the water sparkles. Across the river there are steep hills, covered with houses like in Verona. It is nice to be calm and enjoy such a scene.

We follow Allegheny River Boulevard to Washington, where we must leave the river. After we climb a long hill this same street becomes Fifth Avenue and the houses become mansions. I think of the ones Jesus promises us *if* we get to heaven. Amish, unlike some other Christians, do not say they know for sure they will get to heaven. To say that is proud.

Otto says he knows where all the galleries are, but he does not find them right away. That is all right with me. I look at the mansions and think that if I could live in one, I might never want anything else. That, I think, is the real sin. But there is no worry that I will live in such a place. I have only the ten paintings, and a friend named Otto who wears a red scarf.

Then Otto turns on Walnut street. "Da-da!"

I remember now. Walnut. It is something to eat, but also a kind of wood. Grossdawdi Hostetler built for me a little rocking chair out of walnut. It was the year after the barn fire.

There are many shops on Walnut St. Otto calls them "up the scale." I think this is because many of the people I see are fat. Otto says this is where the rich come to buy their chatchkes. I do not wish to know what this means.

We must park behind the shops because there is no room in the parking garage. We walk to Walnut Street and begin to look for galleries. I have with me the

cardboard tube and now I am very nervous. If we find
the right shop, will Bridgett Monroe recognize me?
And what if she does? Perhaps the water color
paintings of a grown woman are of no interest to those
who collect art.

Otto tells me not to worry. He points out the many
things that interest him. He points with his chin to
two men. I see they are holding hands. In one shop
there is a sapphire ring that costs one-hundred-twenty-
five-thousand dollars. There is a shop that sells coats
made in Peru from llama skins. And over there is a
place that sells only pottery made by Indians. I tell
him Indians scalped my great-great-great-great-great
grandmother Hochstetler, but he laughs. These are
Indians from New Mexico and Arizona, and they are
too busy watching TV to scalp anyone.

Am I hungry, he asks. Over there is a tie restaurant.
I tell Otto I am not hungry enough to eat ties. He
laughs again. There is also a French restaurant we
might try. I know Otto jokes again, because no one
eats French people, except perhaps for cannibals in
Africa. And now I think they are too busy watching
television as well.

"Ah, now there's an art gallery," Otto says.

To The Moon And Back. It is a funny name for a
shop, but we go inside. There are many pictures on the
walls, but they are not photographs, and they are not
paintings. A young man in a one piece suit that is
white stands behind a counter.

"Be with you darlings in a minute," he says, but
does not look our way.

"Impudent ass," Otto says. We start to go, because
clearly this is not Bridgett Monroe's shop, but the
young man hurries to catch us.

"Sorry about that," he says, "but I had a phone
order and had to get caught up on some paperwork."
He looks at Otto and smiles. "How can I help you?"

"What kind of store is this?" Otto asks.

"Our name says it all. We sell enhanced photos of

outer space." He turns. "Like that one there, that was
originally a blowup of the moon landing, but if you
look closely, all the topographical features are made
up of different kinds of cheese. Kind of clever, isn't
it?"

"If you like that sort of thing," Otto says.

I do not know what to think. In Heaven there is still
much discussion about the government's claim that
men landed on the moon. Bishop Yoder does not think
this is possible. God would not allow anyone to get so
close to heaven. Remember what happened in the
Bible with the Tower of Babel? God quickly put a stop
to that, and the tower was not as high as the moon.

"We're running a special this week," the young man
says. "Everything you see is twenty percent off."

Otto looks at the price tag and whistles. "The
twenty percent I'd save would buy me a nice little
vacation in Europe.

"These pictures are very nice," I say, "but we are
looking for an art gallery."

The man in the one piece suit stiffens. "We are an
art gallery."

"Ya, but for paintings and—"

"What she means," Otto says, "is your more run-of-
the-mill pedestrian art. You know, the kind that
appeals to the hoi polloi."

Mr. One Suit smiles. "Gotcha. Well, there's How
Great Thou Art about a block down that way. It's all
religious crap." He winks at Otto. "Don't know how
they survive here."

"That's it?"

"Well, there's Monet's Mind, two blocks the other
way. Pretentious French crap, if you ask me, but you
won't find a Monet. There are a couple of other places
as well. What exactly are you after?" Again he winks.

"We are looking for a woman named Bridgett
Monroe," I say.

He sniffs, like he has a running nose. "Her. Well,
I'm afraid you're out of luck."

"Why is that?" Otto is not happy with the young man.

"Because she's dead."

"Ach!"

Otto puts his arm around me, like a father. "When did she die?"

The young man shrugs. "I don't remember exactly. A couple of years ago, maybe. I'd just started working here. She was hit by a car, right out there, crossing the street. Man, it was gruesome. Brains splattered all over the—"

"Shut up," Otto says.

The clerk makes a face. "Well, you don't have to get nasty."

"Just tell us one thing," Otto says. "Is the shop still there?"

"Yeah, it's still there. The Artful Dodger. Right next to the Thai place."

Otto makes me leave before I can even say thank you.

Otto asks if I want lunch first, and I say yes. I am not hungry, but I feel I need some time before I can visit the shop which Bridgett Monroe once owned. True, I did not know Bridgett Monroe very well, so I am not really sad. But now my future does not seem so good. Besides, the restaurant Otto wishes to visit is the one that serves ties, and I am anxious to solve this riddle.

It is not such a difficult riddle. The Pattaya does not serve ties—it is owned by people from Thailand. This is near China, I think. Chinese food is my favorite.

Many English think the Amish eat only Amish food. The seven sweets and the seven sours. I do not know what these sweets and sours are, but I do know that Mamm's sweet and sour chicken is the best in Heaven. The English do not know that Amish cooking comes from the Swiss German, but borrows from many other traditions. There is no need for the Elders to disapprove of cook books, because they do not lead believers astray.

The Thai cooking I think I like even better than Chinese. Otto orders for me, since we will have the same, and this is my first time in a real English restaurant. In Heaven there is a Mennonite restaurant which is called a buffet, and I ate there during my rumschpringe. But the cooking was like Mamm's, and there were no menus. And just paper napkins. The Pattaya has cloth napkins that are stiff and made to look like crowns. The menu has many things and is written both in English and in foreign, and you must pay for each dish separately.

Even Otto says it is hard to decide, but he orders first the satay with spicy peanut sauce and cucumbers, and a soup with shrimps called Tom Yum Goonk. It is my first time for shrimps. Next comes a noodle dish called Pad Thai, and then when I am so full I think I will burst, there is a green curry. The flavor is very good, but the food burns my mouth. The Amish, I think, borrow from English cookbooks, but leave out the heat.

When Otto pays the bill I feel much shame. So much money would feed Mamm and Daat for a week, maybe two. To eat at such a place again I think would be wrong, even if I am to consider myself English.

Otto does not seem to mind. He takes me next door to the Artful Dodger. I see right away that it is the kind of gallery Bridgett Monroe would own. The paintings I can understand, and the workmanship is very good. There is sculpture as well. This I try not to look at, although I no longer believe such things are idols.

We admire a few paintings and then Otto asks the clerk, who is a lady, if we can speak to the owners.

"I'm the owner," she says.

The woman is maybe just ten years older than I am, but she is dressed in very expensive clothes, more expensive than Penney's I think. And she has much gold jewelry, a wide necklace and many bracelets and rings.

"Well," Otto says, "then you need to meet this young lady, Anna Hostetler."

I put out my hand to shake, but she does not take it.

"Hostetler," she says, "the name sounds familiar."

"Many years ago I gave some drawings to Bridgett Monroe."

She steps back. "Ah, so that was you."

"You remember?"

"I'm Alison Monroe. Bridgett was my aunt. You're all she talked about at one point. How could I forget?"

She does not look like Bridgett, but it has been many years. I only stare at the woman. I do not know what to say.

But Otto does. "Then you're in for a treat," he says. "Anna, show her what you've got."

I start to take the paintings out of the tube to show to Bridgett Monroe's niece. "Don't bother," she says, and there is ice in her voice. "I didn't like your work then, so why should I like it now?"

"Hey, give the kid a chance," Otto says.

"Look, I'm busy. There are people in here who want to *buy*."

This is when I have a thunderstorm of the brain. "Bridgett Monroe said she had a trust fund in my name. Can I see it?" I am not sure what this trust fund is, but I hope it will cause her to change her mind.

Alison Monroe's face turns white. "There isn't any trust fund. Now if you'll be so kind as to leave . . ." Already Bridgett Monroe's niece has turned her back to help another customer. There is nothing else for us to do but leave.

We visit three more galleries. In one of them the owner is not there, but the clerk says if we leave the paintings, he will show them to the owner when he returns from Europe. In the other two shops the owners are present, but they will not look at the painting of a girl who taught herself from a book purchased at Armbruster's hardware.

When we leave the last shop Otto puts his arm around me again. "Don't worry, Anna, we'll think of something."

"Anna," Otto says to me the next morning at breakfast, "don't think I'm trying to get rid of you, because I'm not. I love having you here. But now that you know Bridgett is—well, dead, there is no reason for you to stay in Pittsburgh."

The bite of omelet I try to swallow sticks in my throat. I must take a big sip of orange juice and swallow again.

"Where would I go?"

He shakes his head. "You're not hearing me," he says. "I want you to stay. But you don't have to, you know. There are other cities with art galleries."

As silly as this may sound, I have thought of this. I have had only one dream; to paint and sell my paintings with the help of Bridgett Monroe.

"Which other cities?" I ask. Unser Satt Leit believe that too much knowledge can ruin the soul, but I have discovered that there is no such thing as too much knowledge. If God did not want us to think, he would have created us with small brains, like turkeys. It is said that they will drown in a heavy rain because they do not remember to close their mouths.

Now it is Otto who must swallow twice. "Well, New York, of course. Chicago, L.A., Houston. Atlanta. Even Philadelphia."

I try to imagine Anne Hostetler in New York City, or even Philadelphia. If I had not met Brandy on the bus, or Otto that first night I walked up the hill, I could be dead by now. Jacob and Elizabeth Schwartzentruber had a son, Enoch, who ran off to New York City on his rumschprism. Three months later they had a visit from two of Heaven's policemen.

Enoch had been found dead in an alley, his feet sticking out of a garbage dumpster. The New York doctor—I think he is called a coroner—who examined Enoch, said he thought the boy had not had a good meal in many weeks.

"Don't be silly, Otto," I say. "Why would I go anywhere else, when I have you to cook for me?"

He smiles. "I'll take that as a compliment. But there's something else, isn't there?"

"Yah. I think I have a brother who lives in Pittsburgh."

"No sh— I mean, you're joking, right? No, that's right, you don't joke. Anna, what's this all about?"

"The day I left Heaven the bishop said I had an older brother in Pittsburgh."

"And you didn't know about this?"

"There are many secrets in Heaven."

Otto must swallow again, even though he has eaten nothing since the last time. "What's his name?"

I shrug.

"Are you saying you don't know?"

"I know his last name is Hostetler."

He shakes his head. "Man, you're full of surprises." We sit quietly for a minute, then Otto pours himself another cup of coffee. "Anna," he says, "is it possible this bishop of yours was lying?"

"No."

"You're sure of that? No offense, Anna, but religious leaders lie all the time. I was raised Catholic. I'm sure you know about the abuse scandals in the church."

"Yah, I know." Amish believe it is wrong to gossip about other faiths, but of the sexual abuse there has been much talk. The bishop said it proves Jacob Amman was right when he said that clergymen should be allowed to marry. Just like he was right when he said infants should not be baptized.

"So you think your bishop might have made up this brother thing?"

"Otto, Bishop Yoder is a strict man, and sometimes he has little patience, but he does not deceive."

Otto pushes his coffee aside and puts in front of him the Pittsburgh telephone book. "In that case," he says, "we have some detecting to do."

But it does not take us long. There are eight Hostetlers living in the Pittsburgh area. By supper time we have spoken to all of them. They are, of course, all related to me through our ancestor Jacob, but many generations back. None of them has even heard of Heaven.

"One of them could be lying," Otto says. "Do you want to pay each a surprise visit to see if there is a family resemblance?"

I do not. If there is a brother in Pittsburgh, he does not wish to be found. I must respect this.

In any case, Otto has left his telephone number with each of the men listed in the book. If it is God's will that I connect with my brother—if he even exists—then it will happen. In the meantime, Anne Hostetler, the person I am becoming, must make it alone.

BOOK TWO

CHAPTER
16

I have lived with Otto Goldschmidt on South Street in Verona for the past nine months. During that time I've changed a lot. Otto says the biggest change is my English. The day I started using contractions, Otto baked me a cake. A very small cake. He says he's taught me all the slang he knows, and far too many curse words—although my word order is still a little strange. This I do not think is so.

My biggest challenge has been finding a job. My eight-grade, one room schoolhouse education doesn't qualify me for anything except cleaning houses and working as a "bag girl" at Giant Eagle, although I'm thinking about getting my GED. The house cleaning I hate, because so many English—I mean people in general—are slobs. And they own vacuum cleaners! Anyway, I enjoy bagging groceries because I get to meet people. Well, not actually meet them, but observe them, which can be a lot of fun.

Otto says I vent five hundreds years of repressed aggression on the customers, which really isn't true. It was just that one time. The woman deserved it, and all I did was pack a jar of Paul Newman's Own spaghetti sauce on top of a loaf of bread. She got back at me anyway by complaining to the manager.

Life is good; as good as it can be when you're cut off from your past and have a hole in your heart as big as the Commonwealth of Pennsylvania. When I'm not working, I hang out with Otto, or with Sergeant Bright, whose first name is Tracy, and who has become a very dear friend. I'm also friends with Lucia, the girl from the hair salon down on Allegheny River Boulevard. Believe it or not, I haven't seen Brandy since the morning of the great escape. I haven't seen Gloria or Jim either, thank God, although they're still living at the top of the hill. But I have seen Mickey Hanahan, the handsome man who was Gloria and Brandy's friend.

One Sunday Otto and I go to church. It is called the House of the Living and Resurrected Jehovah. Otto no longer attends church, but it is his idea that we should go. He said he didn't know Jehovah had died, and wants to check this out, but I know he does this for me.

Otto thinks that I am spiritually adrift, and that there is no one in the lifeboat with me. He does not mind being alone in his boat, but for me there must be company. These are his words.

I tell Otto that I am not ready to attend an English church, and that although I still believe in God, I am not so sure the idea of religion—any religion—agrees with me. Religions are invented by men, not God, and men must control the believers through fear of Hell or, if that doesn't work, with promises of riches in Heaven. Maybe it is the other way around. These are my thoughts. They are not the thoughts of a good Christian, I am sad to say.

We arrive at the church only a few minutes late, but already it is very crowded. We must stand in the back. For this I am thankful; it means that we are not noticed by many, and are free to leave when we please. I am taller than Otto and tell him that I see empty benches in the front, on both sides of the aisle. Otto says that maybe those seats are saved for vee-eye-peas. My English is almost one hundred percent, but this is an unfamiliar phrase. I am embarrassed, so I do not bother to ask.

It is very hot in the room, but the others don't seem to mind once the music starts. They clap their hands and sing loudly, and very fast. In the Amish church one song can take twenty minutes to sing. Here they sing ten songs in the same amount of time.

Just when I am getting tired of so much singing, it stops. Suddenly a young man runs in from a side door at the front of the church. He carries with him what I think is a very large Bible. Even from this distance I can see that he has greasy hair, a shiny brown suit, and wears sneakers on his feet.

"Say hallelujah," he shouts.

"Hallelujah," we shout. Everyone except for Otto.

"Say amen!"

"Amen!"

"Brothers and sisters, do I have something for you tonight!"

"What?" It is mostly women who respond.

"What?" The preacher shouts every word. "I'll tell you what! I have proof that God wants you to be rich! Not just spiritually rich, you can get that word at any church, I mean money rich. Yes, brothers and sisters, it says right here," the preacher slaps his Bible with his free hand, "that God wants you to have abundance! Oprah Winfrey-style abundance." He slaps the Bible again. "And what do you need to do to get that abundance? Nothing! Nothing at all! What did I just say, brothers and sisters?"

"Nothing!" Everyone roars again. "Nothing at all!"

The preacher jumps from the stage and lands on one of the empty benches—pews, I think they're called. "Brothers and sisters, what does God want you to be?"

"Rich!" They shout in one voice.

"That's right." Now the preacher does something so amazing, that at first I don't believe my eyes. He puts one foot on the back of the pew, shifts his weight, and then lifts the other foot. Now he is standing on the back, which is only an inch or two wide. It is clear why he wears the sneakers.

"Son of a bitch," Otto says. A woman turns and stares. Otto returns her stare until she looks away.

The preacher creeps across the back of the pew, stepping with the confidence of a cat. "God wants to give each and every one of you his love, forgiveness, and *money!*"

"*Money!*"

The preacher moves faster and faster, then he is running along the back of the pew. When he reaches the aisle, he leaps across and lands on the back of an empty pew. The people scream, whistle, and clap their hands.

"Brothers and sisters, could I have done that without faith?"

"No!"

"You better believe I couldn't! And you must believe to receive."

"Amen," someone yells, but it is not the response the preacher wants.

"What did I say?"

A woman shouts through cupped hands. "That you couldn't jump like that without faith."

From where I stand the preacher looks annoyed. "Wrong answer."

The first person tries again. "Believe to receive!"

Now the preacher smiles. "Yes! And the best part is that the more you believe, the more you will receive."

"The more you will receive," the crowd chants.

The preacher raises his arms and gazes at the ceiling. There is a water mark above his head. I try to imagine that God is somewhere above the watermark—maybe as far above it as the moon—and that the preacher knows which direction he should look.

"Brothers and sisters, in a few minutes the ushers will begin passing baskets. God is watching and will see what you put in those baskets. The amount you put in is directly proportional to the amount you can expect to receive when the Lord begins to bless you."

"Bullshit," Otto mumbles.

Several people turn to give Otto the evil eye. He does not seem to care. But I do. Their stares anger me. But mostly I am angry that the preacher is taking advantage of these people, and that no one dares to stop it. Are they all so foolish? Or perhaps their need is very great, and they do not wish to see the truth, because believing gives them hope. This I understand.

I understand what goes on, but I do not wish to be a part of it. I will no longer try to imagine God beyond the water stain. I will look for God in the hearts of people—people like Otto, my friend who swears and breaks the laws of Leviticus. If I were to put his heart in the offering basket, and the words of the preacher were true, I would be the richest woman in the world.

I lay a hand gently on his sleeve. "I want to go home, Otto."

"Are you sure? He might follow this with a trapeze act. I noticed some suspicious wires hanging from the ceiling."

"Shut up," a woman says. Several people are quick to say "amen."

Otto and I push our way to the entrance of the church, where the air is sweet and cool.

Mickey calls me four months after I move in with Otto and asks me out on a date. Boy, am I surprised. At first I turn him down. In fact, I turn him down five times. But finally my excuses for turning him down so often get to be funny, and we laugh and laugh until I said yes. You see, I am afraid he will mention Gloria and Brandy, maybe even show up with them, but he never says a word about them.

It is my first date that doesn't involve a buggy. Mickey takes me to a fancy restaurant on Mt. Washington, and afterwards we ride the inclined railway to the bottom and walk around the shops at Station Square. On the next date he takes me to see

my first movie. He said it is rated PG and shouldn't
bother me. I can't believe how big the movie screen is
and how real it all looks. If there are any parts that
are supposed to be offensive, I totally miss them.

After this we go out eight times; twice more to the
movies, twice roller skating, once bowling, and the
rest of the times just out to eat. Otto keeps track.
When I get home I must tell him everything, like he's
my father. He always asks if Mickey behaved himself,
and then sounds disappointed when I say yes. Believe
me, I'm disappointed too. Mickey hasn't even tried to
kiss me, although maybe that's a good thing, because
he's a lot better looking than Daniel Weaver.

Otto says he must live vicariously through me. I
think that's the word. He says that he is too old and
unattractive now to have dates—at least with other
men. Women aren't as picky, he tells me. After a
certain age they will date anyone, even him, but of
course he isn't interested. On two occasions Otto has
gone out and stayed very late, but I don't know who
with, or what they did. On that account he is very
private. I respect that.

Today is my birthday. Tonight I'm supposed to go
out with Mickey to celebrate at the La Dulce Vita,
which is an Italian restaurant on Rodi Road up in Penn
Hills near the shopping center. In the meantime, Otto
has a surprise for me. But first he makes me call in
sick at the Giant Eagle, and cancel my three o'clock
appointment to clean Mrs. Iona Crabtree's house on
Second Street. I tell Otto this is impossible, that I
need the money, but he tells me to trust him on this
one.

After breakfast, which Otto makes, he tells me to
get in the car. We're going for a ride to see my
surprise. Before I leave the house I must put on a
blindfold, which is really only one of Otto's scarves,
and which smells strongly of his aftershave.

My first thought is that he's found a gallery that
has agreed to show my work. However, instead of

turning on Allegheny like we're headed into the city, Otto crosses it, and turns right on Railroad Avenue. So then I think we're headed for the police station, maybe to see Tracy Bright, my sergeant friend. But Otto stops halfway there and pulls off the blindfold.

"Here we are."

I see nothing but some stores, one of which is empty. "Very funny, Otto. Now what is it, really?"

He gets out and comes around to open my door. "Madame, if you'll come this way." Then he takes my hand and helps out of the car like I'm an old person, or too weak to walk.

"Otto, what's going on?"

"You'll see in a minute." He pulls me into the empty store.

"Surprise!"

Tracy, Lucia, and Mickey are all there. Even Mrs. Crabtree and some of my coworkers from the Giant Eagle.

"What on earth?" Although I know Otto's curses, I don't use them.

"Voila," Otto says. Your very own gallery, Anna."

"My *what*?"

Otto hands me a piece of paper. "Here it is. Your six-month lease."

"But I don't understand."

"Well, if Muhammad won't come to the mountain, then the mountain must come to him. Here's your mountain, Anna."

I look around, past the people. It's a small room, barely larger than my bedroom at Otto's house. The walls are bare. The floor is bare too, just concrete painted green. There is, however, a large window that faces the street, and this I like very much. Railroad Avenue is never busy, so a window will not help a lot with sales, but it will keep me from feeling boxed in.

Tracy puts her arm around me. "What do you think, Anna?"

"Who is paying for this," I whisper.

"Mickey."

"Mickey?" I say it so loud he turns and grins.

"I own it, Anne." Mickey is the only one who calls me by my new English name.

I pull free from Tracy. "But Mickey, you can't do this—"

He puts a finger to my lips. "The building was empty, anyway, Anne. Just sitting here. Besides, you'll be paying rent. It's all in the lease, which by the way, you need to sign."

I study the paper. "Ten dollars a month?"

"If you can't afford that—" He laughs, and the others join in.

"We're here to help paint," Lucia says. "Make you a sign, whatever you want."

I am overcome with emotion, and think I might cry. I can feel my chin quiver. So much kindness from people I have known for less than a year, barely more time than it takes for a baby to be born. And where did Otto get enough money? He was a school teacher. I've heard that public school teachers make less money than the garbage collectors.

"There, there," Mickey says, and kisses me, but on the top of my head.

"So what color paint do you want?" Lucia asks. She giggles.

"Egg shell white," I say. "Anything else will throw off the colors in the paintings. And the floor must also be white, or else a neutral gray." I bite my lip, but find myself unable to hold back the greed. "Carpet for the floor would be very nice."

"Now *that* I'm not springing for," Mickey says.

"That's my gift," Otto says.

"But Otto, you have already done so much." Now the tears flow freely.

"There, there," Otto says, and he too kisses me on the top of my head. But he must stand on tiptoes.

Everyone laughs.

"Otto said you would want to get started right

away," Lucia says. She skips off and opens a door I
haven't even noticed. There is a little storeroom
behind this shop. In a minute Lucia is back with paint,
brushes and rollers.

"We thought we'd paint first, and carpet later,"
Otto says. "I ordered a cream Berber. They're
installing it tomorrow. Or would you prefer I change
it to gray?"

"Cream is very nice." The voice sounds like mine,
but I am not sure that my lips move. This is what it
must feel like to be in shock.

"Don't forget the sign," Tracy says, and winks at
Mickey.

Now he disappears into the storeroom and returns
with a piece of wood that appears to be about two feet
by six feet. "What do you want to name your gallery,
Anna?"

I shrug. Nothing comes to mind—well, nothing that
isn't silly. Pretentious, even.

"How about this?" Mickey says and turns the wood.

It is a sign, with gold letters on a sapphire blue
background. *HEAVEN.*

Someone has read my mind. But still, it is a stupid
name for a gallery, and says nothing about what is for
sale inside.

"This is just a mockup," Otto says. "If, you
approve, the real one will be metal. If I call today,
they can have it ready by the end of the week. We
were thinking of adding smaller letters underneath,
maybe in black, that read Fine Art Gallery. Or
something to that effect. What do you say, Anna?"

"Thank you." The tears continue to flow.

Heaven. I have tried hard not to think of it, but of
course that's impossible. Everything about Verona and
Pittsburgh remind me that I'm not in Heaven. When I
see my friends around me with smiles on their faces, I
remember my baptism, the day I crossed the dividing

line between childhood and becoming a spiritually
responsible adult.

Amish believe that only adults who have made a
conscious decision to obey Christ's teachings, should
be admitted to the church. Young men and women join
between the ages of sixteen and twenty-one, with
women generally joining earlier than the men. But
whatever the age, the applicant is expected to have
gotten rumschpringe out of his or her system.

The Saturday prior to my baptism I met with Bishop
Yoder, Deacon Stutzman, and three of the elders. I sat
on a straight back chair at the end of Mama's kitchen
table, and they sat on benches at either side. The
Bishop and the Deacon sat on my left, the elders on
my right. Although it was cool in the room, sweat was
trickling down my sides, and little beads were popping
up on my forehead, each one feeling like a thumbtack
pressed into my skull. I had been praying about this
day for months, and practicing my answers for an
entire week. I did not want to appear nervous.

"Daughter," the Bishop said, "do you feel in your
heart that you are ready to renounce the ways of the
world and obey the rules of the Ordnung."

"Yah, I am ready." My rumschpringe is over. I did
not race cars, go to the movies, wear lipstick, or
bundle with boys. I did not get my hair cut at the
Mae's House of Beauty, like Rachel Gingerich did,
and read the magazines with the half-naked women on
the covers. I never smoked a single cigarette, or had
the smallest sip of beer. I was the model Amish
teenager in every respect, except for one. I took the
talent God gave me and used it.

I painted up a storm. Because I was in the
sanctioned period of rebellion, Mamm only pleaded
with me. She would have been within her rights to
punish me—confiscate the paints, make me do extra
chores—because the limits of rumschpringe are set by
the parents, not the rebelling child. But a wise parent
knows that to pull back too hard on the reins, is to

make the horse bolt when given its head. And I think Daat had a lot to with Mamm's restraint. Daat with the sad eyes, who never spoke about anything unless it was the weather, crops, or, on rare occasions, God.

To my credit, I did not flaunt my sin. Daat looked the other way while I painted in the loft. Both parents turned a blind eye when I started selling the pictures at the blooming fence. Mamm's concession to this wild period in my life was to retire back to the vegetable garden, leaving the sale of quilts up to me again.

At first I didn't make as much money as I hoped, because my technique was poor. The how-to books I bought in Armbruster's Hardware seemed to leave out a few steps. Or perhaps I had the wrong kind of paints.

Then one day on a whim, or perhaps it was more than that, I looked up the word art in the telephone book outside the public library. I dared not go inside the library itself, because there were books in there no Christian should read, even an English one. But in the phone book I found the words *Art Supplies*, and for that the only listing was *Armbrusters*. Just above that was a listing for *Art Classes, Miss Mavis Bonecutter teacher.*

"Praise God," I said, which even now I think is a sin to have said. But then I thought I had found another Bridgett Monroe.

La Dolce Vita is the nicest restaurant I've been to. It's not as expensive as the one on Mt. Washington, and it doesn't have a view, but it has plenty of atmosphere. To get from the parking lot you have to walk through a little garden with a fountain which has four lion heads. The water pours from their mouths. There are also plenty of idolatrous statues of humans, all of them life size, and most of them naked.

Inside there is a wall which is really nothing but

one big fountain, the water pouring down it in a single sheet. Arches set on round pillars frame the fountain. Silk grapevines climb the pillars and from the ceiling dangle bunches of purple plastic grapes. And of course there are more idolatrous statues, which by the way, don't bother me in the least—although it is obvious someone has taken offense. The statue nearest the door has had her arms broken off.

"Tacky, isn't it?" Mickey whispers.

"Oh, I think it's wonderful."

"You would, Anne." I introduce myself now as Anne, although Otto and most of my friends call me Anna.

The maitre d' takes us to our reserved seat next to the fountain wall. This is perhaps just a bit too close because now I can see dust on the grape leaves and pale green scum on the wall behind the water, but still, I am enjoying it immensely.

The waiter comes to take our drink orders. Mickey orders a glass of the house wine, and I order a diet coke. It does not even bother me that Mickey drinks alcohol. He does not ask me to join him, and what he does with his body is his business. Anyway, even Jesus drank wine, Mickey says. It's in the Bible— although I don't think it's in our German Bibles back in Heaven.

Our first course is the antipasto, and then Italian wedding soup. Finally the pasta, which is so long you have to wind it around your fork like knitting yarn. We do not order dessert, because we will be having cake back at the house with Otto. While we are waiting for our pasta, Mickey says he has something important to ask me.

I dig my nails into my palms. My nails are no longer short, and are painted what Mamm would call harlot pink. At any rate, I am not expecting Mickey to propose, and I would say no if he did, but I am expecting something along those lines. At the very least I'm expecting him to want to make ours an exclusive relationship. Mickey dates other women, a fact which he has never tried to keep secret.

"Anne," he says, looking me straight in the eyes, "will you allow me the honor of helping you with the grand opening."

"Grand opening?"

"Every gallery needs a grand opening." He smiles. "It's practically a law."

I have learned that if I ask about what I don't know, English riddles disappear like dew in the mid-morning sun. "What is a grand opening?"

"A kick-off party. I was thinking you could invite the owners of the other galleries, patrons of the Andy Warhol Museum, the Frick Museum, and the Carnegie, and, well—just about anyone whose picture has appeared on the society page in the last year. Of course we'll need to find a good caterer, someone who specializes in heavy hors d'oeuvres. And champagne—" he stops and bites his lip. "Will that be a problem? The champagne, I mean."

I am both disappointed and very excited. I want to be Mickey's girlfriend, but a party like this is beyond my wildest dreams.

"Champagne is like wine, yes?"

"Think of it as wine with bubbles."

I don't think the bubbles would have bothered Jesus. Besides, nobody in Heaven will know.

"How much will this cost, Mickey?"

He smiles. "That's for me to know, and you to find out."

"What does that mean?"

"It means I'm footing the bill."

"You will pay?"

"For the whole shebang. It will be my pleasure, Anne. Think of it as my 'welcome to the twenty-first century' present."

"But I can't allow you—"

"Hey, don't look a gift horse in the mouth, Anne. You're going to need all the cash you have to get those pictures framed, right?"

Frames! I had forgotten all about them. In all of the galleries in Shadyside, in all Pittsburgh—and believe me, Otto has taken me to every single one—pictures are either framed, matted, or on stretched canvas. Never have I seen them for sale rolled up in a tube.

"How much does it cost to frame, Mickey?"

He shrugs. "That depends on how much you're willing to spend. I had a page from a calendar I wanted framed. Took it to one of those professional framing shops and they wanted ninety-five dollars, and that was without a mat. Ended up cutting the picture down and stuffing into a ready-made frame from Wal-Mart. Got by for ten. But of course you'll want the best for your paintings."

I nod, but my stomach is turning like Otto's spin dryer. I've painted nine more pictures since I left Heaven. My pictures are probably larger than Mickey's calendar page and at least six of them need frames and mats. At the very least, this will cost me two thousand dollars.

"What's the matter, Anne? You don't look so good."

"The antipasto has given me heartburn."

"Look, if money's a problem, I'd be more than happy to spot you a loan."

I am reluctant to take Mickey's offer. However, if I don't, Otto will want to lend me the money, and Otto cannot afford it. Besides, Mickey has already warned me not to look a gift horse in the mouth, although this is one mouth I do not mind looking at.

"I will pay it back with my first sales."

"Treat yourself with something nice with the money from the first sale. But if it will make you feel any better, I'll draw an agreement you can sign. It will be strictly business, just like the lease."

Strictly business is not what I want from Mickey. For a moment I think I will tell him that, and then the pasta arrives.

CHAPTER

17

Otto wants to teach me how to drive, but I'm not ready. Even he sometimes gets nervous. If you follow Coal Hollow Road to Frankstown Road, it looks like you'll fly right off into space. Some of the roads in Penn Hills are so curvy, homeowners have to put mirrors at the ends of their driveways just to get out on the main road. As long as Otto will drive for me, I'm happy.

First Otto calls all over the city to see which framing store has the best rates, and then we visit a few to see some samples of their work and talk to them in person. The store that satisfies us the most is in the Waterworks Shopping Center across the Allegheny from Verona.

I can get the whole shebang done to my satisfaction, cutting no corners for two thousand and thirty-six dollars plus tax. I am very pleased and offer to treat Otto to a snack at Fudge All You Want, a gourmet candy store next door. Otto has a weakness for sweets, especially chocolate, which he claims is a fruit, because it originally comes from trees.

Just as Otto reaches to open the door, out comes Brandy. At first I don't recognize her because her hair is regular brown and not in spikes. And, she is wearing army clothes. Fatigues, I think they call them.

"Well, wodey-bo-bo," she says, "if it ain't Aggie and her sidekick the Kraut."

"Brandy?"

"As big as life and twice as ugly, not that I've ever been ugly, but ya know what I mean."

"Are you in the army, Brandy?"

"Nah. Got these from an army surplus store. Whatcha think? Sweet, ain't they?"

"She means cool," Otto says.

"Don'tcha be telling me what I mean," Brandy says.

"Bitch," Otto says, then he takes a step back. The door has opened again and Dog Boy and the other smoker come through. I have forgotten their names.

"Woo, woo, woo," Dog Boy says. "Who's this pretty mama?"

"That's Shaggy Aggie," Brandy says. "Remember, from the bus?"

"Holy shit," the second smoker says. "She didn't look like this then."

"Shut up, Justin." Brandy grabs my arm and pulls me aside, leaving Otto with the smokers. He looks as miserable as a chicken in a rainstorm.

"Hey Aggie," she says, and her breath smells like bubble gum, not cigarettes, "you really do look good."

"Thank you. How's your grandmother?"

"Court made us put her in a state-supported home. Gloria's really pissed 'cause she no longer gets Gram's Social Security, but Jim's definitely okay with it."

It still blows my mind, as Otto would say, that Brandy calls her parents by their first names. I called Mamm by her first name when I was seven. Just once. Mamm made me eat a spoon full of shortening which kept me on the two-seater most of the following day.

"How's Jim?" I ask.

"Okay. Strung out as always—oops, you knew that, right?"

"Otto explained it to me."

"Otto! What do you see in that faggot, Aggie?"

"He's my friend, Brandy."

"Yeah, but ya know what he is?"

"He's kind, and he's generous, and—"

"Yeah, yeah, I get the picture. But me and him have never gotten along. He looks down on us, can ya believe that?"

The last thing I want is to get caught up in the feud between Brandy and Otto. I know that Otto dislikes Brandy because he disapproves of her family altogether. He considers them outsiders to Verona, which at first surprises me, because the town has people from many different backgrounds. But most of them grew up there and everyone knows everyone else—except for Brandy's family. Otto says Brandy and Gloria are sluts and probably drug dealers.

"Brandy, if you and Otto got to know each other better, I'm sure you'd both change your minds."

"No way, Jose. I ain't speaking to that creep. Say Aggie, when I first met ya, ya talked all funny like. Now ya sound regular—just like anyone else. How come?"

"Otto—"

"Screw Otto!"

I decide that the best way to avoid an argument is to change subjects. "Why are you with them," I say, and point with my chin to Dog Boy and Justin. I am relieved to see that they are talking quietly with Otto, and that Otto even smiles.

"Believe it or not, Aggie, it's pure coincidence. I met them in Marshals. You remember them, don't ya? From the bus?"

"Yah, I remember."

"Lenny's kinda cute, don't ya think?"

She means Dog Boy. It is time to change the subject again.

"Brandy, I'm having a grand opening of my gallery—"

"Speak English, Aggie."

"Ach, you don't know, do you?"

"I know that you're weird."

This makes me laugh. "Yah, maybe I am. But what

I want to tell you is that I'm an artist."

Her face is as blank as the last page of my sketchbook.

"I'm a painter, Brandy. Not houses—but the kind you hang on walls."

"You're shitting me."

"It's the truth. Remember that cardboard tube I had with me on the bus. There were ten paintings rolled up in that."

"Nuh-unh!"

I nod, feeling sinfully proud of myself. "That's why we're here, to get the pictures framed. So anyway, Brandy, I'm going to have my own art gallery on Railroad Avenue. Would you like to come to the grand opening?"

It is obvious Brandy is impressed. "What kind of grand opening? Ya mean like when they tie balloons in front of the place and give ya coupons for discounts? 'Cause I gotta tell ya, Aggie, I ain't into art all that much."

"It doesn't matter. And there won't be any coupons. This is really more like a party, with champagne and everything. Please say yes, Brandy, because I'd love to have you."

"You're shitting me again."

Although Otto swears, he says people who swear a lot do so because they have deficient vocabularies, himself included. I used to think this was a joke, but for Brandy I think this is true.

"Will you come?"

She smiles. "Can I bring a guest?"

I try not to look at Dog Boy, but Brandy reads my mind. "Don't worry," she says. "It ain't him."

Otto and the smokers walk over. "You wouldn't believe it," he says, "but I used to baby-sit for Lenny here."

"You're kidding," I say. It is one of Otto's favorite expressions.

"No, they used to live next door. Lenny was what—

six or seven then?"

Lenny nods and smiles, but his dog eyes are on me. "Woo, woo, woo." He says this softly, but everyone can hear.

Otto ignores him. "As a matter of fact, I taught Lenny to ride a bike."

"Down South Avenue?" I ask. "Perhaps Lenny fell on his head going down the hill. That would explain a few things."

Everyone laughs.

"Good one," Brandy says.

"Actually, it was Second Street," Otto says, "which, as you know, parallels Allegheny River Boulevard, and is relatively flat most of its length, except for when you get to . . ."

I no longer listen. I am remembering the only bicycle ride I took, and a brother I'd thought I'd forgotten.

Maybe he wasn't my brother, but he was tall and blond, and not as old as Daat. He was definitely not Elam. This man smiled a lot, and he put me on his shoulders, because I was too young to walk through the stubble of the harvested corn field without tripping.

"Anna, see that bird over there? It is called a crow."

The crow is big and fierce looking. "Will it hurt me?"

"No, Anna."

The man squatted, with me still on his shoulders, and held me steady with one hand. With the other he searched for a rock. All he could find was a stick, the stem of a fast growing weed that survived amongst the corn. He tossed the stick at the crow, but instead of flying away, the crow hopped along the ground in our direction. I screamed and tightened my legs around the man's neck.

"Do not worry, Anna. It will not hurt you. It is only curious. Crows are very smart birds. I have seen them drop acorns on the highway so that the wheels of the English cars will crack them open. Did you know that crows can be taught to speak?"

I didn't care if crows could be taught to sing entire hymns from the Osbund in perfect High German. I didn't want that creature any closer.

"I am afraid." I began to cry.

"Yah!" the young man shouted and clapped his hands. The crow flew away, but the movement caused me lose my balance, and I tumbled forward. Fortunately the man caught me.

"Let me down," I whined. "I want to go home."

"But we are almost there."

I had forgotten where we were going, only that I was promised a surprise. But if getting there meant encountering wild beasts and scary falls, I wanted no part of it.

"I want to go now."

He ignored my demands and hoisted me back up. "Anna, if you cannot stay on my shoulders, how will you balance on a bicycle?"

I though I had heard wrong. "A bicycle?"

"Yah. You know what a bicycle is?"

"It has two wheels." I had seen bicycles in the town, in Heaven. Always they belonged to the English, for unser Satt Leit did not allow them. They were worldly, Daat said. First the bicycle, and then the car. Then where will it stop? The bishop forbade them, Mamm said. In her opinion, that was all we needed to know.

The man walked faster. "Yah, I have a bicycle. But you must not tell this to anyone. This is our secret, Anna. Do you understand?"

I shivered with excitement. "Yah."

He carried me to a place where the field was bisected by a small stream and there was a line of trees. Leaning against an oak was a blue bicycle, with a piece of clear plastic sheeting draped over it.

"It is a bicycle!" I clapped my hands.

Brother, because that is surely who he was—even though I can no longer remember his name—pushed the bicycle through yet another cornfield until we come to a small paved road. I had the impression it was a road no one uses anymore, or if they do, only at planting and harvest times.

There was a little platform behind the seat and Brother set me on that. "Hold on tight to my waist, Anna. As tight as you can. If you get scared, close your eyes."

Brother started to pedal, and I closed my eyes as tightly as when Mamm washed my hair. When I felt the wind in my face, I opened my eyes. Just a slit at first. We were moving faster than I ever had in my life.

Trees whizzed by, but with my arms tightly around Brother, I felt as safe as I did with Daat or Mamm in the buggy. Brother turned on to another small paved road and I shrieked with delight. We sped as far as the main highway that lead past our house. That's when Brother slowed to a stop.

"Go down that road," I said. Already I had forgotten my promise to keep the bicycle a secret. I wanted Elam, and the other children that lived along Herztler Road, to see me on the wonderful English invention.

Brother shook his head. I didn't realize it then, but that bicycle, ridden only on two back lanes among the cornfields, was his rumschpringe. That was how daring Brother could get, and still not give Mamm a case of the nerves. No car hidden in the haystack for him, no trip into Philadelphia or New York City to see topless dancers, like everyone knows the Keim boys did during their sanctioned period of rebellion. Just an old blue bicycle and two miles of asphalt. Brother was either very considerate or, as Brandy would say, lacked cajones.

Back at the strip of woods, Brother carefully tucked the plastic around the bike and lifted me back to his shoulders. "Remember, Anna, this is our secret. If you do not tell anyone, then we can do it again."

"I will not tell," I say.

But it didn't matter. That night the barn burned and I never saw brother again. The next spring Daat, who was apparently totally unaware of his oldest son's rebellion, discovered the bicycle among the trees. I remember, because I was with him. Already Brother's face had grown fuzzy to me, but even now, after all these years, I remember Daat's face when he discovered the forbidden machine. He looked sad, not angry. I watched while he pushed the bicycle through the half plowed field to a bass pond on the far side of our property. Grunting, he threw the offending bicycle as far into the pond was possible.

"Do not tell Mamm," he said.

I never did.

Lucia, Tracy, and Mrs. Crabtree all come over to Otto's to help me get ready for the big night. Lucia "teases" my hair, which means she fluffs it with a brush. She must use half a can of hairspray to hold it in place. Tracy says I look like a blonde lion. When Lucia is through fixing my hair she paints my nails— harlot pink. Because it is a special occasion I consent to pink lipstick as well. Immediately I do not like the feel. It leaves my mouth oily, like I have been licking out a sardine can.

While Lucia does my hair and makeup, Mrs. Crabtree puts the finishing touches on the dress I will be wearing. It is a formal dress that belongs to Lucia, but she is two inches shorter than I am and the neckline is cut too low. Fortunately there was extra material in the hem, and Mrs. Crabtree, who used to do a lot of sewing, has a piece of lace to sew across the V of the neck. The lace is navy blue, and the dress is midnight blue, and they don't quite match, but it is close enough.

For a week Otto has been asking me about my dress, and I've been telling him I have one all picked out and ready. I am thinking about a dress I bought at Penney's, but Otto thinks I mean a dress I ordered when I was out with Mickey. On the morning of the opening I show the dress to Otto, and I think he will have a heart attack. This is a "shindig," he says, my golden opportunity to knock the socks off Pittsburgh society. God forbid I should look like I'm going to church.

Tracy watches while Lucia does my hair and Mrs. Crabtree tries to press the old seam from the hem. Fortunately Lucia has all the same measurements as I do, except for the height—although I think maybe my waist is smaller.

"I don't know what all the fuss is about," Tracy said. "It's just a party."

"It's the party of the year," Mrs. Crabtree said, even though her mouth holds half a dozen pins.

"Well, none of *us* are wearing gowns."

"Anna is the guest of honor. Besides, none of us is dating Mickey."

"Tracy doesn't like Mickey," Lucia says.

This surprises me. "Mickey? Tracy, why not?"

She shrugs.

I feel a need to defend Mickey. "He's a very nice man. Very considerate. And cute, don't you think?"

Lucia sprays one last time, but without warning me, so that it gets in my eyes. "Tracy here bats for the other team."

I squeeze my eyes tightly shut for a moment, hoping to make tears. "You play baseball, Tracy?"

"She's a lesbian," Lucia says. "Not that I'm judging or anything."

"Although it is a sin," Mrs. Crabtree mumbles.

"Spoken like a true Catholic," Lucia says.

"I am confused," I say.

"Don't you get it, Anna? Tracy has a crush on you."

Tracy is blushing. "Hey, that's not fair."

What a Dummkopf I am not to have seen it. Tracy has come over many times to visit Otto and me, but always by herself. Sometimes she comes over when Otto is not home, and we sit and talk about many things, although never about sex. When she shops at Giant Eagle she always comes through my line, even if there is a long wait. But all this I think is just friendship.

"I wonder how many people will actually show up," I say. Otto and I sent out seventy-five invitations. Sixty-two people said they would come, but Otto says to allow for at least a ten percent no-show.

"Anna, can I speak to you alone?" Tracy asks.

"Better watch yourself, Anna," Lucia says, but she is laughing.

"A sin," Mrs. Crabtree says, but she too smiles.

I follow Tracy out to Otto's back porch. It is cold, even for April, and I must hug myself to keep warm. Tracy still blushes, and the air makes her cheeks even more red.

"God, Anna, I'm so embarrassed I could die."

"Don't worry, Tracy. I take it as a compliment, yah?"

"Well, just so you know, I would never hit on you—unless I thought the feeling was mutual." Her voice rises just enough to make it a question.

"I'm sorry Tracy, but I like men."

"I'm okay with that. But Anna, are you sure Mickey's the one for you?"

"I like him very much."

"But how much do you know about him?"

"I know what his favorite foods are, I know that his favorite color is blue, I know that when he was a little boy he had a dog named Skipper, I know—"

"Do you know what he does for a living?"

"He's an investment counselor."

"For what company?"

This I do not know. But why should I? Mickey and I never talk about work. It wouldn't be fair, would it? What interesting thing could I say about bagging groceries at Giant Eagle, or cleaning houses?

"We don't discuss his business, Tracy."

"I thought so."

"What do you mean by that?"

"It's just a suspicion I have—based on my law enforcement nose. I can't prove anything, you understand."

CHAPTER

18

Tracy will not say anything more about Mickey. Now when I look at her she blushes. Fortunately there is not much time to look.

Mrs. Crabtree slips the dress over my head and then makes more stitches. Now I am sewn into the dress like an Amish doll. Lucia has loaned me her "pushup" bra. It does not do exercises. Instead it takes the bosoms God gave me, which I think are plenty big enough, and makes them appear twice as large. Lucia wants to put dark eye shadow in the cleavage to accentuate them even more, but I tell her enough is enough. I do not want to look like a Holstein. Even half a Holstein.

Now that she is done with my hair, Lucia works on my face. She plans to sculpt me into a classic beauty. Tracy tells her not to mess with perfection, and then blushes again. Meanwhile, I must wear a towel around my shoulders to keep the makeup off my dress, while Mrs. Crabtree makes the last stitches at my waist. I pray that somebody besides Otto will be around after the party to help me take the dress off.

I am wearing my first pair of high heels and I wobble like a foal. I want to wear sensible shoes, but all the women say this is not to be done. The shoes are new—Otto picked them up at Payless at the last minute—and they are not an exact fit. Mamm once said that English women think they are free because

they can wear what they want, but then they hobble
themselves. They are like horses put out to graze in a
pasture without fences.

Lucia is the last to finish with her job. She hands
me a mirror.

"So? What do you think?"

I do not recognize the woman I see. There is brown
under my cheekbones, pink on top, and even sparkles,
like a thin layer of frost. There are many shades of
brown and gray above my eyes, and they are lined
with black. My eyelashes are black too, and in the
mirror, which makes everything appear larger than it
is, they look like clumps of spiders with long, curving
legs. Even my lips have two shades of red and shine
like a polished apple.

"Oh my god!" Otto says. He slaps his hands to his
face. "You look marvelous!"

"Do you really like it?" I ask. I look like the
Whore of Babylon. At least that is what Catherine
Beiler would say if she could see me now. Mamm
would for sure have a case of the nerves and cry, and
Daat—it is better not to imagine the look on Daat's
face.

"Darling, it's at times like this I wish I was
straight."

"Or out of the closet," Lucia says. "Otto honey,
give me an hour more and some hot wax, and I could
have you looking like this too—well, maybe not
exactly like this."

"In a pig's eye," Mrs. Crabtree mutters.

A car honks and Otto runs to look out the window.
"For that kind of money," he says, "you'd think they'd
at least ring the doorbell."

The women giggle, even Tracy. "Who is it?" I want
to know.

Otto pulls up the blinds, but it is dark outside and
from where I stand, afraid to walk on the silly shoes, I
see only our reflections. The Whore of Babylon and
her four friends. The window mocks me.

Then Tracy turns off the light and now I see a long white car, as long as two regular cars. A limousine they call it. I have seen them before outside churches while weddings are held, and on prom night. Prom, along with high-school graduation, is the English equivalent of baptism. This is how I would explain it to Mamm if I had the chance.

Lucia shows me how to walk down the front steps by holding my dress up with one hand, and I make it to the limousine without falling. The sidewalk from Otto's house to the street is cracked and chunks of it have been pushed up by the frost of many winters. Of course I stumble a few times, and everyone laughs when they know I'm going to be okay. We will all be riding together, and even Mrs. Crabtree is excited.

"Who would have thought I would ever ride in one of these? Too bad the windows are tinted. My friends won't be able to see me."

Otto laughs. "If we pass any of them along the way, I'll make sure the driver pulls over, and you can roll down the windows."

"It's only six blocks to the gallery. I doubt if we'll pass anyone I know."

"Don't be so sure about that. Anna needs to make a grand entrance, so I have arranged for us to take a spin around town first. You know, so we can be fashionably late."

The driver of the limousine, who wears a uniform, comes around and opens the door for me. I am to enter first.

"Like Cinderella going to the ball," Lucia says. I think I hear envy in her voice.

I have not yet met Cinderella, but I'm sure I will, sooner or later. Because she's a hairdresser, Lucia knows everyone. When I meet her, Cinderella and I will share our feeling about what it is like to ride in such a big fancy car. In the meantime I have my friends to share my joy with, and I am grateful to Otto.

We drive up and down all the streets of Verona. We even drive over to Oakmont where, according to Mrs. Crabtree, the hoity-toity people live. We go all the way up Hulton Road, past the house where Hellen Keller used to spend her summers, and turn right on 10th Street. It is now a quarter past seven, but since it is April, it is still light out and people are walking. Even I can tell that they are dressed in expensive clothes, and that they are not walking to get anyplace, but for exercise. A few even walk just for pleasure.

We approach a couple about Mamm and Daat's age. They walk close together, holding hands. I am sure my parents love each other, but this is something I have never seen them do.

Otto tells the limousine driver to pull over. Then he rolls down the window.

"Pardon me," he says. "Do you have any Grey Poupon?"

Everyone laughs, including the driver. Even the strange couple. I am the only one not to understand this joke.

The woman steps closer and looks inside. "Anyone famous in there?"

This time Otto stops the laughter. "As a matter of fact there is." He pats my arm. "This is Anna Hostetler, Pittsburgh's newest art sensation."

"Performing arts?" she asks.

"An actress," the man with her says. Now he steps forward. "I've seen you on Baywatch, haven't I?"

Again everyone in the limousine laughs, except for me. "She's a painter," Otto says. "A damn good painter."

The woman's eyebrows go up. "I don't believe I've heard of you."

"That's because she's new on the scene."

"What sort of work do you do?"

The man doesn't wait for an answer. "We knew

Andy Warhol. Pittsburgh boy, you know. Do you paint like that?"

I don't know much about Mr. Warhol. I look at Otto.

"No," he says. "She paints better than that. Real evocative stuff. Has to do with life on Amish farms. She was Amish, you know."

"You don't say." I can feel him looking at me. It's as if his eyes are inside my clothes.

"I love Amish art," the woman says, but she is tugging gently on the man's arm.

"This isn't Amish art," I say. "It's about the Amish."

"She has her own gallery," Otto says. "As a matter of fact, tonight's the grand opening. We're headed right there now." He hesitates, but only for a few seconds. "Would you like to attend?"

The couple exchange glances. Now the woman steps forward.

"Where is this gallery?"

"Railroad Boulevard." He does not add Verona, but the husband and wife know. They sniff the air like hunting dogs and back away from the limousine.

"I forgot we have plans for this evening the woman says." Already they resume walking.

Otto rolls up the window. "Arrogant bastards."

Tracy pats my knee. "Don't let them get to you, honey. That's Oakmont, for you."

"You think Oakmont's bad," Lucia says. "Try Fox Chapel."

The driver heads back for Verona without being told.

I see the sign first. *HEAVEN*. It is back-lit, as Mickey says, so that it can be seen at night, but is still tasteful. But there is no one outside to see it. There is one van and one car parked on the street, about half a block away. No other cars. Tracy pats my knee again. This time she lets it rest there.

"Don't worry, Anna. They'll show up. Probably just can't find Railroad Avenue, that's all."

"Yeah," Lucia says, "this ain't exactly Fifth Avenue."

I move my knee away from Tracy's hand. "This makes me feel better?"

"You see," Otto says, "what you ladies have done?" He tells the driver to pull up to the curb right next to the shop. Then like there are a thousand people watching, like I am Queen Elizabeth getting out of her golden carriage, he helps me out of the limousine.

Tracy and Lucia clap loudly. Even the driver, whose face is now pink, claps a little.

Otto runs ahead and opens the door. He extends his arm and bows so low his fingertips scrape the sidewalk.

"Entrée, Madame."

Otto has shown me Audrey Hepburn movies. He calls her the epitome of womanhood and grace. I try to sweep into my new gallery like Audrey Hepburn in the final scene of *Roman Holiday*.

Inside there is clapping as well. It is Mickey Hanahan and the caterers. The caterers are wearing white jackets, but Mickey is dressed in a black tuxedo with a black silk shirt and a white bow tie. He smiles at me.

"God, you're a vision of beauty."

"You can say that again," one of the caterers says.

I must look away from Mickey. At first I cannot believe what I see. There is a long table running down the middle of my shop, and another, a smaller one, across the door that opens to the storeroom. On the long table there is more food than you will find at an Amish wedding, but of course it is of a different sort. I see little sandwiches, of various shapes, all with the crust removed. There are warm pastries with fillings, and cold pastries with fillings. There are hot-dogs smaller than my little finger wrapped in dough, and pies that will fit in the palm of my hand. Kitsch, I think they are called.

In the middle of the table there is a sculpture made of ice. A horse's head. I think how shocked Daat and Mamm would be, but how it would please Daat that the sculpture will melt in just a few hours.

On the smaller table there are drinks of many kinds, and I think some of them Jesus did not drink at the wedding in Cana. Just looking at this display would send Mamm to her bed for a week with the nerves. But while I feel guilty, I cannot deny I feel pleasure too. I am no longer the Anna who must obey the Ordnung. Maybe I will have a glass of champagne. That will serve Bishop Yoder right. Catherine Beiler too. No, in memory of Catherine I will drink *two* glasses of champagne.

When Mickey leaves to speak to one of the waiters, Otto steps to my side. "Geez, you'd think he was one of the boys. I'm surprised that damn horse's head isn't a statue of a peeing boy."

"Otto!" But I am no longer surprised by what he says.

"Sorry, Anna, but I still don't think that guy's good enough for you."

Now I am surprised. I have known from the beginning that Otto does not like Mickey, but always this has been implied. I think that's the word.

I look at Mickey. His back is turned as he speaks with the caterers. He has very broad shoulders and narrow hips, but his buttocks are firm and round as cabbages. But this is only a guess, you understand. I have not yet squeezed Mickey's cabbages.

Now Lucia takes my arm. She steers me away from Otto, and in the direction of drinks.

"Anna, I hope you realize how lucky you are."

"Yah. Mickey treats me very nice."

"I'm not just talking about your studmuffins, Anna. I mean *this*." She waves her arm to include everything in the room. "Man, I can hardly believe it. Not even a year ago you walk into my shop, speaking all funny like, and acting like you ain't never been anywhere, and now look where you are. You've got your own gallery. Something like that would never happen to me."

"But you don't want a gallery, Lucia. Do you?"

She sighs. "Of course not. But that ain't the point. I'm never going to amount to anything, Anna. Just cutting hair, a few perms, a color job now and then, that's all I can ever ask for. Hell, the old lady probably doesn't even have me written into her will."

The old lady is Lucia's mother. Mrs. Martin has blue hair and the powder on her face is so thick it looks like she dipped it in flour. Twice a week, on Tuesdays and Fridays, she helps Lucia in the shop. The rest of the time she sits above the business in her apartment and smokes, watching her TV shows. Sometimes, when the weather is nice and Lucia has the shop door open, you can hear her mother laughing through the open window. But it is only the TV she laughs at. If they have a choice, customers always pick Lucia.

"Oh, quit your bitching," Tracy says. There is laughter in her voice, but I know she does not like to see me alone with Lucia.

Mrs. Crabtree joins us as well. "So, who's going to clean my house now, Anna?"

"What do you mean?"

"Well, now that you have your own business, you're going to drop your clients. Right?"

I have not thought of this. There are six houses in Verona I clean, and nine in Oakmont. All but two I clean once a week. For the past two weeks, while Otto and I have been getting the gallery ready, I have had to juggle the hours of my cleaning, but I have not dropped any of the houses from my schedule.

"I will still clean your house," I tell Mrs. Crabtree.

"I just bet you will." Mrs. Crabtree is like a crabapple; small, hard, and bitter. She is a good friend, but you must not compare her to a sweet apple for eating.

There is the sound of the door opening—Otto has tied a string of cow bells to the door—and loud voices. I am afraid to look, in case it is just my imagination.

"Well, I'll be damned," Tracy says. "Look what the cat dragged in."

I turn to greet my guests.

CHAPTER

19

"Brandy!"

She wears a black velvet dress that is so short I think she will not have to raise it to go to the bathroom. Her platform shoes are black and have straps that wind up the legs all the way to the knee. Today her hair is black as well and piled on her head in a million ringlets, held loosely in place with a black velvet ribbon. Even her lipstick is black.

"That's obviously a weave," Lucia says.

"What?" I ask.

"A hairpiece. Like a wig."

"At least she matches," Tracy says. "Got to give her credit for that."

I wouldn't care if Brandy is wearing green and purple. She is not alone. Behind her, and looking as nervous as hens in a fox den are Gloria and Jim. I can't believe my eyes.

"Welcome to Heaven," I say. I cannot control the enthusiasm in my voice.

Gloria looks from Brandy to me, and back to Brandy. "Can I smoke in here?"

Otto appears suddenly at my side. "No," he says.

"Figures." Gloria has a cigarette in her hand, but she does not return outside. Instead she pushes past Otto and starts moving slowly around the room, her eyes only on my paintings. She does not even look at the table, where the horse's head now drips, like the

animal has been ridden too hard and is sweating. Jim
follows her, as close and silent as her shadow. Brandy
clops along behind them, her platform sandals making
as much noise as any horse's hooves.

"Bitch," Tracy say. She is referring to Gloria, but I
do not think this is a professional way for a police
woman to behave.

They walk around the room clockwise, taking time
to study each painting. Brandy walks with them, and I
see her arms moving wildly, but I do not hear what
she says.

Mickey is done with the caterers and he stands with
his hand resting lightly on my shoulder. I can feel
both Otto and Tracy staring at my back. They are
wishing Mickey Hanahan would disappear like the fog
that lifts each morning from the Allegheny River.

But we all turn when the door opens, It is not the
art critic from the Post Gazette, or any of the many
other gallery owners Otto and I have spoken to. This
man's arrival is a mistake.

He wears blue jeans and a brown sports jacket that
has patches on the sleeves. He is shorter than Mamm,
who comes only to my shoulder. To be short is, of
course, not his fault, and it is not his fault that he is
almost bald. In fact, he would look a lot like Otto,
except that he chooses to wrap what little hair he has
around the top of his head like the coils of a cinnamon
bun.

He nods at us, but does not say hello. Then he
starts to walk around the room the opposite way of
Gloria and Jim. Brandy is not with her parents, but
has stopped to flirt with the waiters.

The stranger takes more time than Gloria and Jim,
and when he is only a quarter of the way around the
room they meet at a painting titled *Sudden Storm*.
Gloria and Jim hold drinks in their hands, and they
and the short bald man have a long discussion, but
about what, I do not know. At one point they all turn
and look at me, and Gloria shakes her head.

"You can bet that water seeks its own level," Otto says.

"Probably some street person," Lucia says. "Should we have posted a guard?"

"Street people don't hang out in art galleries," Mrs. Crabtree says. "Besides, this guy's kind of cute."

"Ooh, gross," Lucia says. Everyone laughs, including Mickey.

The stranger starts to move around the room again, and then Gloria and Jim join us. "Do you know who that is?" Gloria demands.

"Obviously a friend of yours," Otto says.

"Screw you," Gloria says. She pulls Jim by the hand and they walk over to the refreshment table. Jim still hasn't said a word.

Brandy comes flying over like a mother hen whose chicks have been threatened. "What the hell just happened?"

"Your parents can't take a joke," Otto says.

"Woo, woo!" It's Dog Boy and Justin. Who invited them, I want to know, but I ask it politely.

"They are not my friends." I say it quickly, and in a whisper.

"Hey, Aggie," Dog Boy says. He comes and stands next to me, on the side opposite Mickey. Dog Boy wears the man's perfume, which is called cologne, like the city in Germany. I think I prefer the smell of *huafa mischt*, horse manure, to this. Meanwhile Justin heads straight to the table with the drinks.

Mickey still has his arm around my shoulders and he gives me a squeeze.

"So, Aggie," Dog Boy says, "you really do all these pictures?"

"Her name is Anna," Mickey says. He squeezes my shoulder tighter. "Or Anne."

"Yeah, whatever." Dog Boy hasn't even looked at my paintings, and I think he never well. His eyes have found Lucia, and hers him. They regard each other like two dogs in heat. Without saying a word they split from the group and head together to the food table, where the ears have melted from the horses head, and the once flowing mane is now just a ridge on the shrinking neck.

"This party really sucks, ya know that," Brandy says. She looks at Mickey and me. Her eyes are filled with a mixture of resentment and pride, but not hate.

"If that's how you feel," Otto says. "Then get the hell out of here."

"Fine! I will!"

But she doesn't, because now five men enter the gallery. They are wearing suits. Even I can tell that they are expensive suits, because they are shiny like a preacher's, and don't have patches at the elbows. Mickey gives my shoulder a final squeeze and hurries to meet them.

"Who in the Sam Hill are they?" Mrs. Crabtree asks.

"They look like pimps," Tracy says.

"Like ya would know," Brandy says.

Tracy puffs up her chest like a pigeon. "I just might. I *am* a police officer."

"Like I can forget."

"It's not my fault you have a rap sheet a mile long."

"All small stuff," Brandy says. "And most of it before I turned eighteen. No fair bringing that up here. Ya know, I oughta sue ya, or something."

"Just try it," Tracy says. "You won't be able to cross the street at a green light without getting a ticket."

Brandy looks at the rest of us, "Younz heard that, right? That's police harassment."

"Please," I beg. "Please don't argue."

I have not gotten used to the way the English argue, raising their voices in public. In Heaven disagreements are gentle, and almost always in private. If peace cannot be achieved, a third party is called in to mediate. There are exceptions, of course, but they are just that. *Exceptions.*

And then there is Catherine Beiler. She disagrees with no one, but her tongue is sharper than a plow blade. A comment here, a comment there, as gentle as a purring kitten, and never to your face. A good blade, like a good knife, Daat says, will cut you and you won't know it. The blood and pain come later.

"Brandy," Otto says, "I want you to leave."

"I don't care what ya want," she says. "This is Aggie's party." She turns to me. "What do ya want, Aggie?"

"Her name is Anna," Tracy says.

Brandy shows Tracy her middle finger, which she calls flipping the bird. "I call her what I want. Besides, she don't mind, do ya, Aggie?"

I nod. "Actually, Brandy, I do."

Brandy looks surprised. "Ya do? Then why didn't ya say something?"

"I did say something. You didn't listen."

Brandy shrugs. "Well, it was just a silly name. It's not like it hurt ya or anything."

"You don't know that," Otto says.

She flips him the bird as well. But I feel sorry for Brandy now. My friends are united in their dislike of her, and Dog Boy and Justin are too busy eating to notice. So I think it is a good thing when Gloria and Jim finally leave the food table to join us. Jim looks at me, and then down at his feet, but Gloria pushes Brandy aside and looks right into my eyes.

"Why the hell didn't you tell me you were capable of this?"

"There was no reason."

"Bullshit." She faces Otto. "The food's crap by the way, but I want a piece of this gallery."

He laughs.

"I'm not joking. Anna owes me."

"For what?"

"We wouldn't be standing here if it weren't for the kindness of my husband and me. We took her in when she first came to this miserable town."

"You took her in to use her."

I do not hear Gloria's response. I am shocked that I
have forgotten to ask about Mrs. Scott. While Gloria
and Otto argue, I take Jim aside. Brandy wants to
follow, but I forbid it.

"No way, Jose," I say.

These are words Brandy understands. She
skedaddles, as Otto would say, to hang out with Dog
Boy and Justin.

I walk Jim to a quiet spot near the storeroom door.
"How is Gloria's mother?"

He will not look me in the face. "She's in a group
home down in Pitcairn. It's not the best, but it's all
she can afford on Social Security."

"Gloria does not help?" This is what Otto calls a
historical question, because the answer is already
known.

"Anna," he says, "I didn't get a chance before to
thank you for what you did for my mother-in-law."

"It was nothing."

"Thank you, Anna."

"I did what had to be done." But I think I would not
do it again. Not if I knew the helpless goat eyes would
turn into hard glittering lumps of coal, and that I
would be accused of trying to kill her.

"I should have done something," he says, and his
voice trails off like he wants me to disagree.

"When you see her again," I say, "tell her hello
from Anna."

"I will do that."

We have nothing more to say so we return to my
friends.

"Well Anna," Brandy says—this is the first time
she has called me by my name, "your party has really
been a bust. Next time you might want to invite your
friends." She laughs, but no one else does.

I look around. Mickey and the men in shiny suits
have disappeared. So has the man with the cinnamon

bun hair. The caterers stand with their arms crossed, waiting to clear away any food left behind by Dog Boy and Justin. The horse's head is now just a small ball of slush, just about the size and shape of a road apple. *Huafta mischt.*

I look at Otto, who fights back tears. "Sorry, Anna. People must have had plans for tonight. I'm sure they'll flock into here tomorrow to see what they've missed. And don't forget, there is the limo ride home. I hired it for the whole evening, you know. We can drive it over to Fox Chapel and pretend we're rich."

"Bullshit," Brandy says. "People will just think we've got the prom date screwed up, or somebody got married. Ya wanna pretend you're rich, then let's ride downtown, or out to the airport."

Otto's lower lip quivers. "Who say's you're coming?"

"Hey, I'm Anna's friend too."

"I want to go straight home," I say. The thought of spending any more time this night with these friends is making my stomach sick. I prefer even to walk back up South Street, than to get back in the car that is long enough to be two cars. It is cool outside, and when I get back to my room at Otto's, I will open the windows and crawl under my covers. I will pretend that I am back in Heaven, in Mamm and Daat's house. I will chose to remember a time when I was still innocent. When I was one of the unser Satt Leit. One of our people.

CHAPTER

20

But I cannot return to innocence, even in my dreams. In my dreams I sit on the peak of Daat's barn roof. Below, on all sides of the barn, are the members of Heaven's Amish community. Not just Bishop Yoder's church, but all the congregations. It is a sea of black clothes and white faces all turned up to look at me. At the beginning of the dream I am dressed as everyone else, but then suddenly I am naked. Totally naked. I have not even fancy English underwear to cover my areas of shame.

"Come down from there," someone calls.

"Yah, come down," others call, and soon everyone is calling to me. But the first voice is always the loudest and I recognize it as the voice of Catherine Beiler. At that point the white faces turn black and unser Satt Leit become a flock of crows.

Their cawing becomes unintelligible. These crows have not had their tongues split. They call louder and louder, and then one of them flies up and brushes me with its giant wings. Its feathers are rippled and hard, like the surface of a washboard. It wishes to knock me to the ground where the rest of the flock will feed on me. It is all I can do to hang on to the roof, gripping with toes as well as my fingers. When the crow's head passes close to me I recognize its eyes as those of Catherine Beiler.

I wake from my dream shivering and must close the

window. The red letters on my alarm clock read four-thirty, the time Daat gets up every morning to milk the cows. Daat doesn't need an alarm to get him up. He has been getting up at this hour since he was sixteen, since Grossdawdi gave him his first freshened heifer to begin his own herd.

Mamm sleeps in until five. Then she starts a fire in the wood-burning kitchen stove. There are Amish who use propane gas for cooking, but not Bishop Yoder's congregation. While Daat finishes the milking and feeds the pigs and chickens, Mamm fries potatoes, ham, and eggs. She slices bread made yesterday. Today's dough will not begin to rise until the kitchen is warm enough to activate the yeast. When breakfast is ready Mamm will wake Grossdawdi Hostetler. He is old now and must be helped to the table. The three of them will eat together, and they will think of me, whose place at the table is empty, but they will not mention my name. Anna Hostetler is dead.

Dead in a bed in Verona.

I drift back to sleep and wake at seven-thirty. The smell of Otto's coffee would wake even the dead, I think. With my coffee I have a bowl of raisin bran, the kind with two scoops. Otto eats only oatmeal, which he says is good for his heart. While we eat I think of Mamm and Daat, and Grossdawdi Hostetler, but I do not speak of them.

To give words to my feelings, is to make them even stronger, and I am not sure I can bear the pain. Otto is a good friend and does not ask what I am thinking, but waits for me to volunteer. Today we talk about the weather, which has turned cold overnight. Beads of snow whip against the windows, even though daffodils bloom along the patio.

Otto pours me a second cup of coffee. He puts in hazelnut creamer, which he knows I love.

"Well, Anna, today's the big day."

"That was yesterday." I am in no mood for jokes.

Otto shakes his head and smiles. "Yesterday was

only the beginning. Today is what counts. Today we see if John and Jane Doe walk in off the street."

"They are customers?"

"We hope so. That means your average gal and guy. The hoi-polloi, so to speak. The great unwashed masses—although the great unwashed probably don't buy a lot of fine art. So back to the average gal and guy."

My English is excellent now, but still there are riddles. The answers do not matter though, because I will not go into the shop. I tell Otto I have given up on my dream to be a successful painter.

"Don't be silly," he said. "You had a dream Anna, and this is it. Dreams don't come true all at once, you know."

"Yah, but maybe I had the wrong dream."

This is the first time I have dared say these words, even to think them to myself. But it is something I must consider. Perhaps it was never meant to be. What if Bridgett Monroe was sent to me as a test? If that was the case, I failed the test, and there is nothing to be gained from persisting in this foolishness.

"Nonsense," Otto says.

But I had opened the gates of doubt, if only for myself. "Daat can use my help. Mamm's nerves keep her inside most of the time."

"Anna, you can't be serious! You're not planning to move back. I mean, you can't." He takes a gulp of his coffee. "They won't let you back, will they?"

"If I repent. The sinner who repents can always go home. It is the story of the Prodigal Son."

"Repent? Hells bells, you haven't done anything wrong!"

"I wanted fame. To be known for my work. That's pride, and pride is a sin. In fact, it is the worst of sins."

"Worse than murder?"

"To take someone's life, is to act as if you are equal with God, who gave the life. Isn't that pride?"

"Maybe. But you're not equating your beautiful paintings with murder—are you?"

"If I return to Heaven, and prepare myself to submit to the Ordnung, perhaps I can believe in what is right."

He drains his cup. "You mean convince yourself that you've done wrong"

"One can choose salvation, Otto. Sometimes belief comes only after the choice has been made."

Otto takes my mug even though I am not finished. He stacks the dishes in the sink without care. I wonder how many chips will appear when they are washed and put away.

"Anna," he says, his back turned to me, "I can choose to be straight, but that ain't going to happen. Not in this lifetime. I may only be a lapsed Catholic, and I don't claim to know that much about the nature of God, but it seems that He—or She—made us who we are for a reason. I haven't figured out why I'm gay, but it's a no-brainer that you were given this incredible talent to share with the world. Don't you think that hiding it—under a bushel, so to speak—has got to be some sort of a sin?"

"That's why I am here, Otto. But if God—and God is a He, Otto—wanted me to be a painter, than he would have . . ." I cannot think of words to finish my sentence.

"He would have what? Lined customers up around the block? Wasn't it enough that he sent you here to me? Aren't I responsible for getting the gallery open in the first place?" His tone has gone from anger to hurt.

"Yes, but Otto—"

"No buts, Anna. Unless it's to get your butt down the hill and to work on time. Otto Goldschmidt is not a coward, and he doesn't waste time on people who are. The night I met you I saw that you are a winner." He turns and looks me in the eyes. "And you know what? I still see it."

"Really?"

"Really. I've never lied to you Anna, and I never will."

The Bible says that we are to give hospitality to strangers, and that by doing so we may be entertaining angels unawares. But here is a man who has given me hospitality, and yet *he* may be the angel. A gay angel in Verona, Pennsylvania—well, with God all things are possible, are they not?

Otto does not quite read my mind. "God is a She," he says, and winks. "If you don't believe me, ask Tracy."

I choose to laugh, rather than correct him. I choose to get dressed and go with Otto down the hill. I choose against Heaven, Pennsylvania, and for Heaven, Verona.

Otto reminds me how the cash register works, and tells me if I have any problems, any problems at all, I must call him. Then he kisses me on both cheeks—for luck, he says—and goes off to do errands.

When the door closes behind him I feel weak again, and must sit on the stool behind the register. What have I done, I ask myself? Why couldn't I have just been a good girl, an obedient woman? Life is so much more simple for those who do not question authority. Blessed are the meek and the humble. But I have been proud, more proud even than the English woman Madonna who Otto listens to on the CD.

The cowbells ring. I look up in fear. I would deserve it if the devil himself walked through Heaven's door. Or even Catherine Beiler. I certainly do not expect to see Landon Frasier, the man who gave me a ride home from the mall.

"Hello Anna," he says, as if we have just spoken to each other the day before.

"Hello, Mr. Frasier."

"Please, call me Landon." He glances around the

gallery, and then excuses himself to take a closer
look.

I watch him as he studies my work. He is taller
even than Mickey, and maybe a few years older. I
guess thirty-five. His hair is dark and he has a deep
tan, even though it has been a late spring. Landon is
wearing a pale blue sweater, Mickey wears only suits.
I cannot help but notice Landon's buttocks when he
bends to examine a painting. Like Mickey's, they are
round and firm as cabbages, although his wallet makes
a bulge.

He looks at each painting before turning to me.
"Anna, these are very good."

"Thank you."

"No, I mean *very* good. Do you do murals?"

I shake my head. Lucia has suggested that I do
murals, paint clouds on the ceilings of nurseries if my
paintings don't sell. She suggests even painted flower
pots, with daisies and puppies, and sayings like *I Love
Pittsburgh*. Bridgett Monroe would never approve of
this, not that it matters. I would rather die alone,
living in the Grossdawdi house on my brother Elam's
farm, than do such a thing with the talent God gave
me.

"Good," Landon says. "Not that there's anything
wrong with painting murals. I'm just glad to see that
you take your work seriously."

"How did you find me? I mean, this gallery?"

"Your friend told me. Whiskey, I think her name
is."

"Brandy?"

"That's her."

"How do you know Brandy?" Sometimes I can be as
snoopy as Catherine Beiler.

"She's up on the boulevard passing out flyers." He
pulls a sheet of folded paper from his wallet.

I grab it from his hand. *Beautiful paintings.
Originals. Support starving artist.* It says this in large
black letters on yellow paper. At the bottom of the

page there is a drawing of a woman that looks a little bit like me, even if she is as thin as a skeleton.

"Please, wait right here," I say. I take three steps for the door and stop. "I can trust you, yah?"

He smiles and throws me his wallet. "Here, take it with you as collateral."

Brandy stands outside Goldylocks, the hair salon where Lucia works. This is fitting, because this morning Brandy's hair is gold. Her skin is gold too, and it shines like metal. Her clothes are gold, as are her platform shoes. She looks like the Oscar statue Otto says I would win, if I decided to become a movie actress. She looks like an angel without wings.

"Brandy, what are you doing?"

She turns and smiles. Only her teeth are white.

"Aggie—I mean, Anna—what do ya think I'm doing? I'm drumming up business for ya, that's what."

I remind myself to think before I speak. "This is very kind of you, Brandy, but you don't need to do this."

"I know I don't. I'm doing it because I want ta."

"Yah, but—"

"What's the matter, Aggie—I mean Anna—"

"Please, Aggie is fine." I truly do not mind anymore. The hollows of my arms are now as smooth as Otto's head.

"Whatever. My point is, Aggie, are ya embarrassed? Is that it?"

I shake my head.

"Ya are so. I can see it in your eyes. Well, let me tell ya something, Aggie—"

A car drives by and the driver honks. The children in the back seat turn and wave. I realize they wave at Brandy, not at me. I am ashamed for being embarrassed, and for lying.

"How did you turn gold, Brandy?"

"Body paint. This getup cost me a few bucks,

Aggie, but hell, you're worth it."

"Thank you." I am torn between my desire to hug Brandy, and my upbringing, which does not encourage the expression of sentiment. I think that Catherine Beiler would not approve of the hug, so this is what I do.

"Jeesh," Brandy says, "ya don't have to get all mushy on me, Aggie. Besides, you're gonna get yourself all messed up with paint."

She is right. There is gold on my hands and arms where they have touched her back.

"Ach!" I don't know where to put my hands.

"Don't worry," Brandy says. "Obviously it comes off easily."

I have not noticed until now that Brandy's dress is very low in back, like a V, almost to the waist. "Who put the gold paint on, Brandy?"

She smiles. "That's for me to know, and you to find out."

I want to find out, but someone shouts from across the street. We turn and see Lucia. She is standing at the corner near her beauty shop, and waving her arms like Mamm and I do when we try to herd the geese into the barn at night to keep them safe from foxes and raccoons.

Lucia doesn't have any geese to herd. "Hey," she shouts louder. "You get away from Anna."

Brandy hears now too. "Bite me!" she screams and holds up her middle finger.

Lucia turns as white as goose down and tries to fly across the street even though the light is red. She does not see the car that hits her when she is only a third of the way across. I hear a thud, and now she is really flying. She lands almost on our side of the street, with her head only inches from the curb. The sound of her hitting the asphalt is like that of a hand slapping water.

The car does not stop. It is what Otto calls an SAV, a suburban assault vehicle. Perhaps the driver did not even see Lucia, but surely he heard the thump. I remember too late that I must read his license plate. All I know is that the car is green and is an assault vehicle.

Brandy and I do not have time to scream. We run to Lucia, who is lying as still as the deer the English hit with their cars. Daat would make the horse gallop fast past the deer, which almost always looked peaceful, like they were sleeping. I pray that Lucia looks peaceful too. I think I will faint if her head has been cracked open like a pumpkin dropped from the back of the field wagon.

But Lucia does not look peaceful. Her head is not cracked open, and there is only a little blood, which seeps from her mouth, but her body lies facing different directions. She is like a cloth doll that has been twisted in the middle.

"Oh my God," Brandy says.

I drop to my knees and reach to touch her. I want only to turn her hips so that her body faces all in the same direction.

"Don't touch her!" Brandy shouts.

"But Brandy—"

"Her back could be busted, or something."

A crowd appears from nowhere. They surround us, like curious cows, pushing and shoving, but doing nothing to help. Daat slipped in a muddy field once and broke his ankle. The cows stood around him all day until it was milking time, then they wandered off to the barn on their own.

It is Brandy who takes charge. "Somebody call 911!"

The rescue squad is only two blocks away. I hear their sirens just seconds later, but they are not as loud as the screams of the blue-haired lady who pushes through the crowd. It is Mrs. Martin, poor Lucia's mother. She scoops her daughter into her arms and sits down on the pavement. It is too late to tell her not to touch, and besides, it would do no good.

Mrs. Martin rocks Lucia like she is a colicky baby. She screams at her daughter to wake up, but Lucia's head wobbles from side to side and her mouth hangs open. Her body is still twisted in the middle, and I see now that her left leg is bent under her as well.

The sirens scream in my ears and the crowd parts like the Red Sea, but it isn't Moses that comes through. It's Delbert Zelnick from the Rescue Squad and two other men. I know Delbert because he is Tracy's friend.

The instant the noise stops Mrs. Martin points at me. "You! It's all your fault!"

My knees go soft, like someone has punched them from behind. I do not know what to say.

"Hey," Brandy says, "ya can't talk to her like that."

"I wasn't talking to her." Mrs. Martin is crying the words. It is like singing with no tune. "I was talking to *you.* You're nothing but white trash. This wouldn't have happened if it weren't for you."

I think I should feel anger on Brandy's behalf, but feel only fear for Lucia. Her mother seems to have forgotten it is a broken body she holds in her arms.

"Mrs. Martin," I say, "you must be careful—"

"I'll sue," she sobs. "I'll sue, I'll sue, I'll sue."

Delbert Zelnick and one of the men he has brought with him lay a stretcher in front of Mrs. Martin. Now I can see only their backs, so I turn to Brandy. She is gone.

CHAPTER

21

One man must hold Mrs. Martin while Delbert and the other put Lucia on the stretcher. Then Delbert helps Mrs. Martin climb into the back of the ambulance. Meanwhile the crowd is talking like sausages, as Daat used to say. This means they say nonsense.

"Did you see that? She just threw herself in front of that truck."

"I always knew she was going to commit suicide, someday. Them Martins were never a stable bunch."

"But I saw the whole thing, and it wasn't a truck, it was a bus. Someone should call PAT."

"It swerved to hit her, you know."

"She was jaywalking. Paid the consequences, if you ask me."

I am disgusted by the talk. It is possible some of these people witnessed the accident, but no one stepped outside of the shops to help until Brandy and I reached Lucia. I think maybe I should set the record straight, but then I remember my gallery. Landon Frasier is alone in the shop—or maybe he's gone, and the shop is unattended.

As I try to slip through the crowd, someone grabs my elbow. "Anna, just a minute."

"Tracy!"

She's in her uniform, but she points to her badge anyway. "This is official business, Anna."

"Yah." I let Tracy steer me through the crowd,

around the corner from the Greek restaurant, to where there is a Thai restaurant. Ochas. I know the place well now; Otto and I have eaten at Ochas many times. We stand under the awning and talk.

"Anna, were you an eyewitness?"

"Yah."

Tracy removes a small pad and a pen from the pocket of her uniform. Her hands tremble.

"Please, tell me everything you saw."

I tell her everything. I leave nothing out—not even the comments from the crowd. "Rubberneckers," Tracy calls them. They are what holds up the traffic for miles on the highways when there is an accident. Many times they cause even more accidents by stopping to stretch their necks.

Tracy asks so many questions that I begin to think maybe she suspects there has been a crime involved. I ask her this.

"No Anna, this is strictly routine." Her cell phone rings. "Just a minute."

She talks in low tones, so I know the polite thing is to turn away and pretend not to hear. I read the menu that is posted in the restaurant window. The Pad Thai is the best I have tasted, and thanks to Otto, I have tasted many variations of this dish. If I ever cooked for Mamm and Daat again, I would try to make this dish. Mamm might not like it, but Daat I think, would.

Most of the ingredients I could buy right there in Heaven. The noodles would not be the same but . . .

"Anna," Tracy says, "that was a call from Delbert. I'm sorry to be the one to have to tell you this, but Lucia is dead. She was pronounced dead upon arrival at St. Margaret's."

I am surprised only in that I feel nothing, not even relief that Lucia is out of pain. Maybe it is because I did not see her suffer, but maybe it is because I am no longer capable of emotion. Perhaps that is the case, because I am not even bothered by this realization. All I want to do is enter the Ochas restaurant and order

Pad Thai, and a strong chicory coffee to which condensed milk has been added.

"Anna, are you listening?"

"I heard you, Tracy."

"Well, I've got to go—have a report to file. But I'll call you when I get more details, like about the funeral and such. Maybe we can go together."

"Yah, that would be nice."

Tracy pats me on the arm and then leaves, but I do not go into the restaurant. I remember again the shop.

Landon Frasier smiles when I return. I am relieved to see that he is there, not only because he has guarded my shop, but I have his wallet in the side pocket of my dress.

"I'm sorry, Landon—I—uh—well a—"

"There's no need for you to explain, Anna. I didn't mind time alone with your beautiful paintings. In fact, I'd like to buy this one."

He has already on the counter a small watercolor. I call this one Grossdawdi's House. It is a joke no English person is expected to get. A Grossdawdi's House is a cottage for grandparents to live in after they retire and turn the farm over to one of the children. The house in this painting is not a grandparent's cottage, but what the English call an outhouse—an outdoor toilet. Grossdawdi Hostetler spends so much time in this place that Daat once said that when Jesus returns for the Second Coming, that's where he will find my grandfather. Daat told this joke during a game of horseshoes with his friends, but Bishop Yoder heard about it. The next meeting Sunday, which we hosted, Daat had to get down on his knees before the congregation and confess his sin of blasphemy.

"Do you like this painting?" I ask in surprise.

Landon laughs. "Enough to pay six hundred and ninety-five dollars for it. And ninety-nine cents. Does that include tax?" He laughs again.

"I'll give you a ten percent discount, Mr. Frasier. That will take care of the tax."

"I accept your kind offer. But Anna, please, call me Landon."

I nod. "Do you want this wrapped?" Otto has helped me think of everything.

"No, I want to prop this up on the front seat beside me and gaze at it all the way home. I get a real charge out of this."

"I do not take credit cards, Landon. Only cash—and checks." Otto has taught me to look closely at the photo I.D. *and* compare signatures.

"No problem—if you'll be so kind as to return my wallet."

Daat says my cheeks look like ripe tomatoes when I blush. He exaggerates, so perhaps they are only pink now, even though I feel them sting.

"I am so sorry, Landon." I hand him the wallet, which is heavy with money.

Landon opens the wallet, but he does not look inside. "Anna, what's wrong? Is it that silly flyer that has you so upset?"

I cannot look at him or I will cry, and I will not cry in front of a man who is practically a stranger. Or maybe I will not cry, and that is worse. Although my cheeks burn, my heart feels numb with cold.

"My friend Lucia is dead."

"I'm sorry. When did she die?"

"Just now, when I was outside."

"I'm afraid I don't understand."

"She was hit by a car. I saw it happen. That's what took me so long."

"You're kidding," he said. By now this is a meaningless phrase the English use along with historical questions.

I take his money and give him the receipt. There is nothing left for me to say. When he leaves I will close the gallery and take a walk. It does not matter where.

Maybe along the river. My soul requires peace.

"Do you like picnics, Anna?"

"Yah." In Heaven we made many picnics, especially in the summer when it was too hot to eat in the kitchen. Mamm and I filled a wicker basket—what Otto calls a hamper—with fried chicken, macaroni salad, watermelon pickles and shoofly pie. Most of the picnics we made on the banks of the bass pond, which was on our farm, but sometimes we would join other families at Miller's Creek, where there was a small waterfall. Because the creek ran through the woods it was much cooler, but if we stayed too long the mosquitoes would come out. Mosquitoes were just one more thing that set Mamm's nerves off.

Landon gives me a wide smile. "Give me twenty minutes, and I'll take us on a picnic you won't forget. That is, if you don't mind closing up your gallery."

I do not mind at all. I am happy not to think of anything that will remind me of Lucia. Besides, I have already sold one painting, which is more than I expected.

I lock up while Landon gets the picnic. He returns with two paper bags, and a plastic bag through which I can see there are bottles. It does not look like a picnic to me, but I have much yet to learn of the English ways.

He tells me it will be a long drive, and asks if I mind. I tell him the longer the better. He laughs and asks if I am interested in driving through an Amish community he knows about, and which is only a little out of the way. To this I must say no.

I have many cousins who live in Amish communities scattered all over America, some even in Belize and South America. Ours is not a major religion, and we must marry our own. Because of this we are, as Otto says, inbred. All the Hostetlers in this country descend from the patriarch Jacob Hochstetler, whose wife was scalped in the massacre of 1750. All the Yoders come from two brothers. The Masts, the

Millers, the Kauffmans—we are all one big family. Otto says I am my own cousin. He says I need only a sandwich and I am a family picnic.

"You sure you don't want to buzz through," Landon asks? "It's really quite interesting. There's a country-style store and everything."

"I am very sure."

There are not many things that Landon and I can discuss along the ride. Like me, he wishes not to speak of his family. I know nothing of sports, but I pretend to be interested when Landon tells me he predicts the Pirates will have an awesome year. At least I know now that they are not the same men who rape and steal at sea.

Finally there is nothing more we can say, so Landon turns on the radio. The music is loud, with many notes, much like the music Brandy plays.

"Do you like this?" Landon asks.

"It's okay," I say, remembering to use contractions. I do not use them when I think, because I think still in dialect. I dream in dialect as well.

"Do you prefer something else?" Landon asks. He wants only to please.

"Classical is very nice," I say. The classical I have learned to like from Otto. He says that a man named Mozart, who is very much dead, is the chief composer in Heaven. He means *the* Heaven, of course. Heaven, Pennsylvania, does not produce people of importance.

Landon's face tightens just a little bit, but he switches to another station. First I think that I should feel guilty about making him listen to music he does not like so much, but I think, *what the hay*. This expression I learned from Brandy. It means many things I think, but now I wish it to mean that Landon is a grown man who has offered me a choice, and it is not my responsibility to choose what he would like. To ignore his gift of a choice, would be disrespectful.

It is not Mozart we listen to, but Beethoven. This is the song that has the cannons at the end, and Landon

pounds the steering wheel with his fist along with
each boom. I think now he likes the classical music
more.

It is a long ride, but I do not mind. There is
countryside to see, and this I have missed since
moving to Verona.

The land becomes less steep and I see a field with
cows. They are not black and white Holsteins like the
ones on Daat and Mamm's farm. These are brown, and
I think they are the Swiss breed I have heard so much
about.

"Landon," I say, "do you know what breed of cows
those are?"

He laughs. "Cows are cows, aren't they?"

"Oh no. Just like with dogs there are many breeds."

He wears now the polite smile of one who must
listen, but who has left his heart at the front door.
This is what Daat says of Mose Augsberger, who
thinks only of his next sentence. It is not *unser Satt
Leit* for Mose to act this way, but he can hardly be
blamed. His great grandmother was born a Lutheran.
Very few from the outside convert to the faith, for the
Ordnung can be a heavy burden. I know that of which
I speak.

Landon turns off the radio and we ride in silence. It
is not a comfortable silence, and I am very much
relieved when we leave the highway.

"See that sign," he says. "Goat-milk fudge. That
means we're almost there. You ever try goat milk
fudge, Anna?"

I shake my head. I do not like the taste of goat in
any form.

"You have to try it," he says. He pulls over onto a
gravel parking lot in front of a shed. A plump woman
in a ruffled apron smiles at Landon, and it is a smile
of recognition.

"Back for more, I see."

"Can't stay away," he says.

"Brought your daughter this time, did you?" She

points to me with her chin.

"Nope, just a family friend."

She nods. "Got a special going this week. Buy one pound, get another at half price."

Landon buys two pounds. One we will eat on the picnic, the other is for his sister. When we are back in the car he offers me a piece. It smells to me of goat, but I eat it so as not to offend. It is sweet like Mamm's fudge, but tastes like it smells. My stomach wishes it were back in Verona.

Just when I think I may taste the fudge for the second time, Landon pulls into a parking lot. There are only a few other cars, and no people.

Landon says we must follow the path down the hill through the woods. He takes with him the plastic bags of food and an old blanket from the trunk of his car. I do not mind walking. The hill is not as steep as the one in Verona, and the trees remind me of home.

We hear the river before we see it. It is called Slippery Rock Creek, Landon tells me, and it speaks loudly because it contains many rocks over which the water must fall or pass around. There is an old grinding mill on the water's edge, and nearby a wooden bridge that is covered, and looks somewhat like a country mailbox. I think this is the most beautiful place I have ever seen, and I would like very much to paint the sights.

The mill house is empty, except for a skinny woman in pants that are neither long nor short, as is the fashion in this part of Pennsylvania. It is a warm and sunny day—too warm for April—and on top she wears only a cloth tube. An accident waiting to happen, I think, but Landon's eyes say he approves. With the woman are two boys, maybe ages eight and ten, who are as fat and round as piglets. They waddle from side to side when they walk. I must stop myself from the sin of judgment. Amish children help with the chores when they are as young as three. Amos Beiler, whose left leg was deformed, was the only child I knew who was overweight.

The woman smiles and says hello. We greet her in return, but the sons are not interested in being polite. There are exhibits inside the mill house and the boys waddle from sign to sign, and at each the older boy reads aloud to his brother.

Landon steers me by the elbow until we are outside. He is anxious to show me the covered bridge. They are getting scarcer than hen's teeth he says. He asks if we have any like this in Heaven.

We do not, but I think maybe it would be a good idea. In the spring, when the water is high, the horses are nervous whenever they must cross Miller's Creek. Two years ago Levi Zug lost control of his horse and the buggy went over the edge. Rachel Zug was eight months pregnant. No one was hurt, thank God, but the baby came early, and it is common knowledge that baby Jonas screams whenever he sees water, even if it is just to drink.

After we admire the bridge we follow the path along Slippery Rock Creek. At first it is paved, so that even those in wheelchairs can enjoy the beauty. But after a ways it turns into a dirt path that twists around the trunks of trees and rocks as big as the outdoor toilet in the painting that Landon bought. My legs are sturdy but Landon insists on taking my hand and helping me "over the rough spots." His hand is very warm and the first time he touches me, I feel like I have been shocked by static electricity. Because the Amish do not have carpets, this I did not feel until I moved in with Otto.

There is a flat rock almost in the middle of the creek, and there are smaller stepping rocks laid out to reach it. This, I think, would make the perfect place for our picnic, but Landon wishes to remain in the shade. He leads me up a narrow valley which he calls a ravine. A small stream passes through the ravine on its way to meet the creek, and we must cross it several times. There are many small rocks in the ravine and walking is very difficult. This gives Landon many opportunities to grab my hand, and sometimes it seems that he does not want to let go.

At last we reach the top of the ravine where the stream makes a fall of perhaps three feet. Our own private Niagara, Landon says. He spreads the blanket over some ferns and sets out the food. Roast beef sandwiches from Subway and bottled water. Daat would laugh at the bottled water, and Mamm would call it a waste of money. The Subway sandwiches too.

I try not to think of Mamm. If she knew I was sitting among the ferns with a man, even now that I am no longer of the faith, she would suffer a very bad case of the nerves. Landon is not a boy in rumschpringe, but a grown man who knows the ways of the world. Oh, if only Catherine Beiler could see me now.

"What are you smiling about?" Landon asks.

"It's nothing." I have remembered the contraction.

"It had to be something. Come on, share."

"They were wicked thoughts."

He smiles. "I find that hard to believe, Anna. Wicked thoughts coming from an angel like you." He takes my hand again, even though we are sitting, and it is impossible for me to fall.

Now my face feels as hot as Landon's hand. I must say something before he gets the wrong opinion.

"I was thinking about an old lady back in Heaven. She would not approve of a picnic in the woods."

"Is that so?" He pulls my hand to his mouth and kisses the back of it.

I am so shocked, I sit as still as Lot's wife after she became the pillar of salt. Landon does not seem to notice. He kisses my hand again, and then the soft place on the inside of my elbow. I remain frozen, as he scoots closer, and then his lips are on my neck. I can smell his deodorant and the goat milk fudge. The smell of fudge is not so bad when it comes from Landon's mouth.

Because I do nothing to resist, I am saying yes to his advances. This I know in my head. At the same time I cannot believe I allow him to kiss me on the same day my friend Lucia dies. Perhaps it is because there is room for only one set of thoughts in my head, and I want them now to be of Landon. Otto hates movies in which there is great sadness followed by passion. He says they are totally unrealistic. I think now maybe he is wrong, because the mind wants always to escape.

Landon's lips reach mine and I feel more electricity. This time it shoots all through my body, even to those places I am not supposed to touch. I am not afraid, because I know I will stop when the time is right. There is a big difference, I think, between kissing in the woods and lying together as man and wife.

Then I think maybe I am wrong. If Daniel Weaver had kissed me like this...

"Ooh, yuck!"

I jerk my head so fast I bump Landon's lips. I learn later that he cuts them on his teeth and bleeds. All I know now is that the piglets from the mill are squatting in the ferns, just an arm's reach away.

"Damn kids," Landon says. He stands, holding one hand over his mouth.

The piglets crash through the woods grunting. Between grunts they shout disgusting words I try not to hear. I stand also. It is then that I see the blood.

"Oh, Landon, I am so sorry."

"It wasn't your fault, Anna. Where the hell is their mother?"

It does not matter where she is. The picnic is over. Landon's lip has already swollen to twice its normal size, and although the bleeding slows, the cut is very deep. Like a little ravine, I think.

Otto says he will give me driving lessons when the time is right, which he says is the same as the twelfth of never. Because I cannot drive, Landon must do so. I ask him if he thinks we should find a hospital, but he isn't interested. Lips heal faster than any other part of the body, he says, otherwise mankind would starve to death. By tomorrow he will be fine.

In the meantime I will not let him speak, so on the way back to Verona we listen only to the radio. A woman sings about a somebody-done-somebody-wrong song. I think there are many people who have done me wrong, but there is no point in keeping track. To hold a grudge hurts only the person holding it. This is what Otto says—but he has not met Catherine Beiler.

The radio announcer interrupts the somebody-done-somebody-wrong song to say that the traffic across the Hulton Bridge is backed up due to a fire.

When we cross the lavender bridge into Oakmont, the traffic moves very slow, but still it moves. When we reach the little bridge that crosses into Verona, it stops altogether, and there are no cars coming the other way.

We get out of the car to become rubberneckers. Something is happening in Verona. What could it be, we ask the people in the car in front of us.

"Haven't you heard?" the woman asks. "It's been on the radio all afternoon."

"We have heard there is a fire."

"Not just *a* fire. Half the downtown. They say it started in an art gallery, or someplace like that."

CHAPTER

22

Landon turns the car around and parks it in the nearest spot where they will not tow away. Then we walk across the little bridge, past Daily's Bottling Company, which makes juice, and into Verona. There is much smoke, and it is both hard to see and breathe. When we are only a few feet from the bridge, a policeman tries to make us turn around.

"We don't need rubberneckers," he says.

"She's a property owner," Landon says. "The art gallery."

"Don't care what she owns. This is no place for civilians."

"It's her place that's burning," Landon says. He grabs my arm and pulls me around the policeman.

The policeman grabs Landon's shirt. "Look buddy, you aiming to spend the night in jail?"

"They're okay," someone says.

"Tracy!"

Sergeant Bright puts her hand on my back and gives me a gentle push, past the policeman. He looks unhappy, but what can he do?

"Anna," she says, still pushing, "you heard the news?"

"Someone said it was my shop—and half of Verona."

Her laugh is bitter. "It isn't half, but it may as well be. Ferguson's dry-cleaning shop, the pool hall,

Hubbard's Cupboard, that cute little antique store that opened less than a year ago—and your place. Sorry, Anna. They had to call in Oakmont, Harmarville, all the Penn Hills stations—even Wilkinsburg. Never been a fire this big in Verona."

Sometimes the mind cannot handle all the information it receives. If Mamm saw the movie Otto rented when he thought I was going to stay overnight at Lucia's on her birthday—well, Mamm's mind would have splattered like an egg dropped on the porch steps from a second story window. That is how my mind felt now.

"Is the gallery totally burned?"

Tracy patted me. "For now at least it looks like it started there. Hey you guys, I gotta go. I'll give younz a call when I learn anything. Actually, I'll be calling younz anyway. They'll be wanting to ask questions."

Landon squeezes my arm. "Who will be wanting to ask questions?" he says to Tracy.

"Both departments, fire and police. But don't worry. It's standard procedure."

"You don't have anything to worry about," Landon says, as if I cannot hear.

Tracy pats me again and leaves. One of the cars is trying to get around the barricade, even though an officer is blowing a whistle and waving. Perhaps this person lives in Verona and is worried about his home; I do not recognize him as a shopkeeper.

"Come on," Landon says. Landon lets go of my arm and takes my hand. He pulls me up the nearest side street. It is not as steep as the one that goes past Otto's house, but it too is cobble stones—I know now that gobble stones come only from turkey gizzards. We turn right on the street that goes past Mrs. Crabtree's house. Many neighbors stand on the sidewalk, talking in little groups. Mrs. Crabtree is among them, and when she sees us she leaves her group and approaches.

"You have a lot of nerve," she says.

"What did you say?" Landon says.

"I wasn't talking to you, young man." She points at me. Her finger is as crooked as Grossdawdi Hostetler's. "It's her fault and she knows it. First Lucia dies and then this terrible fire which is destroying the town. You're like a curse, Anna. The sooner you get out of town, the better. We all think so."

"Bullshit," Landon says. "She isn't going anywhere."

"Well, she isn't coming back to work for me, I can tell you that."

"Come on," Landon says. He pulls my arm.

Mrs. Crabtree grabs the other. "You're right. She's not going anywhere, not until I'm through speaking my mind. You," she says to me, "you come here pretending to be Aye-mish or something, acting as innocent as a newborn kitten, but believe me sister, I can see right through that act now. Could kick myself for giving you a job, that's what. Who knows what all you managed to steal from me. I should have you arrested, and held in jail until I count every piece of silver."

"All of which is dime-store flatware." The voice is Otto's.

"Otto!" I pull away from both Landon and Mrs. Crabtree, and throw myself into my friend's arms.

Otto's perfume is even stronger today, but I do not mind, as it helps to mask the smell of smoke. He holds me tight, and I bury my face in his soft scarf, which today is yellow.

"I'll take over from here," I hear him say to Landon.

"Well, but I—uh—"

"Landon, it is okay. Otto is a good friend of mine."

"She lives with me," Otto says.

Landon grabs my arm again. "Anna, is this true?"

"Don't worry," Mrs. Crabtree says, "Otto here is a faggot."

"Don't talk about him like that," I say. Even though I am angry, I have used the contraction. I like it now; it's shorter.

Mrs. Crabtree brings her head back, like a turkey that has seen its reflection in the water pan.

"What did you say?"

"I said not to speak of Otto in this way. He is a kind man. What he does in private is not your business."

Mrs. Crabtree waves her arms. She is the overfed Thanksgiving turkey trying to fly.

"Do you see how this little bitch talks to me?" she demands of her neighbors. "Like she's somebody. But she's a friend of them that live on top of the hill. The white trash."

"Takes trash to know it," Otto says. He pulls me away from the group, away from Landon who has found someone he knows to talk to. He does not even look when I walk away.

"So Anna, how are you *really* doing," Otto says. "You just putting on a good show, or are you in shock?"

"I have the shocks I think. This is too much for my head all at once."

"I can imagine."

We walk in silence for the length of several houses. "So who's that guy you were with."

"No one. Just a friend."

"So, which is he?"

"A friend."

"What happened to his lip? You give him a punch?"

I feel as if Otto can see right through me to my soul. There is no point in lying.

"We went on a picnic, and then we kissed."

"And?"

"We bumped heads."

"That's all?"

"Yes."

"Did you get a chance to eat your picnic lunch?"

"No. Otto, why is it that I feel so empty inside? Like I am watching someone else's life on the television?"

"Because you're in shock, Anna. It's only natural."

Otto asks no more questions. I have questions of my own, mostly about the fire, but Otto tells me they must wait until later, because it is too early for anyone to tell how it started. And anyway, he must first see to it that body and soul are kept together.

When we get home he cooks fried bologna sandwiches and tomato soup. Comfort food he calls them. I have no appetite, but he coaxes me to eat, like I am a small child. "Just one more bite, for Uncle Otto," he says. And then another bite, until the food is gone.

"And now it's off to bed with you," Otto says.

"Otto, it is the middle of the day!"

"Middle, shmiddle, what difference does that make? You're exhausted, Anna. You need a good long nap."

In Heaven only young children and the very old indulge in such a luxury. The daylight hours were created for man to work, or to praise God. Sunday afternoon was the only exception, because then God napped too, yah? Bishop Yoder even preached a sermon about a man who napped on Saturday afternoon, when there were yet crops to be brought in from the field. While the lazy man was sleeping, a flock of locusts devoured all the corn and half of the soybeans. When the locusts left, nothing remained in the cornfield except for some of the locusts' feathers. This story was only an illustration I think, because the bishop did not realize locusts were insects.

I did not see how God could punish me any more if I napped, and I was so tired, I could barely keep my eyes open. I make Otto promise to wake me if he hears any news of how the fire started, or what, if anything, is left of my shop. He pulls the shade and I fall asleep immediately.

My dream is so real that in it I ask myself if I am

dreaming. I shake myself until I am awake, except that too is part of the dream. I am back on the farm, in Heaven, and I am again three years old. It is only two days since my birthday.

There is a youth party in the barn, and it is part of this thing called rumschpringe. Because of Mamm's nerves, it is not a dance and there are no smuggled radios. Instead, Brother and his friends are singing hymns. These are not the slow Amish hymns from the Ausbund, the ones which can take as much as twenty minutes for each song; these are the fast Mennonite hymns.

They sing a hymn called *Bringing In The Sheaves*, which is very lively I think. The words gush out like water from the kitchen pump. I know this because I am hiding in the loft.

There are two things I am forbidden to do; climb up into the loft without Daat or Brother's help, and touch the long wooden matches Mamm keeps in a drawer by the stove. Tonight I do both. I do them because I am angry. Brother has told me a secret. There will be a singing party in the barn after supper, but I am not allowed to attend because I am too young. Even our brother Elam has not been invited.

Elam would not be invited to my party either, but I am Brother's only sister, and he is very fond of me, and I of him. It is not right that Brother's friends should be there, and not me. Brother has even invited Amos Beiler, who has one leg much shorter than the other and walks in a funny way.

Because I am angry I will do the two things I am not allowed. As soon as Mamm puts me to bed I sneak out the window. My room is on the second floor, as are all the bedrooms, but the roof slopes down to a mulberry tree that Daat does not trim anymore. In my dream, which does not seem like a dream, I understand that Daat leaves the tree untrimmed so that Brother can leave the house at night without disturbing Mamm. I also realize that if I manage to

get down to the ground, I will never be able to climb
back up again. I simply do not have the strength. As
for the matches, I have two hidden under my mattress,
where they have been ever since my birthday when
Mamm spanked me for sticking my tongue out at her
because she would not let me lick the icing bowl.
These are the matches that do not need a box to strike,
only something hard. I have seen Mamm use them
many times, but have yet to try one myself.

Although I like the Mennonite hymns very much, I
am eventually bored, and decide to try and strike the
matches. There is in the loft a pitchfork made of
metal. The first match I try makes only sparks, and the
stick breaks in half. The second match lights the first
time I rub it across the metal. This excites me so much
I almost drop it. But I am able to hold the match and
admire the flame I created, until the flame gets so
close to my fingers it burns. Then I drop it.

I do not expect many things when I am three years
old. Life is a continuous string of surprises. The fact
that the hay burns so quickly is just another surprise. I
do, however, expect Daat to be mad that his hay
burns. There is nothing I can do to stop the flames,
but if I leave the barn at once, maybe Daat will blame
the fire on the teenagers below.

Just as I thought, I am unable to climb the mulberry
tree. It is very cold outside, so I have no choice but to
come through the front door, which is never locked,
but which we seldom use. It is my intent to sneak
upstairs unnoticed.

I can see into the kitchen, and that Mamm is
standing in front of the sink with her back turned.
Daat is at the table reading the *Budget*, which is the
Amish newspaper that is popular wherever our people
live, even as far away as Paraguay. I have my foot on
the first step when Daat looks up.

"Perhaps our Anna has something to tell us," he
says in a soft voice.

CHAPTER

23

"Hey, hey," Otto says, shaking me. "Wake up, Anna, you're having a nightmare."

Daat's face becomes Otto's, and then I am awake. "Oh Otto, it was terrible."

"Tell me about it." He climbs on the bed, and I do not mind. Every woman should have a gay man for a friend.

"It's fading fast and I am not sure, but Otto, I think I did something very, very, wrong when I was a little girl."

"What did you do? Put your bonnet on inside out? Forget to say your prayers? Accidentally watch an X-rated movie?" He laughs.

"I burned down the barn."

He looks at me with surprise. "You're serious?"

"Yah—I think. But maybe it was just a dream."

"I'm sure that's what it was. You wouldn't believe some of the stuff I've dreamed. Once I even dreamed I was married to Prince Charles, but I couldn't figure out if I was supposed to be Lady Di or Camilla, or someone else altogether. In any case, I was definitely a queen." He laughs again.

"I have had this dream before—about the fire, I mean—but this is the first time I dreamt it was I who started it."

"Association, that's what it is, Anna. Your shop burns today, and because you weren't there you feel responsible. So you extend that feeling back to that barn when you were a kid. What you need is to eat again, that's what."

"But I just ate."

"That was four hours ago."

I look at the window. The light that creeps around the edges of the shade is that of early evening.

"What time is it?"

"Almost seven."

"Ach!"

Otto insists that I eat again. This time his comfort food is macaroni and cheese that comes from a box, to which he has added tiny sausages, no bigger than my baby finger. Lil' Smokies, they are called.

After supper he wants to watch television, but there is something I need to do first. "It will only take a few minutes," I tell Otto.

"Anna, you want to talk to Brandy, don't you?"

"She is not responsible for Lucia's death. She must know that."

"And you are not responsible for Brandy."

"It is my responsibility not to cause anyone pain, and to remove pain if I can." These are, of course, the words of a hypocrite. I have caused Mamm and Daat more pain then they can bear. I know this, yet I do not return to unser Satt Leit. I tell myself that in my parent's case it is unnecessary pain, and exists only because they will not adjust their attitudes.

Otto shrugs. "Suit yourself, but the movie starts in half an hour, and it's one of Hitchcock's best." As I go out the door, he calls after me. "If someone from the police or fire department comes—"

"You know where I will be," I say, and then I run up the hill.

My calves ache and I am out of breath when I reach the Scott's house. By now I know that Scott is also the last name of Jim and Brandy. This is a big coincidence

Otto says, but I think not. In Heaven there are many who marry others with the same name. Grossmutter Yoder was a Yoder before she married Grossdawdi Yoder, and Grossmutter Hostetler was a Yoder as well.

I am very relieved to see that it is Jim who opens the door. He is surprised, but smiles. I think he is even thinner than the last time I saw him, which does not seem possible.

"Don't worry, Anna," he says. "Gloria's out."

"And Brandy?"

"She's in her room, but I don't think she wants to see you."

"Jim, it is very important. Please tell her that I am here."

He shrugs and goes off. He shrugs again when he returns. "It's like I said. She wants to be left alone."

Jim does not close the door and he stands partly to the side. His body is telling me to come in and see for myself. At least this is my opinion.

When I walk through the door he does nothing to stop me. "Don't take what she says personally." That is all he says.

Brandy lies in the dark, and I remember that her room has shades and drapes. The light from the hall shows only a dim shape on the bed. Maybe it is dirty clothes, and not Brandy.

"Brandy, is that you?"

The lump moves. "Go away!"

I step into the room, which smells of unwashed feet and used underwear. "Brandy, what happened this morning—"

She sits. "Ain't ya got no ears? I said go away."

Because she does not swear at me, I know she wants really for me to enter. I sit on her bed. It is not in my jeans, as Otto says, to touch others in an affectionate way, but I pat Brandy's legs.

"Lesbo," she says.

"Brandy, what happened to Lucia had nothing to do

with you. It was the fault of the hit-and-leave driver."

"Ya mean run, ya retard."

"Yah, run. But you know what I say is true, yah? That it is not your fault."

"Well, have they caught whoever did it?"

I am ashamed that I do not know. Too much has happened this day, and I have not thought to ask.

"Well, it wouldn't surprise me if they say that I pushed her or something. Blame it on Brandy, 'cause that's the easiest thing to do."

"But no one has blamed you." I am becoming impatient with this pity party, as Otto calls it. "So Brandy, why are you not at work?" I cover my mouth; I have said too much. Of course she is not at work, even though she works night, because she is upset over Lucia's death.

Brandy jumps off the bed. She is wearing just a T-shirt which does not cover much. When she puts her hands on her hips, it covers even less.

"I got fired, Aggie, that's why."

"Fired?" I am ashamed to say I do not even know where it is Brandy works. I think maybe a restaurant with a bad reputation. For that reason I have never asked.

"Damn it, Aggie, do I have ta repeat everything? Ya don't have a hearing problem, do ya?"

"I hear very well, Brandy."

"Then listen to this, but hang on to your socks first, 'cause it's gonna knock them right off. For your information, Miss Nosy, my boss said I made a lousy stripper."

"Stripper? Like for the furniture?"

Brandy laughs so hard she falls on the floor. Literally. Right at my feet.

"What is so funny, Brandy."

"Woo-woo," she says, just like Dog Boy. "Ya really are a trip, Aggie, ya know that?"

"Yah," I say, just so she will stop with the teasing.

"A stripper," she says, "is someone who takes off

her clothes in a bar and dances naked."

I have heard tales of others' rumschpringe. In communities less strict than Heaven, the boys sometimes visit English bars and get drunk. But I have never heard of these strippers. This does not mean they do not exist, but only that I have been sheltered. Perhaps my friends did not tell me these stories, because they were afraid I would get the nerves like Mamm.

"Aggie, if ya don't close your mouth, something big, like maybe a bat, is going to fly right into it. Ya gonna choke, ya know? And ya better not do that, 'cause I don't know any damn CPR."

"All your clothes?" It is what my mind wants to know first.

"Except for a G-string, which is this big—" she makes her thumb and first finger into a circle, "—which, don't even cover up what you see now."

I turn my head, suddenly embarrassed. This is TMI, as Tracy says.

"Gotcha!" Brandy shouts. She howls like Dog Boy again.

"Brandy, please—"

"Damn, but you're dumb, Aggie, Ya really believed that stripper bit?"

"Because you said it was so."

"Well, then screw you, 'cause I ain't no stripper. I work at a hospital, cleaning up puke and piss, that's what."

She surely jokes again. If this is really what she does, why did she not do the same for Mrs. Scott?

"Bet I can read your mind, Aggie. Bet you're wondering why I didn't do a better job of looking after the old lady, ain't ya?"

I will not answer. I do not like this mind-reading.

"Well, it's a good question, Aggie, and the only thing I can say is that I didn't get paid for that, but at the hospital I do."

"Brandy, Otto waits for me to watch a movie. I

must go now."

"Oh yeah, which movie?"

I shrug.

"He better not be trying to corrupt ya with porn. Say, Aggie, where did ya go this morning?"

"This morning?"

"Don't give me that shit. Ya know good and well what I mean? After what happened to Lucia, where did ya go with that studmuffin?"

Now it is I who must squirm like a worm facing the hook. "He is just a friend."

"A little old for ya, don't ya think?"

"He is no older than Mickey—I think."

"Mickey! Damn, Aggie, how do ya do it? Ya come to town as innocent as a baby, then ya steal my boyfriend, next ya help my granny to break out, like she's a runaway con, and now ya end up with the cutest thing with legs this side of the Allegheny."

"But he is not my boyfriend."

"Whatever ya say. Did ya make out with this guy?"

"Brandy!"

"Ya did, didn't ya! Where? At his place?"

There is no point in lying, if she can read the truth in my face. Besides, she is my best friend—well, except for Otto.

"It was in the woods."

"Get out! Did you go all the way?"

I giggled. "No. Some boys disturbed us."

"I hoped he kicked their butts."

"We came home. Brandy, do you think it was wrong to do what I did?"

Her eyes meet at her nose, a sign she is thinking hard. This I can tell even in the dark room because they shine like the eyes of an animal.

"Yeah, it was wrong—what with Lucia just being killed. But hell, I kinda understand. Sometimes I think I'd jump off Hulton Bridge, if it would make me feel better."

"Brandy, are you sick?"

"Inside, you idiot!"

"What is the illness?"

Brandy holds her head in both hands and shakes it. "Jeezles-peezles, but you're stupid. It's a wonder you remember to breathe."

I know that there is a warm spot in Brandy's heart for me, but this does not make it any easier to tolerate the ridicule.

"Goodnight," I say and walk quickly to the door.

Jim holds it open for me. "Cut her a little slack, will you, Anna? She's been through a lot lately."

"And I haven't?" I love now the contractions.

It will take me only a few minutes to walk down the hill as far as Otto's house, but I decide to take a detour. If I turn right on the next street I come to, I can walk around a very long block that is level, and it is only when I get back to First Street that I must descend again. The walking, I think, will help clear the thoughts from my head, so I can better appreciate Otto's movie.

It is dark now, and lights are on in most of the houses. This is what I want to see. These are not fancy houses like in Oakmont. Whenever we go to Oakmont, Otto says, "Well, we're not in Kansas anymore, Dorothy."

I don't care which city I am in. I like looking at lights, because I like to imagine that there are normal people living normal lives behind those curtains.

Sometimes the curtains are open, and I see the normal people. They are watching television, or vacuuming, or once, I even saw a man hit his wife. He was not so normal, I think. In Verona, everyone else that I do not know is normal. Their lives are happy, or at least they have learned to be content with what they have.

I know that I could never become a good Amish wife, but I could be happy in a little house like one of these, with a husband and children to take care of. Just as long as my husband didn't hit me. I could drive the children to their sporting activities, and if everyone agreed, for suppers we would get the fast food, or I could make quick meals from boxes. I could even learn to be happy without my painting—if that was what God really wanted from me. But for that God would have to speak to me directly, in a human voice. One that I could hear with my flesh and blood ears.

When I get back to Otto's house I see a different car in his driveway. "Mickey," I say and run inside.

"Your insurance agent is here," Otto says. He spits out the words like Mamm does when she plucks a chicken and the small wet breast feathers cling to her lips.

"Hey babe." Mickey hugs me tightly in front of Otto. Mickey too wears the man's perfume, but on him it smells better.

"Mickey, I can explain everything."

He grabs my hand and pulls me to the door. In his eyes I see great emotion. If the little house in Verona is to be shared by Mickey, then I would be willing to give up even the painting—if that is God's will.

We go out onto the porch, and Otto tries to follow, but Mickey kicks the door shut with his heel. "Nosy little bastard," he says. "Pardon my French."

He does not mean the language of France. What he says is a youthanism for swearing.

"Babe, I need to ask you a few questions."

"Brandy had nothing to do with it, Mickey."

"Brandy?"

"Lucia saw us standing together and got mad. Brandy did not push her, or say anything to make her run across the street."

He gives me a soft kiss. His lips are hotter than Landon's, and I think they have more experience.

"I don't want to talk about Lucia," he says. "This is important."

"What?" I do not know what else to say.

"What I mean, babe, is that it's more personal."

I know now what he means, and I feel a wave of shame. Catherine Beiler was right; I am the Whore of Babylon. The Bishop and elders were right as well. It is a journey of small steps from the faith of my fathers, to the spiritual wilderness of the English. One does not notice the landscape becoming desolate until it is too late.

The only way for me to keep Mickey is to follow the way of the fathers and confess everything. It is up to him to offer forgiveness, and it is possible he may never wish to do so, but it is my only chance if we are to live in a small Verona house and be happy together.

"Mickey," I force my voice to be strong, "there is something I must tell you."

He does not seem surprised. "I'm listening."

"It was only a kiss, Mickey. It meant nothing."

"Whatever you say. Look, Anne, how many people know about our arrangement?"

"All my friends, I guess. Look, Mickey, at first Brandy was very angry, but I think now—"

His eyes reflect nothing. Just two dark holes, out of which the soul has already poured. I think that if I look hard enough I will see the back of his head.

"I don't give a rat's ass about Brandy. I'm talking about *our* arrangement."

"But we didn't have an arrangement, Mickey." I find myself looking down at my ring finger. The Amish in Heaven don't wear wedding rings. There is no need. For the men the beard suits this purpose. For the women, it is the style of apron and bonnet. An Amish person in Heaven can tell if another is married just by looking at them across the livestock auction.

"That I'm your freaking landlord." Mickey spits when he talks.

"Everyone, of course. I mean, all my friends. They were there when I signed the lease, remember?"

"Yeah," he says. "But if anyone official comes

around and asks, tell them you pay me twelve hundred dollars a month in rent, not ten."

"But Mickey—"

He grabs both wrists. "Do you love me, Anne?"

This is the first time we have ever spoken of love. What a Dummkopf I am, and how foolish of me, to have expected an engagement ring before that word is said. And now that it has been said, that the question has been asked, I do not know the answer.

"Well, do you?"

"I think so."

"If you do, you'll do as I ask. Anne, I mean it. I'm counting on you to go along with me on this. It's extremely important. The damn fools really screwed up on this one."

My wrists hurt, and I smell anger on his breath. I know that sounds like a silly thing to say, but just like some animals can smell fear, I think I can smell anger.

"Mickey, I must go inside now. Otto is waiting."

"Screw Otto," he says. He drops my wrists. "Later. I'll call you—don't call me."

I do not want to go inside and face Otto. But if I wait any longer, Otto will know something is wrong. Perhaps he has already seen us through the window. Mickey says to screw Otto, but it is me who should be screwed—because I am the screw-up. This, I think, is a better word for me than Dummkopf. Everything I touch crumbles, like the clods of earth in the field when there has been no rain for weeks. Sometime I think I should start my own business; one that is not an art gallery. People could hire me to work for their enemies, or even just to be the friend of their worst enemy.

I look through the little window at the top of the front door. The glass is distorted, but I see Otto—well, four Ottos—putting out snacks for the movie. I hear him whistling one of his favorite tunes about a jungle where the lion sleeps tonight. Although Otto is despised by many, I think he is more normal than many whose lights shine on the cobbled stones of Verona.

"There you are!" Otto says. He is always glad to see me. "I couldn't decide between buttered popcorn or plain, but since we already blew our diets at the shindig the other night, I figured what the hell."

The movie is called *The Birds*, and I do not recommend that you watch it—not if you are easily scared like me. In the movie the birds have gone crazy and want to peck to death the humans. The people must barricade their windows and doors—even their chimneys. I tell Otto this gives me the heebie-jeebies, and can we not watch *Breakfast at Tiffany's*, which we have on tape.

There is a time for every season under heaven, Otto says, and tonight it is the birds' time. Audrey Hepburn will have to take her turn.

When I go to bed that night I have birds on the brain. I check my bedroom windows to make sure they are closed tightly, then I pull the shades and draw the curtains. I am thankful I do not have a fireplace in the room. Something brushes the roof and I jump. I do not go to sleep for at least an hour, and when I do, it seems like only minutes before Otto pounds on the door.

CHAPTER

24

"Anna, come on, wake up. They're here."

I sit up in the bed. The clock reads 8:37 A.M. "Who's here?"

The door opens a crack, and then Otto pushes his head through. "You decent?"

"Yah, come in."

"Silly question, wasn't it? You're always decent. Queen of the Girl Scouts in your flannel PJs."

I do not mind that Otto teases. "Well you are not a Boy Scout," I say. "They wouldn't let you in."

Otto laughs. "Touché. Actually I did belong, but I had to do my lusting in private. Anyway, the Inquisition awaits without."

I laugh. "What language is that, Otto?"

"English, I think. It's Tracy and some young hunk from the fire department. His name is Horace something-or-another. You don't run into many Horaces these days, and none that look like him. See if you can get his number, Anna."

It has been a deep sleep, and I have not yet thought about yesterday's troubles. My burned shop, Mickey— I want only to crawl under the covers. When I crawl out again, I will be a little girl once more, one with different choices. Or, if the choices are to be the same, I will make them differently. Is that Mamm's cooking I smell downstairs? Is that the sound of Daat rolling back the barn door, so that the cows, which have been out all night, can come in for the milking?

"Anna, where the hell are you? You sure aren't in Verona, that's for sure."

I want the voice to be Daat's, but it is only Otto. "I am in Heaven, Otto."

He shakes his head and smiles. "You're a long way from Heaven, darling. Come on," he slaps my leg, "get dressed. I'll tell them you'll be out in five minutes. Don't make it any longer than that. I don't want that studmuffin Horace getting ticked off with me from the get-go."

I do not care that Horace is cute, so I do not care what I wear. If I still had my Amish clothes, I would put them on. Then, instead of speaking to the fireman and Tracy, I would climb out the window and . . .

"Earth to Anna!" Otto helps me select what to wear, and turns his back while I dress. The blue sweater I think is too tight, and the jeans—even if Mamm approved of women in men's clothes, she would not understand this low rise. Trust me, this is Otto's idea, not mine. He gives me a little push out the door. "Remember, get his number."

Tracy smiles when she sees me. "Anna, this is Fire Inspector Hobson Fryes. Hobson, this is that gorgeous young Amish girl I was telling you about."

This embarrasses me. "I am no longer Amish," I say. Anyway, it is Hobson who is gorgeous. He looks like Mickey, only younger, and there is a dimple in his chin. No wonder Otto is so excited he has gotten the man's name wrong.

"Ma'am," Hobson says and reaches to shake my hand.

"Hobson is originally from the south," Tracy says. "They use last names for first names."

Hobson shifts from one foot to the other. It is clear that he is embarrassed as well.

"Maybe we should get right down to business." For one so young, his voice booms like thunder.

"Yeah," Tracy says. Now she is embarrassed for not

having kept things professional.

They ask me many questions, taking turns, although I think Tracy feels that she is in charge. It is easy to answer these questions truthfully. No, I was not cooking something in my gallery. I did not have a space heater on. The wiring was inspected, and yes I have a record of the inspection. Otto and Mickey are the only other people to have keys, and finally no, I did not store gasoline in the shop. They ask more questions as well, but these are the ones that jump to mind.

"Excuse us for a few minutes," Tracy says.

I go off to find Otto. Maybe we can make some coffee for Tracy and the fire inspector.

Otto is in his room, watching Regis and Kelly on the telly. That's what he calls it, and he does it every morning that we don't have something special to do. He winks when he sees me.

"You get his number?"

"Not yet, and his name is Hobson, not Horace."

"Who cares what his name is. Did you see that dimple?"

"Yah."

"Think Kirk Douglas mid-1950s. Think The Vikings. I'd like to take that dimple—hey, if you didn't get his number, what are you doing here? Anything go wrong, Anna?"

"They wish to speak privately. Otto, I was thinking maybe we should make them some coffee."

"Capital idea," he says and rushes off to the kitchen, without even turning off the telly. I rush after him, but as we cross the living room, Tracy calls to me.

"Anna, can you step outside for a minute."

I am not worried that Tracy will put the moves on me, but it bothers me that she wishes to speak to me alone. I suspect that as a friend, she wishes to warn me of trouble.

We go outside to the cement patio. The folding chairs Otto keeps there in the summer are still in the shed, so we must stand to talk.

"Anna, you look worried. Don't be. This is good news. We caught the hit-and-run."

I must shift gears, as Otto says. "The man who killed Lucia?"

"Actually, it was a woman. A drunk. Wouldn't confess at first, even though there was ample DNA on the bumper. When we confronted her with that, she had instant and total recall. Even wants to sue the bar that allowed her to get drunk. Give me a break. It was ten o'clock in the morning. The bar had been closed for eight hours. Anyway, the good news is because she made such a detailed confession, and we have the DNA, you might not even have to make an appearance."

"In court?" This had not even occurred to me. Unser Satt Leit—not that I can count myself as belonging anymore—have always shied away from the courts. In Europe the Amish people were persecuted in courts, both religious and secular. In America there have been times when going to court was necessary, like fighting for the right *not* to have the children educated past the eighth grade, and that battle was won in the Supreme Court in 1972.

"Anna, even if that happens, I'll be there."

"Thank you."

I feel that it is time to go inside now, but Tracy hesitates. "Anna, there is one more thing."

I wait quietly for her to continue.

"It's about Landon Frasier. The man you were with yesterday."

"Tracy, that is not your business."

"But Anna—"

I go back inside, and Tracy follows me like a dog at heels. Otto is still in the kitchen putting together the coffee and, I think, some cookies from a box. Hobson Fryes remains sitting where we left him, working on some notes. I march straight up to him.

"Mr. Fryes," I say, although the voice does not

sound like mine, "may I have your telephone number?"

He has green eyes. "Work or home?"

"Home," I say. Behind me Tracy gasps.

"No problem," he says, and gives me the number. "But my job keeps me out a lot. If you have questions that relate to your shop—well, it might be easier for you to contact Sergeant Bright."

"The number is so that I can ask you to the movies, Inspector Fryes. Do you like movies?"

Behind the kitchen door Otto gasps.

"I love movies," Hobson Fryes says and smiles.

I smile back.

"I can't believe you did that." Tracy and the fire inspector have left. Otto is stacking the cups and plates in the dishwasher. Because he is angry, he does not judge so well, and one of the cups chips when he smacks it against the door of the washer. This makes him even angrier, and he uses words I have never heard before. Then he says, "You see what you made me do?"

I say nothing.

Otto sighs, then he straightens and hugs me. "I'm sorry, Anna. It's just that I feel . . . double-crossed." Then, remembering he speaks to a Dummkopf, he adds, "You know, betrayed."

"Otto, maybe Hobson Fryes really wants to go out with me, not you."

"Don't be silly, darling, I'm not in the mood for jokes."

"I'm not joking."

He picks the chipped piece out of the silverware basket. "You're serious, aren't you?"

"Yah, why not?"

"Well, because—damn Anna, I'm sorry. I really am. I was being presumptuous. Of course he'd want to go out with you. I would too, if I were straight."

"Really?"

The phone rings. I have learned not to answer the phone when Otto is at home, even if I know the call is for me. Otto likes to be surprised when he answers. Because of this, he will not even get the caller I.D., which more and more people have, I hear. Tracy has it, and Lucia had it. Even the Scotts up at the top of the hill have it.

Otto bumps his head on the countertop, but he does not seem to mind. "Hello, Otto's House of Perpetual Pleasure." He says this often, and things even more outrageous, because it gives the telly-marketers "what for."

But Otto blushes. "Who may I say is calling?" he asks.

There is a long silence.

"Knock it off, buddy," Otto shouts. "Just because I played one on you doesn't mean—"

A shorter silence, but Otto turns even redder. "Yeah, give me the number and I'll call you right back."

"Otto, who is it," I ask when he hangs up.

He doesn't answer, but punches the number in and taps his fingers impatiently on the counter waiting for the phone to ring on the other end. Otto often says that Pony Express works faster than Ma Bell, but since I don't know either of these people, I never ask for details.

Finally the person on the other end of the line answers. Now Otto's face loses all its color, like noodles dried too long in the sun.

"Yes, sir," Otto says, and then "no, sir." Then he says "yes sir" three times in a row. He rubs his left hand over his head, which he keeps shaved, smooth as a peeled egg. "I don't know, sir, I'll have to ask her." Then he says "no" several more times, and "yes" one last time. Trying to guess what they speak about is like trying to guess if it will rain by looking at just the weather report. When the conversation is over

Otto drops the phone so hard that I think it is a wonder it does not chip, like the coffee cup.

"Holy shit!" he says and grabs me. Before I can tell him no, he is dancing with me around the kitchen. This is my first time to dance, and I can tell you this; the Mennonites are wrong. Such an activity cannot possibly lead to sex. Otto has already stepped on my toes three times, and his breath smells of bologna that has lain out in the sun with the egg noodles.

I push him gently away. "Otto, what has happened?"

"You've made it!" he cries, and tries to dance again.

Old bologna does not like to be pinched, I discover, and Otto stops his foolishness. "Otto, please make sense."

"Oh but I am, Anna. That was a Mr. Bonsavage. He's an art critic for the *New York Times*. Abby, he was at your grand opening!"

"But how can this be? I didn't invite him."

"Fate, darling! He has an aunt in South Hills. He was visiting her, saw the flyers in one of the antique stores downtown, and just showed up. Do you remember a short bald man the night of the open house?"

"That was you Otto—" I did not mean for that to slip out.

"Touché, darling. But this guy is even shorter than moi. Think, Anna."

It seems like weeks ago since the grand opening. "Yah. His head looked like a cinnamon bun. He was the only stranger."

"Yes, but not the only strange one. Anyway, Anna, he loves your work. Says it reminds him of Ansel Adams's early work. He wants to write a piece on you. Says he's got a backlog of articles now, but he's thinking maybe sometime in September. Wants to know if he can send a photographer over sometime early August to do a shoot."

"But Otto, there are no paintings." I feel like Elijah

Bontrager, whose wife made him a new Mutzi, a sort of coat, and the next day Elijah had his arm taken off by the thresher. Poor Elijah never got to put both arms through those sleeves.

Otto's face still shines with happiness. "How long does it take you to do a painting?"

I must think. I have never timed myself. The paintings have always been works of love, and if they took a week or a year, they were finished when they were finished. But if I worked steadily, and didn't have to hide anything from Mamm, I could do one a week, a week and a half at the most.

"Two weeks," I say, just to be on the safe side.

A flicker of disappointment and then Otto's face shines again. "What if you knew exactly what you were going to paint? Would that make any difference?"

"Well, maybe, but Otto—"

"Don't but Otto me, darling. This is fate. Let's see, it's mid-April. If you started right away, you could squeeze in one this month yet, and then two each for May, June, and July—that only makes seven. You sure you can't work any faster?"

"Otto, I don't know! I have never worked under such pressure. Besides, where would I paint?"

He pushes aside the dinette table and two chairs. It is where we take all our meals, unless it is me who has cooked, and we have guests.

"What about here?" he asks, and waves his arms.

"In the kitchen?"

"You painted in a hayloft, didn't you?"

"Yah." I look around. The light is definitely much better in the kitchen. The hayloft had only one window. The kitchen has two, but it also has electricity. And on pleasant days it would be simple to carry the easel outside—if I only had an easel

"I have no supplies, Otto."

"Darling," Otto says, "you and I are going shopping."

CHAPTER

25

Otto wants me to paint the same paintings the fire destroyed. I tell him this is impossible. I am not a copy machine.

We set my new easel up in the kitchen and spread the rest of my supplies on the dinette table and counters. He says the plan is for us to eat carry-out only until the collection is complete again. For this I breathe a sigh of relief. It has been my fear that Otto will volunteer to do all the cooking, and a skeleton cannot paint.

I start my first painting that same afternoon. My intent is to duplicate, as close as possible, the one I did in Heaven of an old rusty plow in an abandoned field. On the fence in the background there is a For Sale sign. Now I find that my hand insists on adding a clump of black-eyed Susans. They peek from behind one of the blades. In a loud voice they cry, "there was a woman on this farm!"

She planted flowers that have now gone wild. The farmer and his wife have died and the land is for sale, but memory of the woman lives on in the flowers. Soon the land will be farmed again, with a new plow, and the man may be forgotten, but the woman will live on in the flowers, which will grow anywhere the land is not disturbed.

Otto watches while he waits for delivery from Domino's Pizza. He paces like the leopard in the

Pittsburgh Zoo.

"What's with the flowers, darling? I don't remember them from the other one."

"They are something new."

"I can see that. But aren't they a little—well, trite is the best word I can come up with. You know what that means, right, darling?"

"The inside of a sheep's stomach," I say, but I am only joking.

"Anna, I'm serious here. This is the opportunity of a lifetime."

"I'm serious too, Otto. I must paint what is in my heart."

Otto grumbles and glances at the clock. The pizza delivery boy always has trouble finding our house.

"Hey," he says suddenly, "how much longer do you have on that?"

"Just here in the sky, it needs to be evened out."

"But Annie, this took only one afternoon"

"Yah." Even I am surprised.

"If you can do two paintings—okay, let's say one a day, well then—"

"No, Otto. I can't do any more than I can do. Don't you understand?"

"Yes, of course, but since we're ordering in, and I promise to do all the housework—"

"Otto," I say in Mamm's sternest voice, "don't count your eggs until they are laid." I know this is not the right expression, but Mamm didn't.

Otto laughs, and then I must laugh. Together we laugh so hard we almost miss the doorbell. The pizza boy is already halfway to his car before Otto catches him.

The next day I do only half a painting. Otto nags like a teenager whose rumschpringe has come, but whose parents will not honor such a custom because of the nerves. Can't I hurry it up just a little, he begs. What if he plays soft music, maybe some Mozart? He will even lie on the floor and rub my feet if that will make me paint faster.

I tell him to take a hike, a real one. Walk down the hill to the Giant Eagle and get us some canning rings. What are canning rings, he wants to know? But I will not say. If he does not know what they are, it will take him longer to find them. Of course we have no use for rubber rings, but he will discover that only after he sees them, or asks for help.

He leaves me alone, but refuses to walk. Mankind, he says, is born with a limited number—he uses the word finite, which at first I do not know—of heartbeats. Use all these heartbeats up, and then you die. Otto says he learned this from a nature show on the telly. They counted the heartbeats of an elephant, which is the largest land mammal, and of a shrew, which is the smallest. Both have the same number of heartbeats, but the elephant, with its slow heart, lives more than fifty years, and the tiny shrew only two.

Otto is back in less than twenty minutes. He has with him only two Lean Cuisine dinners and a half gallon of Breyer's Butter Pecan ice-cream. "The Lord giveth, and the Lord taketh away" he says when I tease him about mixing diet foods with rich fatty ones. "And the Lord doesn't give much better than Breyer's ice-cream."

"Yah, maybe, but where are the canning rings?"

"In the car, of course. They weighed close to a hundred pounds each. Had to get three bagboys to help me get them to the car. You don't expect me to schlep those in by myself, do you?"

I drop my brush, which splashes blue paint in an area that is supposed to be green. I hurry to clean it off, but already it is too late, and I will have to think of something which is bluish green for that spot.

"Ooh, sorry, Anna. I didn't mean for that to happen."

"Ach, it's all right. Otto, what is this about canning rings that weigh a hundred pounds?"

He laughs so hard that he must put down the ice-cream and frozen dinners, and hold his stomach with both hands. The top of his head turns vermilion red, so I think it is only fitting that I should add some white and blue.

Otto laughs harder. "Stop, stop, you're killing me."

But I do not stop until Otto Goldschmidt has the American flag stretching from ear to ear. He moves so much, it is not a very precise representation, but Otto says that is because the flag is flapping in the breeze generated by my gums.

In some ways the day after Lucia's death is the happiest of my life. I know that is because I have so much work to do, and that my work brings me more joy than anything else in life. I know that it is wrong to feel this way—one must never put the love of work before the love of friends—but that is how I feel.

The night before the funeral Mrs. Martin calls and asks us if we will be there. She is worried that the church will be empty, and what will that say about Lucia? That she was a nobody, that's what. The service will be at St. Thomas Memorial Episcopal Church in Oakmont, and the interment will be in the cemetery at the top of the hill. Otto assures her that we will be there.

"Imagine that," he says, "the Martins are Episcopalians. Who would have thunk?" Otto is fond of using made up words if they suit him better.

Aside from the visit with Otto to the Church of the Living and Resurrected Jehovah, I have not "thunk" about church at all since moving to Verona. No, that is not true. I think about the Amish church all the time, and I grieve that my place on the women's bench will always be empty, but I do not think about joining a new church. If God gives me a gift that is not compatible with my religion, then it is up to him to find me a new church. Just not the church with the jumping preacher.

But what Otto means is that the Episcopal Church in Oakmont is where one would expect to find the doctors, lawyers, and successful business men. It is not where one would expect to find the blue-haired owner of a beauty parlor and the daughter who works there.

Otto says that the Episcopal Church is like the Catholic Church, but without the Pope. I think this means there will be many statues, and I am ashamed to say, I find this idea exciting. I hope there are many statues, and that most of them are of the Virgin Mary. It is childish of me, but I know this would upset Bishop Yoder and Catherine Beiler to no end.

To unser Satt Leit there are degrees of Christianity, and Roman Catholics are at the bottom of this ladder. There are even those among the Amish who do not believe that Catholics are true Christians. This is because of the Amish Church's history with the Catholics.

There are no statues of Jesus' mother in St. Thomas Memorial Episcopal Church, but there are wooden carvings of men around what is called a pulpit. This is where the sermons are preached. I have never even seen a pulpit; our minister stands with nothing between him and the congregation when he preaches.

St. Thomas Memorial Episcopal Church is made of stone, and the windows are stained glass. The benches have backs, and there are little stools upon which to kneel. The Amish I know meet only in each other's homes, and sit on benches without backs. When it is time to kneel, Amish people have only the hard wood floor.

Otto points out the altar, which I think does not look like the altars in the Bible on which sacrifices were performed. Otto tells me that modern altars are where the mass is said, although this means nothing to me. The Amish worship service is three hours long, but it contains only the slow hymns and much preaching.

Even on communion Sundays there is no mass.

In front of the steps that lead to the altar is Lucia's coffin. It rests on a cart with wheels, and is covered by a simple green cloth. The box containing my friend's body draws my eyes like it is a powerful magnet, and my eyes are nothing more than metal balls. I look at the things Otto points out, but always I must look again at the coffin.

Inside that box Lucia's body will explode with gasses, then rot, and finally will turn again to dust. It is what will happen to each of us, but to have it happen to someone so young, so pretty, so full of life, that is what compels me to look.

The service is supposed to start at noon. It is half past already, and there are only a handful of people there; two young men, and three women the age of Mrs. Martin. As for Mrs. Martin, I do not see the blue hair anywhere. The two young men, Otto whispers, are with the funeral home. One has buns of steel, but it would be ghoulish to fantasize about him at a time like this, wouldn't it?

Finally, a door at the back opens and in walks Mrs. Martin. She leans heavily on the arm of a man who dresses like a crow. He has on a black gown that reaches to his shoes, and over this a white circle of cloth. The priest, Otto says. The Episcopalians call them priests, just like the Catholics do. But these priests can marry. Otto whispers a joke I do not understand. "Abstinence makes the church grow fondlers."

Mrs. Martin sees us and smiles, but she sits in the front row with one of the older ladies. Then the mass begins. The ritual is very interesting to me, although I am uncomfortable, but in an excited sort of way. Everything about Amish worship is plain. Episcopalians are just the opposite, even if they do not have the Pope. Mamm would have a bad case of nerves in this church, and even Daat could not sit through such a service.

When it is time to go up for the communion, to receive the body and blood of Christ, only Mrs. Martin and the friend sitting next to her go. As a lapsed Catholic, Otto has no interest. The priest says that anyone who is baptized is welcome, so I would like to go up and see what it is all about.

"Please, Otto, come with me."

"No way. I've had God in my tummy a hundred times, and it hasn't made a difference. But hey, that shouldn't stop you."

Of course it does. I do not want this experience alone. I am irritated at Otto when the priest drinks the rest of the wine from the silver cup and wipes it dry with a white cloth. Who knows when I will have another chance at having God in my tummy.

The church doors are very heavy and I hear one open and close. I turn my head but I do not see anyone. In my bones I feel that Brandy has arrived.

The priest makes an announcement that the burial will happen immediately after the service in the cemetery at the top of the hill. During the last hymn, which sounds terrible because there is no one to sing it, the two men at the back come forward and wheel the cart with Lucia and her coffin out to the hearse.

The priest rides with Mrs. Martin and her friend. Otto and I drive behind them. The other two women have disappeared. Otto thinks maybe they work for the church, or maybe one of them is the priest's wife.

"Eleanor Rigby," he says.

"Otto, sometimes you make no sense."

"Name of a Beatle's song. No one came to her funeral either. Lucia was young and pretty. Had a lot of regular customers at that shop. You'd think *someone* would come. That busybody Mrs. Crabtree at least. I know Tracy had to work today but, hell's bells, don't they give time off for this sort of thing?"

I cannot argue. In Heaven, when one of unser Satt Leit dies, everyone will come to see him or her off to the next world. It does not matter if they have a tongue like Mrs. Beiler, or if they are shy, or ugly, or not very well liked, or if it is so cold that the horses' breath freezes, or so hot that the men in their black mutzis and the women in their black capes, have a renewed fear of Hell. Whatever the circumstances, the community will be there. Elizabeth Lehman gave birth in the cemetery the day her Grossdawdi was buried.

Lucia's grave is near the center of the cemetery and she will have a nice view of the Allegheny River, and Fox Chapel which lies beyond. Her name is already on the marble marker, along with her father's name, and Mrs. Martin's. Mr. Martin died ten years ago, and he is the only who has dates after his name.

The priest says a few words about Jesus being the resurrection and the life, but my mind wanders. It is too nice a day to be buried. The sun is warm for April and there are daffodils blooming beside many of the graves. The smell of lilacs is in the air. A sparrow flies over from a nearby bush and lands near my feet. It cocks its head, as if it is used to being fed.

Without being obvious I look around to see if Brandy has followed. But I see nothing more than headstones, bushes and a few small trees. Perhaps Brandy is hiding behind one of the larger bushes. Maybe she stays in bed, with her covers pulled up over her head. That's what I would have done, if I didn't have Otto to set me straight.

The priest says the final words, and Mrs. Martin makes a noise like she is trying to cry, but doesn't know how. Then it is over. The gravediggers must wait until we are gone before they finish their work. At an Amish funeral it would not be strangers filling the hole, but family and friends.

We must struggle to think of things to say to Mrs. Martin. Her breath smells of liquor. She does not invite us to her house, and we do not want to invite her to ours.

"If you need anything—anything at all," Otto says.

I pray that she needs nothing.

CHAPTER

26

Otto is in a hurry for me to resume painting. He will make a big pot of SpaghettiOs for lunch, with real grated cheese on top, if I will get right back to painting. I slip off my funeral dress, put on a pair of jeans, and one of Otto's long-sleeved denim shirts. It was a gift, he says, something he would never wear in a million years, so it is all right to get paint on it. Perhaps the shirt will be worth thousands of dollars some day.

I start on a new painting, and it is like nothing else I've done. The paper on the easel soon becomes an Amish graveyard on a cold, windy day. A long line of black buggies is leaving the cemetery. Although at first I do not intend it to be so, the last buggy to leave belongs to Daat and Mamm. The wind blows so hard the canvas sides bulge, and horse's ears, mane, and tail point in the same direction. There is no snow on the ground to symbolize purity, to give a touch of beauty to a world filled with pain. There is only gray and brown, and the black of the buggies. Life goes on, life goes on; the hooves clop out the rhythm, but no one thinks to ask why life must go on.

Otto says it's a horrible painting, but he can't take his eyes off it. Maybe I'm entering a dark phase like Goya, he says. I do not know who Goya is, not that it matters. I am not in a phase. I am painting the inside of my heart. After supper I begin yet another painting.

"Is that a barn-raising?" Otto asks.

It is not. It is what is left of the barn after a fire has burned most of it to the ground. Just a few black beams stand, barely enough to be silhouetted against the winter sky.

"Annie, darling, you need to go to bed. Uncle Otto will read you a nice bedtime story—something with a happily-ever-after ending, and then you will dream about sugar plums and all that good stuff, and tomorrow you'll wake up eager to paint water pumps and rusting plowshares."

For supper Otto has served me fish sticks with ketchup, and rice pudding from a can. I do not think I want to dream about sugar plums. When I have my pajamas on, he tucks me into bed and reads to me from an old book called *David and the Phoenix*.

"This was my favorite book when I was a little boy," he says.

I fall asleep before he gets to the end.

The next morning I begin to paint copies of the paintings that were burned in my shop. I do not do this for Otto's sake, but because it is what is in my heart today. Otto is so happy that he grabs the broom and dances around the kitchen. He refuses to talk, only to sing.

"How about a mushroom omelet for lunch, darling?"

"Otto, please, you break my concentration."

"Can't have that," he sings.

"Otto, where will we show Mr. Savage these new paintings?"

"That's Bonsavage, and you're absolutely right, darling." He grabs the *Post-Gazette* off the top of the microwave and spreads it on the floor. "We'll rent another shop—even if it's just for a week. We'll tell the noble savage the demand for your artistic treasures was too large for the space."

"Where will we get the money, Otto?"

"Insurance, of course. That's what it's for, darling. You did speak to your agent about it, right?" His words have hard edges, and I think they could stand alone if you set them just so on the floor.

"Yah, he will handle everything."

"Details," Otto says. "You need details, darling. Give him a ring."

How far Anna Hostetler has come in just one year. I know Otto means to call Mickey, not a ring on the finger. I put my brush to soak, wash my hands, and give Mickey a ring. I give him fifteen rings.

"He's not answering?" Otto says.

I want to be sarcastic and give a silly answer, because this is a historical question. Of course Mickey is not answering. But I feel fear creeping into my body, first into my stomach, then upwards to the throat. Mickey has an answering machine, and it is not answering either.

"Hey, your thrill for the day isn't home. Leave a message." That is what I should be hearing, not ring after ring.

"Maybe you dialed the wrong number, Anna."

I look in the back of the phone book where the number is written and try again. More rings. I wait until there have been thirty, then I hang up."

"Give me the phone," Otto says.

I hand him the receiver. "Who do you call, Otto?"

"Someone I should have called two days ago."

The man at Speedy Pay Insurance Agency says he has no record of an Anna Hostetler. There is, however, an Anna Hostman. Could that be me? Otto laughs when he hears that Anna Hostman is sixty-five years old and that her policy is for cruise cancellation insurance.

"Try Mickey Hanahan," he says.

"Yeah—cut him a check this morning. Just like the name says, we at Speedy Pay, pay speedy."

"You at Speedy Pay are a bunch of asses," Otto says. He slams down the receiver.

"It's okay, Otto, really it is. They are only paintings, and I am replacing them, yah?"

"This is fraud," Otto says. He picks up the phone, which still works, and calls Tracy. He tells her what has happened, and then he listens a long time. "But, but," he says a dozen times. When he is done he returns the phone gently to its cradle. "I still say these insurance chop houses shouldn't be allowed to exist."

"What did Tracy say?"

"Basically that if Speedy Pay was stupid enough to cut Mickey a check without conducting their own investigation—well, there's nothing the police can do."

"But Mickey lied." He lied with his eyes when they said I was the most beautiful woman he had ever seen. He lied with his hands when he touched me and said I sent electricity running through his body, just as I felt the current coming from him. He lied with his lips when he asked me if I loved him, because my ears heard the word love and were deceived. He lied just by being him, because everything about Mickey Hanahan said he was a man I could trust.

Otto does not care that I feel betrayed. "Where did you meet Mickey, Anna?"

"You know," I say irritably. "At Brandy's."

"Touché."

He says this word a lot, so I know its meaning. It means "I told you so," but in a fancy French way. For Otto the discussion is over. What's done is done. Now I must get back to painting, and he will make the mushroom omelet.

"Would you like that with mole sauce?" he asks.

"What?"

"It's like a chocolate sauce, but not sweet. I found it in the Mexican food aisle of Giant Eagle."

"Whatever," I say. It is also an expression I learned from Otto.

The mole sauce is terrible, but it helps to take my attention away from Otto's omelet, which is even worse. All afternoon I paint, and then all evening, even though the light is not so good. I am like a woman possessed, Otto says, and he is happy for the demons. Still, he gets tired of watching and wanders off to see a video, the one with the witches and the scary flying monkeys. I think we have seen it a million times.

I quit painting when it is almost midnight. The day, which has been warm, is edged with frost, and I sit on the front porch and stare at the lights. All the happy homes, I think, where no one has had to choose between family and heart. I wear only a light jacket and no shoes. My feet are tucked under me. There are not many cars at this hour, and each one that passes makes me draw back deeper into the shadows.

"Ya ain't gonna just disappear, ya know?"

It is a wonder that I don't jump out of my socks. "Brandy!"

"Nah, it's a goddamn flying monkey."

She stands by the porch; the bushes which Otto is too lazy to trim, come up to her chest. "I seen Otto watching that stupid movie through the window. Don't he get tired of it? I mean, like that's gotta be older than George Washington."

"It's his favorite, Brandy."

"How come ya weren't watching it, too?"

"I was painting. Brandy, why are you here, looking through the windows?"

"Had ta wait until that old fart went ta bed, didn't I?"

"Brandy," I say sharply. I will not tolerate her speaking badly of Otto.

"All right, all right. Look, Aggie, I need ya ta take a walk."

"Brandy, I am very busy these days. Like I said, I

am painting again."

"Well, I ain't talking about walking in the daytime anyway. I'm talking about now."

"*Now*? Brandy, it is almost the middle of the night."

She laughs. "The night's just getting started, Aggie."

Suddenly I am very cold. "I will not walk with you tonight, Brandy."

Brandy stands there in the bushes. She is so still she becomes one with them. Her silence speaks much louder than her voice.

"Okay," I say. "But I must get a jacket first, and some shoes."

When I return she has not moved. "Thanks, Aggie."

We head downhill in silence. At first I think Brandy wants us to visit the spot where Lucia was killed, or to see where the great fire has burned. But when we reach the street where Mrs. Crabtree lives, Brandy turns right. Most of the lights we see are street lamps, but there is a light on in one of Mrs. Crabtree's back bedrooms.

"Bitch," Brandy says.

I am ashamed that she has read my mind. I walk faster and get ahead, although I do not know where she plans to go.

"Face it Aggie," she calls after me, "you ain't too good at picking friends."

I stop. "You are my friend."

"Yeah, and lucky for you. So, how was the funeral?"

I shrug. I cannot shake the feeling that Brandy was there—somewhere. Watching.

"Betcha nobody came. Am I right?"

"Did you?"

She laughs. "Hell, no! What makes ya say that?" She does not wait for an answer. "In case ya were wondering, we're going to Riverfront Park."

"In Oakmont?"

"Ya know another?"

The park is at least a mile away, at the foot of the lilac-colored bridge. Otto has taken me there to sit on the benches by the river and feed the Canada geese. But always we have driven.

"Brandy, that is too far."

"Sorry, Aggie, but that's where we gotta go."

"Why?"

"Because there's someone I want ya to meet."

My heart pounds. I do not want to meet someone in a dark park by the river. Not someone Brandy knows.

"Who is this person? It's not Mickey, is it?"

"Ha," she says, but does not laugh. "No, it ain't Mickey."

I stop. We are down on Allegheny River Boulevard now, at the edge of town where there is a little war memorial. Behind us are the buildings which still stand after the fire, although we have not looked in that direction. Although it has been several days, the smell of smoke is thick, and not pleasant, like the smell of burnt wood. Only two buildings were actually destroyed, Tracy tells me, but there is damage to four others.

"Brandy, I am going back to Otto's."

She grabs my arm. Her nails which are black, and each of which has a skull painted on it, dig into my flesh.

"Aggie, ya *gotta* come."

"Not until you tell me why."

"'Cause there's an Amish man waitin' there to see ya," she says.

CHAPTER

27

I must gulp for air. "Brandy, you're joking!"

She shakes her head vigorously. "Am not."

Perhaps I have heard wrong. "An Amish man?"

"Yup, beard and everything. Even has B.O. Jeesh, Aggie, don't youse believe in wearing deodorant?"

Now I grab her arm. My nails are short, but my hands remain strong from milking cows.

"What's his name, Brandy? How did you meet him"

"Look, Aggie, I ain't supposed to be telling you any of this shit. You're suppose ta find this out for yourself."

"Says who, Brandy?"

"I ain't supposed ta tell ya that, either."

I squeeze so hard that Matilda, our most gentle milk cow, would have kicked me through the back of the stall. "Brandy, you must tell me everything."

"Love ta, Aggie, but ya wanna find out more, ya gotta ask him yourself."

Maybe I am a fool, but I begin to run toward the park. Brandy tries to keep up, but the shoes that are platforms do not cooperate.

"Hey, ya gotta wait for me."

I ignore her. There is a sidewalk that runs along the cobblestone street, and here where the land is flat, I can run very fast. Brother used to say I was the fastest thing on two legs. I think I remember that.

"Ya speak ta him alone, ya gonna spook him,"

Brandy shouts. "Ya don't look Amish anymore, or
have ya forgotten?"

She has a point and I slow down enough to allow
her to catch up. "Jeesh, Aggie, what are ya, some
kinda Olympic runner?"

Maybe I am not such a good runner, because I am
breathing hard. "Brandy, how did you meet this man?
Where?"

"Told ya, I ain't allowed to tell." She pants louder
than I. "But ya know that guy ya been dating?"

"Mickey."

"I ain't talking about Mickey. The other one."

"Landon?"

"Faggot name, ain't it? Which is funny, Aggie,
'cause he's married."

Married? How does Brandy know this? Does she
follow me everywhere? Does she dig into the lives of
everyone I meet? Surely she talks like a sausage—but
what if it is true? If so, then I have gone too far with
the liberation of Anna, even by my own standards.

"How do you know Landon, Brandy?"

Apparently sarcasm does not take much energy. "Ya
think I'm blind, Aggie. I was there in the mall the day
you met him."

"But I didn't see you. That's why Landon drove me
back."

"Yeah, he drove ya to Otto's. Trust me, Aggie, he's
married. That's all ya need ta know."

I cannot think why she would make up a story like
this. What a Dummkopf I have been, will always be. If
the piglets had not disturbed us in the woods, who
knows what sin I might have committed.

"Brandy, do you spy on me?"

She refuses to answer. We walk from the corner of
Delaware to the edge of the park, and she will not say
a word. She pants heavily now. Brandy has never
milked a cow, never lifted bales of hay up onto a
wagon, never even pumped water. Her mouth is what
gets most of the exercise, and now she gives it a rest.

The park is dark, and the picnic tables and playground equipment are strange black shapes that jump out at me when I am only a few feet away. The river makes a soothing sound, but it too is as black as the cola Otto prefers to drink instead of water. I step too close to a pair of sleeping Canada geese. One squawks and flaps away in the darkness, the other hisses like a quieter version of the river.

"Better watch where ya step," Brandy says, her first words in many blocks. "There's goose shit all over the place."

She leads the way now. We follow a concrete path close to the water, below the tennis courts. There is a picnic shelter just ahead.

"Hey," she calls softly to someone unseen, "we're here. We finally made it."

There is no answer.

Fear and excitement are fast turning to anger. "Brandy, so help me," I say. The English way is to threaten, and it comes easier with each day.

"Hey!" she calls louder. "Ya wanna talk ta her, or not?"

A shape too tall for a goose steps away from the shelter and onto the path.

"You took so long, I fell asleep."

"Yeah? Well, we're here now."

I can see that it is a man, but a very young one. Perhaps just a boy. He does not wear Amish clothes, and he does not have a beard. Brandy has made a fool of me again.

I turn away in anger.

"Is that you Anna Hostetler," the young man asks. His accent is English, and perhaps he is only from Oakmont or Verona, but he pronounces my last name with familiarity.

I stop, but do not turn. "Who wants to know?"

"Levi Augsberger."

I turn and step closer. He is blond, his pale hair almost as light as his teeth. I know a Levi Augsberger,

but he is a little boy, still attending the one room
school house in Heaven. "Who are you really?"

"Levi Augsberger—Samuel and Mary's son."

"I don't have time for games, whoever you are.
Samuel and Mary Augsberger have only young
children."

"I am sixteen," he says, and I hear the defiance in
his voice. "I am making my rumschpringe."

Now I am so close I can smell the beer on his
breath. Could it be possible? If so, where have the
years gone? But I have not been paying attention the
last couple of years. No doubt there are many things
that have escaped my attention.

Although this boy has the voice of a man, he is
very short. Levi Augsberger was always very short for
his age. Little Levi everyone called him.

"Tell me the name the Augsbergers give to their
horse," I say. I refer to their favorite buggy horse, a
very spirited animal everyone calls Samson. The horse
got its name because one day, when Little Levi was
angry at his parents, he cut off part of the horse's
mane. Like Samson in the Bible, the horse became
weak after that, but it was not because of the mane.

Finally Little Levi confessed that he had fed the
horse some insect killer he had gotten from the son of
an English neighbor. The horse eventually recovered.
At any rate, in the words of Otto, Little Levi was a
"handful."

"Samson," the night visitor says without hesitation.

"Ach! Is it really you? What are you doing here?"

"Like I said, I'm on rumschpringe. As if to prove
his point, Levi Augsberger lights a cigarette. A goose
seems to whimper somewhere in the darkness.

"Yah, it is you," I say, reverting to my Dutch.

"I speak only English now, Anna. I don't plan to go
back."

And you will fit in very well, I think. I must sit. I
find a bench in the shelter. There is a bag with
pockets, a knapsack it is called, on the picnic table.

"Do you need my help, Levi?" I am afraid of his answer. My life is complicated enough. How can I afford to help a wild thing like Little Levi?

"Don't flatter yourself, Anna," he says. "I came to help you."

"Me?"

"It's about your Mamm," he says. Mamm is the only word which he pronounces like unser Satt Leit.

"What about Mamm?" It has been more than a year, and if I were not already sitting on a picnic bench, I would soon be sitting on a pile of goose droppings.

"She's sick. Some kind of cancer. Stomach, I think. I'm supposed to tell you to come home."

I must admit that for a few seconds—less than a minute—I had a strange feeling of joy. If Mamm died, then I would no longer be responsible for her getting the nerves. I know it was wrong to feel that way, even for a few seconds, but I choose to be honest. Of course this strange feeling was quickly followed by shame, and then the proper sort of concern.

"Who told you this?"

"Bishop Yoder."

"Ach," I say. It is possible the Bishop has set a trap for me. I think this only because I must think that anything is possible. If Anna Hostetler can feel one second of joy that her mother lies dying, then the bishop too is capable of anything.

"It sounds as if you don't like the old man. Can't say that I blame you, putting the ban on you like he did. The Amish ways—well, they might be all right for some people, but not for Levi Augsberger. At least it's a free country, and we get to choose, right?"

"Do we?" I expect sympathy. Levi Augsberger is the only other person in Pittsburgh who can understand.

"Look Anna, my ride is coming by any minute and—"

"Your ride?"

"Friends," he says.

I think this has to do with Brandy. I look around,
but cannot see her. Just the dark shapes of tree trunks,
playground equipment and geese.

"Little Levi, how long have you been in
Pittsburgh?"

He hesitates, and in that moment a car honks at the
edge of the park. "Got to go," Little Levi says, and
then, except for the geese, I am alone in the dark.

I hurry into the light. I do not wear a wristwatch, but I
think it is about two in the morning. I take the road on
the lower side of the train tracks, that parallels
Allegheny River Boulevard. The upper road is mostly
businesses, but even at this hour an occasional car
rumbles down the cobblestones. Most of the drivers
are men returning from the bars. Some of them are
teenage boys who, despite the cold, like to hang out
the windows and yell obscenities. Hey, sweet-stuff,
you want a piece of me? That kind of thing.

The lower road passes a mixture of business and
houses. There is almost no traffic and my only fear is
of dogs which are not chained. Brandy told me about
being bitten by a dog called a pit bull when she was a
little girl. The dog came out of nowhere and clamped
its jaws on her leg. It wouldn't let go, even when Jim
beat it with a stick. It wasn't until the owner came out
of the house and pulled on the dog's collar, that it let
go. Then it bit the owner.

I think that if a dog attacks, I will climb a tree. It
will be the first time. Amish girls in Heaven do not
climb trees, because it is not modest.

But no dogs attack me; none even bark. The streets
of Oakmont below the railroad tracks are very
peaceful at night, like Daat's fields in winter. On
nights that I cannot sleep, I will walk the streets,
instead of staying in bed counting sheep, like Otto
suggests. Who wants to count sheep anyway? It does
not put me to sleep. Sheep smell and they all look

alike. Perhaps I will count the same sheep twice. Much better to count cows, which are very individual in my opinion, and more important than sheep.

I get as far as the war monument before I am hassled, as Otto would say. The car slows and pulls over to the curb. I walk as close to yards as I can, but many of them are surrounded by chain link fences. There could be dogs.

"Anna! It's me, Tracy."

How stupid of me not to have even looked at the car. It is a police cruiser. Tracy drives, and she has with her a young man. Andhra, I think his name is, but everyone calls him Andy. He is originally from India, or maybe Pakistan—geography was not my favorite subject—but is now an American citizen and on the police force. My family has been in this country three hundred years, and Andy's family only a dozen, but except for his accent, I think he speaks better English than I do.

I do not know which embarrasses me more, the fact that I have not recognized my friends, or that I am out so late at night. "I was getting some fresh air," I say. The English custom of telling white lies is very handy.

Tracy smiles. She knows there is more to the story, but she is a friend, and a friend does not push.

"Andy and I are just getting off duty. We're headed over to Eat'N'Park over in Harmarville—it's open all night. Want to come along for a bite?"

I am not hungry, but I do need to talk when the time is right. "Yah, that would be nice."

They must get Tracy's car, which is parked at the police station. Do I want to ride back with them, Andy asks. Since they will be gone only a few minutes, I tell them I will wait.

"Suit yourself," Tracy says, but it is obvious that she is happy I will be joining them.

They are gone only a minute when a long black car—a very expensive make, I think—pulls up beside me. This time, so I will not feel foolish, I turn and face the car. I even smile.

The window, which is electric, goes down and I see a man Daat's age in a suit and tie. "How much?" he asks.

"I'm sorry, I don't understand."

"Don't play games with me honey, the police station is right around the corner. Just tell me how much."

"How much for what?"

"You tell me. Don't you have a list or something?"

"I'm sorry, sir, But I really do not understand. Like you said, the police station is right around the corner. Maybe they can help you."

"Bloody entrapment," he says, and the car roars off through downtown Verona, in the direction of Pittsburgh.

CHAPTER

28

I think I am the slowest mind on the planet, because it isn't until our food arrives at the Eat'N'Park that it sinks in. "He thought I was a prostitute!"

"That's what we've been trying to say." Andy has ordered scrambled eggs, hash browns, bacon and wheat toast, even though it is the middle of the night. He pours ketchup over his eggs to show that he is a real American. "I've seen that car before, cruising down Main Street. Just never had a reason to pull him over. Don't worry Anna, one of these nights he'll forget to use his turn signals, or a brake light will be out. Then what goes around, comes around."

"You're talking about Karma, right?" Tracy eats a hamburger with fries, and a side order of iceberg lettuce, a dish the English insists on calling salad. This is served with bleu cheese dressing in a paper cup.

Andy shakes his head. He does not like references to his past.

"I'm talking about traffic violations. Everyone makes them—but sometimes we're more vigilant than others. He sprinkles salt over everything on his plate, and I notice for the first time that he has an extra baby finger on each hand. These are real fingers, and perfectly shaped. They even have little nails. How could I have not noticed such a thing about a man I have met at least a dozen times, and whose hand I have shook? This is how self-absorbed I am. Pride, that's what it all comes down to, yah? The bishop was right.

I have no real appetite. Still, it is comforting to eat soup, although the beef vegetable soup at Eat'N'Park is not as good as Mamm's. I have made my friends wait until we are eating before I will tell them what I am doing out so late.

"So," Tracy says, her mouth full of lettuce, the cheese dressing oozing from the sides of her mouth, "are you going to spill it, or not?"

"I think not," I say, "the soup is almost gone."

"Not that silly. What were you doing out so late?"

"Brandy—"

"I thought so. Anna, when are you going to learn that girl is trouble?"

"Tracy," Andy says. His voice warns her to back off.

"Okay, okay."

"Brandy took me to see an Amish boy," I say. I speak fast so that no one will interrupt. "He is on rumschpringe—which is like the Amish season of rebellion. But it is difficult to really explain. Anyway, he brings news that my mother has cancer."

They chew their food slowly. It is like a contest to see who can take the longest to swallow. Manners are suddenly very important now that the word cancer has been said.

I give them a break. "I have decided to return to Heaven to see for myself if this is true."

"To stay?" Tracy asks.

I sip a spoon of soup. It is my turn to stall. I do not plan to stay in Heaven, but then I have not really planned any of my life. I have followed my heart, and that has given me heartbreak mixed with a little joy.

Andy wipes the corner of his mouth with the sixth finger of his left hand. Then he licks the ketchup off it.

"So you believe this boy—obviously you knew him.

Right?"

"I knew him when he was little."

"But you said he's some kind of rebel—"

"He rebels from the church. It is allowed, until he is old enough to be baptized."

"Yes, but how old is he?"

"Sixteen, I think. Maybe seventeen."

Andy and Tracy exchange glances. "Then he's a minor," Tracy says. "Do his parents know where he is?"

I shrug. "This is the way of the Amish. Besides, an Amish boy at sixteen—well, he has learned much spiritual discipline, and knows how to work very hard."

"All this spiritual discipline," Tracy says, unable to disguise her feelings, "and yet he runs around at two in the morning meeting people in the park." It isn't even a question.

"Yes, but—"

"We could have him picked up," Andy says. "Officially he's a runaway."

I make an English fist for the first time in my life and strike the table. The silverware jumps and Andy's glass, which was still full, spills over the sides.

"This is not about Levi Augsberger. This is about Mamm having cancer."

I am aware that everyone in the no-smoking section watches. Our waitress, who calls me "Honey," rushes over.

"Everything all right, Honey?"

"Yes. Could we please pay now?"

"Bring the check to me," Tracy says. Her eyes apologize for not having been more sensitive.

"How can we help?" Andy asks. He picks up his water glass to wipe the spill, and I see that he holds the sixth finger out, like Otto does when he sips tea. How could I have not noticed such a thing?

"You know," Tracy says, "I've got a few days of vacation saved up. And the only time I've been to eastern Pennsylvania was to a law-enforcement conference in Philadelphia. I could drive you, Anna. After you see your mom, then maybe we could go to New York. It's not that far from Heaven, is it?"

New York is a long way from Heaven. I appreciate Tracy's wish to be helpful, but this is a trip I must make alone. I certainly have no desire to be a tourist.

"I think I will take the bus," I say. "That is how I left, so that is how I shall return."

"But will you come back *here*?"

"I can not yet say."

"There are lots of galleries in New York, Anna. Museums too. And Broadway plays."

Andy shakes his head. "How do you know, if you've never been there?"

Tracy glares. "It's common knowledge. Besides, I read magazines—even books sometimes."

The waitress returns with the check. She places it in front of Andy.

"Call me old-fashioned," she says, "but the man ought to pay."

Andy looks her straight in the eye as he hands the paper over to Tracy. He did not become an American to be old-fashioned.

"Damn foreigners," she says.

It is time for us to leave.

All the lights are on in Otto's house.

"Oh, oh," Tracy says. She offers to come in, but is relieved when I say I must face the music alone. Andy does not even offer.

The door opens before I touch it.

"Anna, you scared the living shit out of me. Where the hell were you?"

"I went for a walk."

Otto pulls me inside. He wears what is called a smoking jacket. The scarf is shorter than the usual ones and tucks into the jacket, and I think it is made from the finest polyester.

"You could have told me where you were going. Do you have any idea what it's like to sit by the phone all night? Of course you don't. Well, it's agony, that's what it is. You just disappear like that—poof, into thin air. Anna, for all I know, you were kidnapped by a serial killer or, worse yet, those crazy Scotts up the street got hold of you."

"It was the Scotts." I smile inside because I know Otto will be aggravated.

"Brandy?"

"Yes. Otto, an Amish boy has come to town to give me a message. My mother is ill."

"I should have known. I told you to stay away from that—" He puts his hands to his face. He wears clear polish that shines in the light from a table lamp. "Your mother?" he asks in a much different tone.

"The boy said she has cancer."

"Do you know this boy?"

"Yes, when he was little."

He cocks his head. "Anna, how does an Amish boy get to Verona?"

"I met him in Oakmont, at the park, but that doesn't matter. He is in the period of rebellion and allowed to travel—at least it is understood that he will do so. Otto, I must return to Heaven and see my mother."

He nods. "Of course. Let's both get a little sleep, and then I'll drive you."

"You would do that?" My desire to return on a bus has vanished, now that Otto offers to drive. He is my new family, and I will not feel that I owe him.

"Anna, you know I'm curious about your former life." He glances at the window. It will be light in only a few hours. "Maybe we can go the day after tomorrow. That will give me a chance to get the car ready."

"Okay." I do not know how long Mamm has had this disease, so one day will not make a difference. Besides, Otto's car is what is called a clunker. He says it is foolish to throw money away on a new car, when an old car will get you to the same places. Perhaps now he feels different about the subject.

Otto kisses me on the forehead, and I apologize for having caused him such worry.

But when I awake a few hours later, anxious to think about the trip and home, it is my turn to worry. Otto is not in the house or yard, and the clunker is still in the garage. Because Otto is saving his heartbeats I know he cannot have walked very far. But where?

"Ach Dummkopf," I say and slap my forehead. Of course. Otto has gone to see Brandy. He has gone up the hill to tell the bunch of "scalawags" once and for all what he really thinks of them. Brandy will call him a faggot, and Gloria will too, if she is there. Jim, as always, will remain silent. The AIDS he suffers from, or maybe the drugs he uses to fight it, have sucked all the energy from him. Perhaps that is just as well, because now he has an excuse not to argue with his wife and daughter. A beaten man has more peace I think.

I pull on a pair of jeans, a sweatshirt that says "I love PA," and run a brush through my hair. I still wear it shoulder-length, but looking at it has reminded me of Lucia. This is when the guilt hits me.

If I had stayed in Heaven, and not come to Pittsburgh, Lucia would still be alive. She would not have run across the street when she saw me talking with Brandy. And if I had stayed home and been a good daughter, perhaps Mamm's nerves would not have gotten so bad that she came down with cancer. All this, I tell the girl in the mirror, because I could not submit to the will of the community, which is also the will of God.

When I get to the top of the hill, to Brandy's house, I am so angry at myself that I am not even tired. Out of breath, yes, but only a mountain climber would not be out of breath going up such a hill. If Otto is here, he has used up at least a year of his life.

The doorbell does not work, and I will not open the door uninvited. I must knock until my knuckles are sore. Finally the door is opened by Gloria.

"You," she says, as if she has been talking for an hour about me, but without mentioning my name. A cigarette hangs from lips in need of fresh paint.

I see past her into the living room. Jim, Brandy, and Otto stand in a clump. Whatever has been going on, it is three against one. Well, now it is four against one. Anna Hostetler is not a fighter, but if Gloria is the enemy . . . I pray that God will forgive me such a thought.

"Come in," Otto says in a loud voice, as if it is his house. "You are never going to believe this."

As I enter my stomach turns. Otto's house smells of lavender and paint, and sometimes popcorn. The Scott house reeks of tobacco smoke, sour milk, and pain. Yes, I think, pain has its own smell.

"Ya are gonna need ta sit," Brandy says.

Jim stoops to move a pile of dirty clothes on the sofa, but Brandy kicks it off before he can reach it. She nearly hits her father with her clog.

"You're my freaking cousin she says."

"Excuse me?"

Brandy pushes me so hard that I fall on the sofa. Then she plops beside me and puts her arm around me. She squeezes my shoulders.

"It's like really weird, huh? But it's true—Jim swears it is."

I still do not understand. "This is a joke?"

"No joke," Gloria says. She heads to the kitchen, her favorite spot to smoke.

"Actually," Otto says, "you aren't cousins. Anna is your aunt."

"Auntie Aggie," Brandy says and laughs. She squeezes my shoulder again.

This cannot be true. If Brandy is my niece, that

means Jim is my brother. But I have no brother named Jim. Only Elam and the one I call Brother who left Heaven for Pittsburgh, and whose name is not in the phone book.

I look closely at Jim. For the first time I see that despite his illness—or maybe because of it—he looks exactly like Mamm. I close my eyes. Suddenly I am very glad Brandy has made me sit.

BOOK THREE

CHAPTER

29

"Anna. Anna, are you all right? Would you like a glass of water?" It is Jim and he speaks in our native Pennsylvania Dutch.

I look up at Mamm's face. The features are the same, but there is both kindness and sadness in my brother's eyes. In Mamm's eyes, if I remember correctly, there was only anxiety.

"What is the name of your brother?" I ask him.

"Elam."

"And what is the name of Daat's youngest brother, the one who is always playing jokes."

He frowns and switches to English. "He isn't much older than you—so he was just a boy when I left—but I bet that would be Benjamin."

"What was the secret I shared with my oldest brother?"

Now he laughs, and it is Daat's voice I hear. "A bicycle. A crummy, beaten-up hunk of metal I had to hide in the woods."

"Sheesh," Brandy says, "Youse were strict, weren't ya?"

I turn to her, my head spinning with questions. "Brandy, how long have you known?"

"Like forever. Jim don't lie to me."

"Bullshit," Gloria says from the kitchen. I think she is not happy to be excluded from the group, even though she has done it to herself.

But Otto doesn't mind. "So Brandy, when you took the bus through Heaven—with Justin and Dog Boy—you knew then?"

Brandy likes Otto as much as he likes her. She gives him a look that makes this clear.

"I ain't no masochist. Jim made me do it."

We all look at Jim. "I have contacts. Friends who left Heaven on rumschpringe and never returned, but manage to stay in touch with sympathetic siblings and parents. It's against the rules of the Meidung—the ritual shunning, but it happens. Sometimes love is stronger than the law. Anyway, when Anna left I knew exactly what bus she would be on, and I sent Brandy to meet her. Justin and the one you call Dog Boy were not part of my plan."

Our eyes shift back to Brandy. "Sheesh, it's not like I committed a crime, or anything. I wasn't about to go to that hell-hole by myself. 'Sides, they wanted to come."

"But you pretended not to know them," I said.

"Well, they can be a little weird, and I didn't want to scare the piss out of ya, Aggie."

"Brandy," Jim says sharply.

He is too late if he wishes to spare the ears of the little sister he left behind. And what of the parents he left behind? Yah, Mamm and Daat never mentioned his name, but surely they have been hurting inside all these years.

But my mind jumps to another question. "Jim Scott is not an Amish name."

Jim smiles. "New beginnings, a new name. Joseph Hostetler, Anna. That's what my name was."

He was named for our ancestor who was carried off by the Delaware when he was just a little boy. Both Josephs were forced into exile, but the first one returned. The crime of that little boy was that he was the son of settlers, and it was the French and Indian War. But as for the second Joseph Hostetler, what was his crime?

"Why were you banned, Joseph?"

Brandy pokes me with a black nail. "Hey, his name is Jim."

"Yes, Jim," my brother says. "I prefer it now."

"Why were you banned?"

The eyes, which are Mamm's, turn cold. "Maybe another time, Anna."

"I think it was murder," Brandy says. Her eyes sparkle with excitement, and I think I see Daat in her.

"He doesn't have the balls for that," Gloria shouts from the kitchen.

"People," Otto says, and he claps his hands softly, "shouldn't we be planning the great pilgrimage?"

When it is clear no one understands, he tries again. "Our road-trip to Heaven. I'll drive, of course, seeing as how I'm the only sober one with a license. Anna, you'll sit in front, because you have to navigate, and you two in the back. Jim, you've probably been gone too long to remember anything, right? Dog Boy and Justin are not invited." He glares at the kitchen, but makes no reference to Gloria.

"Cool," Brandy says, "when do we leave?"

"Tomorrow. And try not to dress like a slut, will you? Anna's parents are in for enough of a surprise."

"Up yours," Brandy says, although her tone says that she will behave.

Gloria's smoke drifts in from the kitchen, but she says nothing to stop us. The trip is on.

It is good that Jim sits in the back, because he must rest against pillows, and twice Otto must stop for him to puke. This is Otto's word, not mine. The trip to Heaven by car is much quicker than the trip by bus. And Otto does not mind when someone needs to pee, and he only barely minds it when Jim pukes.

I think that Jim and I—especially Jim—are like our ancestor Joseph Hochstetler, and his brother Christian. At the end of the French and Indian war they did not want to be returned to the family into which they had been born. Many years had passed, and they were no longer Amish, but Delaware. Yet they had no choice.

When their father looked up from dinner one evening, he saw two Indian braves sitting on a stump in the front yard. Jacob Hochstetler immediately went out to ask the young men what they wanted. By then his sons' skin had been bronzed by the sun, and they wore their hair in the Mohawk style, and dressed in buckskin. When he got closer the bereaved father noticed that one of the Indians had piercing blue eyes.

"Could it be?" he asked. "Are you my sons Joseph and Christian?"

The boys had forgotten their mother tongue, except for the Lord's Prayer, and they began to recite it in poor, heavily-accented German.

When he heard the prayer, Jacob's heart was filled with love. He hugged his sons, and although they did not immediately return his affection, they were a family again. The faith lived on.

With Mamm on her deathbed, Jim and I have no choice either. We must visit our mother, but we will never be a family again, and the faith will most definitely not live on through us. Perhaps someday Brandy or I will have children, but they will never be Amish. Although a person can become Amish by choice, it almost never happens. Who would take on such a hard life? Surely not a child of Brandy's.

She sits now and counts the dead deer along the highway. There are thirty-nine. At least she does not count bottles of beer on the wall.

Some of the deer are smashed so flat the car does not even bump. Some of the deer beside the road look untouched, as if they have just fallen asleep. Other are being picked apart by buzzards. Brandy says the buzzards look like bald-headed Amish men in black coats. She means the Mutzi, although she does not know the word. It is supposed to be a joke, but no one laughs. From the look on Otto's face, I think he would like to feed her to the buzzards.

We stop at McDonalds's in Breezewood for burgers and milkshakes, and of course French fries, which Brandy says are the best in the whole world. We stop again in Harrisburg for what Otto calls a "coffee and donut pick-me-up," and to consult the map. I know my way to the farm only if we are within ten miles of Heaven, and if it is a road I have been on. The road we travel now is new to me.

But it is no problem, because Otto can read the map. "Holy guacamole," he says, "I looked at this yesterday, but I still can't believe how small the town is. It's a wonder a bus runs through there."

"Heaven has a Wal-Mart," I say in its defense.

We drive by the bus station where Brandy ripped off my sleeves. She starts to say something, but the new Anna reaches behind the seat and pinches Brandy's knees.

"Ya don't have ta get so touchy," she says.

The closer we get to Heaven, the more questions Otto must ask about the Amish. I answer most of them, because there are many things Jim cannot remember. He remains awake now, his head propped on the pillow, his eyes hungrily taking in every detail of the countryside.

"Heaven has really grown," he says.

"Is it big enough to admit Baptists?" Otto asks. When no one laughs, he says, "That was a joke, for crying out loud."

We begin passing horses and buggies. It is my impulse to slouch in my seat so that I am not recognized. I fight that feeling and keep my face pointed straight ahead, but my eyes strain to see at the sides. Since Otto must drive, he keeps his eyes on the road—most of the time. Brandy must be herself and her face is pressed to the window, like that of a child watching the first snow of the season.

I tell no one, but I recognize the Christian Beachy family; Old Abraham Lichty and his wife Sarah; Jacob

the Strong Yoder, who is a nephew of the Bishop; and
Isaac Lantz, the Lemon. It is said that Isaac is called
the Lemon because his hair is yellow, but everyone
knows it is because his expression is always sour. At
any rate, none of these people see me, or that my face
is surely red.

"Hey," Brandy says, "all them buggies ain't the
same."

I explain that there are many groups of Amish, each
with their own customs.

"Hey, there's that man who took ya to the
Laundromat bus station!"

Of course I must turn my head.

"Made ya look!"

I wonder why Jim does not try to control his
daughter. Then I remember that Brandy Scott is really
a Hostetler, and what point is there in trying to
control one of us? Like aunt, like niece. The poor girl
is in for a hard life.

"Turn left just past that sugar maple," I say.

"Which one is it?" Otto asks. "I'm not a botanist,
you know." He grows nervous at the thought of
meeting Mamm and Daat.

After the maple it is only a quarter of a mile down
Hertzler Lane to the driveway. My stomach tightens
and my heart pounds. I want to crawl out of my skin. I
wish Otto would turn around and drive as fast as he
can for Pittsburgh. Perhaps this is what Mamm feels
like when she gets the nerves—except that she heads
always for her bed, not the city.

"Dang, that's a big house," Brandy says, when Otto
turns into the driveway.

"It was meant for many children," I say, "but my
parents were not blessed—"

I stop when I remember that Jim was one of the
children for which the house was intended. His face is
white, but his eyes, which are blue, appear black. I
want to reach in the back seat and take his hand. It
should be me sitting beside Brother, not the foolish

Brandy.

The buggy is parked under another tree, this one a silver maple. The horse is not harnessed, and I think I catch a glimpse of it behind the barn. This means that someone is home.

It has been a long drive, but still there has not been time enough for me to think of what to say. Perhaps, I decide at the last moment, that it is best not to have a plan. I will "wing it," as Otto likes to say. Maybe Jim will speak first.

Too bad we cannot tether Brandy to the front hitch. I knock, but nobody answers. Brandy pounds with her fist, even though I beg her not to.

"Anybody home?" she shouts. Again, Jim does nothing to stop this foolishness. I think that even if he were not sick, he would do nothing. In that, he is like Daat.

Unser Satt Leit do not lock their doors in Heaven. This is Bishop Yoder's influence. Do the mansions we are promised in the *real* Heaven have locks? If there is one so needy as to steal from an Amish home—for there are no luxuries to be found—then it is possible that God Himself sent the thief.

Brandy tires of banging and opens the door. "Grandma?" she calls. "Grandpa? Younz there?"

"Brandy!" Otto grabs her arm, but it is too late.

We follow her into the main room like goslings after a goose. A silly goose.

CHAPTER

30

The house is exactly as I remembered. There is Daat's chair, there is Mamm's. Between them is a pine table that Daat himself made. On the table is a Coleman lantern, a German Bible, and a stack of Reader's Digests. One of Mamm's best quilts hangs on the wall, a quilt that was never for sale. Seeing it reminds me of Bridgette Monroe and a wave of guilt washes over me.

If I had been a good daughter, I would have been home to take care of Mamm. I wonder if Jim feels the same way, too. He has not seen Mamm for almost twenty years. Does he even recognize anything that he sees?

"Nothing's changed a bit," he says, as if reading my mind.

"Old fashioned, ain't it?" Brandy says. "Like a museum or something."

Today Otto wears a lavender scarf, and he flips it now so that both ends hang in the back. "Quaint, that's the word. Anna, I see where you get your inspiration."

None of us seems to be considering that we are, in fact, intruders in someone else's home. Ever since we were banned, Jim and I have not been part of the family, and Otto and Brandy have never belonged. Yet we talk in normal voices, and take no care to walk softly.

It should not surprise us then that someone comes

down the stairs, but we all jump anyway. It is Daat. He does not seem surprised, so perhaps he has heard us. At the landing he stops and looks down at us, and his gaze shifts from Jim to me, and back to Jim. Then to Brandy. He smiles.

"Your Grossmutter is upstairs," he says. I realize at once that he addresses Brandy because, despite her purple hair, he has recognized her as his flesh and blood. Daat is not forbidden to speak to Brandy because she was never baptized into the church, and so the Meidung does not apply to her.

Brandy stares at the grandfather she never knew. "*Excuse* me? Don't you be calling my mother gross, old man. Just because she don't keep them roots covered, and that lipstick of hers is like the pits— well, ya ain't so hot looking yourself."

Daat's smile broadens. "Your Grossmutter Hostetler. Your father's mother."

"This is your grandfather," Jim whispers. Tears stream down his face and fall on the hardwood floor.

Brandy's jaw drops. "No shit!"

"Shhh!" I correct her, since Jim will not.

To my shock, Daat does not even seem to mind the swearing. He looks at Otto.

"You are the English that gave my granddaughter a ride?"

"Yes, sir."

Otto approaches the staircase and Daat steps down enough so they can shake hands. Because Otto is English, he is not part of the problem, and is to be treated with full respect.

"Thank you," Daat says. If Otto's shaved head, bright scarf, and women's perfume bothers my father, he does not let on. The ways of the world are beyond comprehension.

Brandy cannot stand that Otto receives this attention. "So you are my grandpop," she says. "Or should I call ya Grossfather? 'Cause man, this shit's gonna take some getting used to."

"Grossdawdi," Daat says. "Come, I will take you to see your Grossmutter."

Perhaps it is my imagination, but my father's eyes include Jim and me in his invitation. Otto, too. We follow Daat up the stairs. I am crying as well, so it is hard to see, but my feet seem to have their own memory and find each step.

My room used to be the warmest bedroom in the house, because it was directly above the kitchen, but now this is where Mamm lies. Jim muffles a sob when he sees her, propped up on pillows, but he does not go in. We wait outside the door in a tight bunch.

"Go on in," Daat says to Brandy. We all follow her. Only Otto remains outside.

Mamm's eyes are closed, but she stirs when she hears us enter. "Rachel," Daat says, "you have visitors."

Brandy walks halfway to the bed then stops. I think she does this because the room smells too much like old lady Scott's, and brings back bad memories. At any rate, my niece steps aside and allows Jim and me to get right up to the bed.

Although it does not look like Mamm has seen us, she extends her right hand. I take it in mine. It is as light and dry as a turkey foot. Mamm does not squeeze my hand, but neither does she pull back.

"Mamm, it is me, Anna."

She breathes louder, and it is the only indication that she might have heard.

Now it is Jim's turn. "Mamm, this is Joseph, your oldest son."

Mamm's eyelids flicker, but she does not open them all the way. Perhaps the lids are just too heavy.

"I am sorry for the pain I caused," Jim says.

"Me, too," I hurry to add.

But Mamm says nothing. Daat steps beside us.

"It was God's will that she have visitors before she dies," he says. He still cannot bring himself to acknowledge us directly.

"Is she in awful pain?" Brandy asks.

"Yah, terrible pain." Daat does not show physical affection, but he stands so close his sleeve touches Brandy's arm.

Jim leans forward, his lips almost touching our mother's ear. "Mamm, it is all right now to let go. Please Mamm, go home to God."

I have heard that there are those who cling to life until they are given permission to leave by the ones they love. Apparently Jim has heard this, too. I must give him my support.

"Yah, go home to God," I say. It is for her, not for me.

Suddenly Mamm moans. Her body jerks, then she lies very still.

"Is she dead?" Brandy asks.

I watch, stunned, as Daat feels for Mamm's pulse. "No," he says, after a thousand years have passed. "She has not yet gone to be with the Lord."

We stay in Mamm's room for a few more minutes. Jim strokes Mamm's hand, but I stand as still as Lot's wife, *after* she turned into the pillar of salt. Unser Satt Leit do not touch as easily as English, and I have not been in the world as long as my brother. But if I must be very honest, there is something within me that keeps my hands stiff at my sides, something that does not have to do directly with my Amish upbringing.

Surely I love Mamm. Have I not returned to Heaven to see her? And this because of a boy that is barely more than a stranger! But if that were me, dying in a bed in Verona, would Mamm be there? For my own sake I try not to think of this.

Forgive us our trespasses, as we forgive those who trespass against us, the Bible says. It does not tell us why. It does not explain, I think, that to forgive others is the biggest gift we can give ourselves. This I learn from Otto, who must always forgive others because he is a faggot. He forgives even Brandy—although it does not always show.

Without words Daat moves us into the hallway

where Mamm cannot hear. "Your Uncle Elam," he
whispers to Brandy, "has gone to get the Bishop and
some of the women so that your Grossmutter will not
die alone." Daat says this to warn us, as much as to
inform. Soon the house will be filled with people,
none of whom will be allowed to speak with Jim or
me. Are we up to the challenge Daat's eyes ask, but he
asks this of Brandy.

"Isn't there supposed to be a doctor?" Brandy asks.
My niece is a sensible girl.

"Your Grossmutter was in a hospital for six weeks.
Now there is nothing that can be done," Daat says.

"How soon?" Otto asks. "I mean, how soon until
she passes?" He asks this on my behalf.

Daat shrugs. "It is in God's hands. The doctor says
maybe today, maybe tomorrow, maybe a week from
now."

"Are there any motels in town?" Otto asks.

There is never a need for an Amish person to use a
hotel, not as long as there is an Amish community
nearby. It does not matter if they belong to a district
with different customs. Ultimately, unser Satt Leit are
all one people, connected by blood and history. This
is why Daat's answer surprises me so much.

"The White Deer Motel is near the Wal-Mart, on
the other side of town. It is the only motel."

"Maybe we should find ourselves some rooms,"
Otto says. He knows better than to expect Daat to ask
us to stay.

"Yah, that would be good," Daat says. I know that
he has taken the time to find the motel. Perhaps he has
even checked on the availability of rooms.

"I ain't going to no motel," Brandy announces. I'm
staying right here with Grosspop and Grossmom."

Daat's face shows panic, like that of a horse that is
forced to cross a flooded stream. "I think maybe the
beds are not so good."

"They were never uncomfortable for me," I say.
"But using the outhouse, now that is another story.

Daat did you ever kill the snake that hunts for spiders under the seat?"

Daat does not answer me, but he smiles. "The outhouse," he tells Brandy, "can be cold at night."

Now it is Brandy's face where the emotions play. "If Grosspop can pee outside, so can I."

Again, if Daat is shocked by her language, he does not show it. How unfair that grandparents will tolerate from their grandchildren what they will not from their own children. If Brandy had been Daat and Mamm's daughter, maybe they would have become Mennonites if she insisted on painting. I do not think they would have agreed to the shunning.

Because Jim is weak he sits in Mamm's chair and does not participate in the conversation. But Otto smiles at us.

"How many channels do you get on cable?" he asks Daat.

My father looks like a sheep that has been asked a mathematics question.

"Betcha, he gets satellite," Brandy says. Never mind that I have told her many times that the Amish do not even use electricity.

I turn to Brandy like she is the interpreter of a foreign language. "Ask him if he has a television."

"No television," Daat says without waiting for her question.

"Well shit," Brandy says, "there goes that." Then she puts her arms around Daat and kisses him on the cheek. "See ya later," she says, as if she has known him a million years.

Brandy's actions have made me very angry. If I tried to kiss Daat, he would move faster than a field mouse that has seen the shadow of a hawk. I also feel guilty because I have not even thought of kissing. All I can think of is Mamm dying upstairs, and that it is somehow my fault, and that if it were not for Bishop Yoder and the Meidung, she would not be there at all.

"Just a minute," I say, and then I run back up the

stairs.

Mamm has not moved since we left her. She breathes quietly, like a fussy baby that has finally fallen asleep. But her face is not peaceful. Even asleep and so near death, Mamm's face shows that she has always been a victim of the nerves.

If I hesitate I will not do what I came for, so I lean and kiss her on check. Just like Brandy kissed Daat. Just like Judas kissed Jesus.

"I love you, Mamm."

Her eyes fly open. I have forgotten how pale they are, like the sky when it is covered by high wispy clouds. The eyes stay open only for a second or two, but they look directly at me. She does not—perhaps she cannot—say anything, but I have read in her eyes that she has heard me, and that she loves me, too. It may not be the love that other mothers and daughters share, but it is ours. It is the best we can do.

I am gone only a few minutes. When I return I am grateful that no one, not even Brandy, asks what I did. In fact, Brandy makes a joke.

"Hey," she says, "if we don't get our bony butts over to that motel, they might start running out of rooms."

There are no rooms available at the White Deer Motel. Otto does the talking, and it is clear that the old man behind the desk does not like my friend.

"You should have made reservations," the clerk says, and does not even look at Otto.

"Well, for starters, we didn't know if there was a motel. We certainly didn't know the name."

"White Deer's been here for fifty-seven years. No, fifty-eight. Sully Mae and I had this built the year we were married. Anniversary is next month. You ever been married, son?" There is much sarcasm.

Otto must swallow his pride if we are to make progress. "Congratulations on the longevity of your marriage. Like I said, I would have called and made a reservation, but this is my first time in town and—"

"Should have done your research, son. Heaven is the new tourist Mecca for them that wants to see the Amish. Ain't yet overrun like Lancaster."

"Could you please recommend another motel?"

"Ain't no other. Have to go back practically as far as Hershey to find one. No sir, this is the only game for miles around."

This is when I have my brain shower. "Do you have a reservation for Hostetler?"

The old man turns to look at me. "What if I do? That ain't exactly your business, is it?"

"My name is Anna Hostetler. It's possible that—"

He shuffles over to a square of little boxes on the wall, and takes from it two keys on long plastic sticks. "First time I had an Amish man come in and make reservations. You somehow related?"

"He's my father."

He looks at me a long time, then he looks at the others. "Got just two rooms reserved, and I see there's four of you." His dark eyes are full of accusations.

"No problemo," Brandy says. I am glad she has remained silent so far. "Her and me will share a room."

The old man looks directly at Otto. "Them two guys ain't sharing a room. Not in this hotel."

"It's a *motel*," Otto says, "and you're jumping to conclusions."

I am embarrassed and angry that such a man would exist in Heaven, but I know there are many who share his beliefs. I grab Jim's arm.

"This man is my brother, and her father." I point to Brandy. "He can stay with one of us. Mr. Goldschmidt will share with the other."

"I ain't sharing no room with Otto," Brandy says.

So I share a room with Otto. It is my very first time in a motel, or a hotel for that matter, and I find it very exciting. Otto says the White Deer is a dump, but we have our own bathroom, and we each have our own bed! There is a little round table with a chair in one corner of the room, and on the wall, which is a beautiful knotty pine, there is a picture of mountains and a river. The lights by the beds are very dim, and it is hard to read the Bible that someone left in the drawer, but I think Otto prefers to watch television. Imagine that! A television and we do not even have to pay extra.

Even more exciting than the motel room, is the restaurant across the street where we eat supper. It is called Cracker Barrel. It is new to Heaven, and it is better than any restaurant I have ever eaten at. Even the ones Mickey took me to. This restaurant has a store you must walk through, in order to get to the dining room. The store sells beautiful things like fancy lamps and glass vases, sweatshirts, and tiny waterfall machines. Even toys. The food is delicious, too, and I think that if the White Deer Motel was connected to this restaurant, I would never want to leave.

We eat supper, and then just as I expected, Otto wishes to watch television. It is a very old movie called *King Kong*. He tells me I look like the actress Faye Ray, but I do not think this is a compliment. I fall asleep halfway through the movie because I think it is silly. I have been to the Pittsburgh Zoo with Mickey, and I can tell you with confidence there are no apes that big.

That night I dream of Mamm and the pale blue eyes that fly open when I speak of love. I dream that she dies, and that she calls out to me as her spirit leaves the shell of her body. As Mamm ascends to Heaven, the *real* Heaven, her soul takes on the shape of a white bird. Not a dove, but a big bird, like a heron, or maybe an egret, with a long skinny neck, and bright orange legs. These, too, I saw at the Pittsburgh Zoo.

Just as the bird enters Heaven—which now looks somewhat like the inside of Cracker Barrel—it cries out in a loud voice. "Anna, I told you not to speak to

Bridgett Monroe. Now see what you have done!"

I awake shivering. It is early morning, the sky just beginning to lighten. Otto lies face down across his bed. He is dressed in his outdoor clothes, and the television is still on, although the sound is very faint. A woman with blond hair, whose smile is not sincere in my opinion, is demonstrating how to make a picture frame out of the inside of toilet paper rolls.

"This is the day that Mamm has died," I say to myself, and turn off the television.

CHAPTER

31

Jim and I sit in the car with faces of stone. It is
Brandy who cries on the way to the farm. She has put
on even more mascara, and now it smears.

"You look like a raccoon," Otto says, and then he
remembers that it is her grandmother who has passed,
and he should not have said such a thing.

We are not surprised to see that the yard is full of
buggies. Not one of these Amish owns a telephone,
but each has told a neighbor, and now the entire
community knows. Women I recognize are carrying in
plates of food, while the men stand in clumps talking
quietly, perhaps pretending to admire someone else's
horse. Death is awkward at best.

Unlike the day before, I am not ashamed to be seen.
It is my Mamm who has died. I have every right to be
here, as does Jim. So what if no one speaks to us?

But then who do we see the second we get out of
the car. Daat, that's who. He says something to
Benjamin Kreider, the man he is talking to, then he
comes over and shakes Brandy's hand.

"Did you sleep well in the motel?"

"It was all right, Grosspop," she says and throws
herself at him, like she is the towel, and he is the
rack. Daat lets her hug him, while Benjamin and the
other men turn their backs. "I'm so sorry for ya,"
Brandy sobs. The raccoon eyes stain his white shirt.

Daat pushes her gently away. "For what are you

sorry, Brandy?"

"About Grossmom dying, of course. It ain't right that she dies before I get a chance ta know her." She turns to Jim, Her hands makes fists, so that only her black thumbnails show. "Ya oughta told me I was Amish. I coulda visited my Grossmom when ya sent me out here to pick up Aggie."

Jim has only the strength to close his eyes, but Daat shakes his head. "Your Grossmutter is not dead."

"She's not?" I think we all say this, even Otto.

I step into the basement of my soul. It would be easier for me if Mamm were dead. At least I would have my memory of seeing her alive for the last time, and it is not such a bad memory, given the circumstances. But if Mamm is alive . . .

"Why are all these people here?" Otto asks.

Daat smiles. "The people bring food, but it is just kindness. I think maybe my Rachel is better—but we will know soon. The doctor is on his way."

"Only in Heaven do they still make house calls," Otto says.

I look at the black coats and see a flock of ravens. "Is Elam here?"

Otto repeats my question so that Daat will answer.

Yah, Elam is inside." Daat remembers to shake Otto's hand. "Welcome again, friend. Did you have breakfast at the motel?"

"Shit no," Brandy says, "and I'm starving."

"Then come inside," Daat says. "There is plenty to eat."

The Meidung forbids the faithful from breaking bread with those who will not repent, but *anner* Satt Leit—the other sort of people—are not included in this ban. There is, however, something new in Daat's voice. I will not go so far as to call it defiance, but I know that for this one time at least, Jim and I are to be included. So what if someone tells the Bishop? Perhaps the Bishop is already here, although I do not see him. Perhaps he is upstairs praying with Mamm.

At any rate, Daat will be asked to repent, and he
will do it willingly and sincerely. There will be no
lasting consequences—for many others have gone this
way before, so who is there to judge? Except for one
thing; Daat will live with the knowledge that he has
submitted to his own will, and not the will of the
people. Daat will have compromised his principles. In
doing this he will become more of a father, but less of
a man. An Amish man. I think it is more important
that Daat remain a good Amish man, because that's
what he was before he became a father, and that's
what he will be if, heaven forbid, all three of his
children should die tomorrow.

"I will stay here," I say. "Outside."

"Yes, outside," Jim says. His voice is weak, and he
must say this twice for Daat to hear him.

"Suit yourselves,'' Brandy says, and she charges
off to look for the food.

"Be back in a minute," Otto says, and races after
her. I think he goes not so much for the food, but to
keep Brandy under control.

Daat looks at his feet, then walks away.

Brandy and Otto take more than a minute. Jim wants
to sit in the car because he is tired. I no longer care
what the others think of me—at least that is what I try
to remind myself. Unser Satt Leit have gentle souls,
but their tongues, especially those of the women, are
not always so kind. Because I want to look around,
recall some happy memories, I will do so outside with
the men.

Not much changes in a year on an Amish farm,
unless there is illness. It is still too early in the year
to plant many vegetables and flowers, but Mamm has
not even yet prepared the garden bed. I wander past
the empty plots. My feet seem to be drawn to the barn.
It sits exactly where the old barn was, and unless you
were there and remember the night of the fire, it is

hard to imagine that it has not always been on this site.

The new barn is nothing more than a wooden building, where Daat keeps his hay and feed, and where the cows take refuge on cold winter nights. The screams of the children, the crackling flames, the condensation on the windows of the house, these should all be forgotten. Why can't I forget them?

I force myself to turn away, and then I jump. Bishop Yoder is standing directly behind me, not an arm's length away. He is not surprised by my reaction; there is no doubt he has been expecting it.

"Anna Hostetler, it is good to see you."

I am astounded by his words. "Is it? I thought you aren't supposed to speak to me."

"It is my duty to see if you have come home to repent."

"Bishop Yoder, there is much for which I need to repent, but I will not repent for using the talent God gave me."

"I see."

But he does not. If he did, he would turn his back on me and walk away.

"You were looking at the barn, Anna. Do you remember how the fire started?"

"It was a long time ago, Bishop. I was little girl. How can I remember?"

"I think you do, Anna."

"I do not!" I turn away quickly, but it is too late. The tears have started. "I was a little girl."

He reaches to touch my shoulder. I can feel the heat, as hot as any fire, but in the end he does not touch.

"You were a very little girl. For that you must be forgiven."

The knowledge that it was I who started the fire is almost unbearable. I must sit on the grass, so that I do not fall. The dream was true. I played with matches in Daat's barn. I lit the fire. I stood in the house and watched through the frosted window as the barn went up in flames. If that part is true, is it also true that someone died?

"Bishop Yoder," I say through a voice that is thick from crying, "did someone die?"

He looks at me with genuine compassion, of that I am sure. Still, he cannot bring himself to touch me.

"Amos Beiler," he says. "Because of his condition he was not able to get out of the barn in time."

I catch my breath. "One leg was shorter than the other?"

He nods, the huge nose bobbing at the ground like a divining rod.

"Catherine's only son. Her only child. Her husband David was killed in a haying accident before the baby was born. There are those who foolishly say that it was the stress that caused the boy to be malformed. But it was God's will, Anna."

God's will? I have a lot to say to the Bishop about God's will, but there is more to think about now. So that is why Catherine Beiler has not liked me all those years. And why should she? I, Anna Hostetler, am a murderer. At the very least, a killer.

"I am so sorry,'" I say, even though I know that words are not enough.

"Anna, you were too young to be held accountable. It does not matter now." He stares in silence for a moment. "Anyway, the price has already been paid."

"Price?"

"Your brother," he whispers.

I struggle to my feet. "Elam?"

"Ach, not Elam—Joseph."

"Jim? What about him?"

Bishop Yoder glances around. There is no one within hearing distance.

"Your brother Joseph, the one you call Jim, he took the blame for the fire."

My legs grow weak, and I must sit again. "Jim said he did it?"

The bishop nods. "Yah. This is what he told the others—your parents. Catherine Beiler. Joseph thought he would spare you the pain—the consequences—of your action."

"Then how do you know? Did he confess this to you? Privately?"

He taps his chest with a long, thick finger. "I feel this in here. It was the time of his rumschpringe, but Joseph was an obedient boy. He loved his parents very much. He would not have hurt them by turning to worldly ways." He pauses to look behind him again. "Anna, your brother loved you even more than he loved your parents."

Suddenly I am filled with rage; at my parents, at the bishop, at Jim. The bishop's words ring true. I feel it in my chest.

This is so unfair. I did not ask to have someone love me so much that he would sacrifice his life for me. This is what Jesus did, but it is not what a brother should do. How can a sister pay this back?

The anger gives me strength, and I jump to my feet. "Excuse me, Bishop," I say and walk past him, back to the growing sea of buggies and men in Mutzi coats.

"Anna," the bishop calls to me, "why do you not repent?"

"Screw you," I want to say, but this is Otto's and Brandy's way of speaking, not mine. It is the way of the world—some of it at any rate—but it is not the way I choose to live. Instead of swearing, I will say nothing. At least to the bishop.

Jim raises his head when I return to the car, but he does not open his eyes. "You were gone a long time," he says.

"Where are the others?"

"Still in the house, I think."

My brother's voice is weak, but I have no time to waste. Fences must be mended, or else torn down.

"I had a talk with Bishop Yoder," I say.

Jim's face twitches, but his eyes remain closed. "What about?"

"The fire. What else?" I cannot keep sarcasm out of my voice.

"Yes, of course. It would ultimately be about that."

"Why do you say that?"

"Look, Anna, that was a long time ago. Can't it remain in the past?"

"Not until we talk about it."

He sighs. "What do you want to know?"

"I want to know what right you had to sacrifice your life for me?"

Blue eyes flutter open. "Sacrifice?"

"That's what the bishop called it. In so many words."

"But I didn't, Anna."

He can save his protests. "It wasn't fair. I was just a little girl—barely more than a baby. I wasn't capable of accepting your sacrifice. Not then. And I'm not willing to accept the burden of it now."

He reaches out with cold talons that grip my arm with surprising strength. "You've got it all wrong, Anna. I didn't do it for you, I did it for me."

"That doesn't make it fair."

"No, what I mean is that I left the community because I could not accept the Ordnung. I had a drug habit even then. You see, it had everything to do with me, and nothing to do with you."

"You took drugs in Heaven?"

He laughs weakly. "Heaven, had its dark places, Anna. I'm sure it still has. I'd like to say it was because our Mamm and Daat were so strict that I headed straight for these temptations when I turned sixteen, but that isn't the whole truth. The truth is that I was weak. I couldn't resist what the world had to offer—even the bad stuff. Eventually I would have left home, fire, or no fire. It was convenient for me that—"

"That I started the fire?"

"Yes, but nobody believed you did, you see. That was the beauty of it. I took the blame, and it gave me an excuse to get out of here."

"The bishop didn't believe you were guilty. And neither did Catherine Beiler."

"But Mamm and Daat did." He makes no attempt to mask the bitterness.

"So you're not a hero after all, are you, Jim?"

"What do you mean?"

"The big brother who saved his baby sister."

His eyes close. "No, I'm afraid not. Joseph Hostetler was never a hero."

I can think of nothing further to say, which is just as well, because Brandy and Otto have returned to the car. They carry plates piled high with food.

Dusk falls as we get close to Verona. The lights of the city blink on and off, like they hold a secret and are winking at us. When we get to the top of the hill we see that secret is Gloria. She sits on a box, surrounded by other boxes, and piles of clothes.

"Hallelujah," Otto says, "the bitch is moving out."

"Otto!" I say it sharply for Jim and Brandy's sake, but they are not at all upset.

"Hope she doesn't have my CD player," is all Brandy says. She presses her face against the car window. "What the hell!"

Brandy jumps out before Otto can stop the car. She staggers on her platform shoes, but manages to keep her balance,

"Hey, ya can't take my shit!" she shouts at her mother.

"I ain't taking none of it," Gloria shouts back. "I'm throwing it out, that's what."

"What ya mean, throwing it out? That's good shit."

Gloria has a bitter laugh. "I'm throwing younz stuff out. Now do you get it?"

Meanwhile Jim sits in the car, his head back against the seat, his eyes closed. He does not have the energy to care.

Brandy must fight for the both of them. "Ya can't do that."

Gloria lights a cigarette and blows smoke in Brandy's face before answering. "I can do anything I want. I own this dump."

"But it's Jim's dump, too."

Gloria glares at her daughter. "You're a traitor, you know that?"

"How am I a traitor?" There is something in Brandy's voice that makes me think she cares about her mother. This surprises me.

"Because you belong to me, Brandy. Not him."

"Of course I belong to Jim. He's my dad."

"No, he ain't."

"What?"

Otto starts to back the car out of the driveway. "We're getting out of here," he mumbles.

"No, Otto." I grab his wrist and squeeze it hard. "I want to hear the rest," I whisper.

Gloria has the ears of a fox. "Yeah, by all means, stay and listen." She cups her hands to her mouth. "Hey neighbors, are you listening?"

Of course none of the neighbors respond. They are used to the Scotts.

"Now where was I?" Gloria says, and kicks a pile of clothes.

"My dad," Brandy screams, "what do ya mean Jim ain't my dad?"

Gloria stares at her daughter, then laughs. "What part don't you understand? I mean, give me a break, Brandy. You know where babies come from. How they get here."

Brandy stiffens. "Yeah, I know. Watcha trying ta tell me, Gloria, that ya slept around before I was born? That you were a slut? Well, guess what? That ain't news to me."

"That's a hell of a thing to say to your mother." Gloria lunges forward, as she pulls her arm back. The next thing I know Brandy is lying in the driveway. At least the clothes have broken her fall.

Brandy is down, but she is not out of the argument. "How do ya know Jim ain't my father? It could be him, couldn't it?"

Gloria sucks long and hard on her cigarette. The lit end glows bright in the fading light, but the smoke can no longer be seen.

"I suppose it's possible that he's your father—I wasn't that much of a slut. But you don't have his personality, Brandy. Can't you see that?"

"Damn," Otto whispers. "This is better than a movie any day."

In the backseat Jim snores quietly. Brandy points to her father.

"So why'd ya marry him, if ya hate him so much?"

"I don't hate him. He disgusts me." She sucks again on the cigarette, as if she depends on it to supply the words. "He was really cute when we met. All sort of bashful, like he didn't know anything about the world. Wanted me to teach him everything. I tried, believe me, I did. But I couldn't teach him backbone, Brandy. Never had it, never will."

The fight is mine as well. This is my brother and my niece Gloria is trashing. And Gloria is my sister-in-law. What concerns them, concerns me.

"That's what you think," I say. Now it is Otto who has *me* by the wrist. I pull away from him and unfasten my seatbelt. "Jim has more courage than you will ever know," I say, my voice rising, fueled by anger, until it sounds as if I was born English.

Gloria tosses the stub of her cigarette. It lands near a pile of papers, but rolls into grass, which is thick and green.

"You've seen *The Wizzard of Oz*, missy?"

"Yeah, she's seen it," Brandy says. "So what?"

"Remember the tin man who didn't have a heart?

Jim there, never had one. Never had any balls, if you know what I mean."

So strong is my desire to slap Gloria, that I must fold my hands together, as if for praying.

"He gave up his life as an Amish man for me." I say this for Brandy's sake, even though I know it isn't true.

"Bullshit."

"But he did. The bishop told me."

Gloria fumbles in the pocket of her jeans for another cigarette. It is bent, and she straightens it with shaky fingers. "Believe what you want, dear. But that story's a bunch of crap."

My folded hands shake. "You don't know that."

She lights the cigarette and drops the match. It lands on one of Brandy's sweaters, and she must stamp the fire out with her foot. "I suppose you're referring to that stupid barn burning. Man, like I haven't heard that a million times."

"Well, I haven't," Brandy says. "Tell me."

Mother turns to daughter. I see for the first time that Brandy does not resemble Gloria at all. She looks more like Jim, but only a little. She could be anyone's child.

"Your auntie seems to think that just because she burned down a goddamn barn, Jim gave up his life as an Amish man."

Brandy's eyes widen. "Get out!"

"It's true, Brandy," I say. Lies do not matter now.

"The hell it is," Gloria snorts. "I met your precious brother the week he left that hole you call Heaven. I was working downtown. On the street," she adds, spitting out each word. "He was already hooked on heroin. Was desperate to get some more—"

"You're a liar!" I shouted.

"Real cute, he was then. I wasn't connected with anyone—outside of business—so we hooked up. He needed someone to show him the ropes. And it was refreshing to have someone need you like that. I mean really need you. We married about a month later."

"She's lying," I shouted again. "Brandy, don't believe her! Otto, say something."

Otto has nothing to say. He gets out of the car and helps Brandy put her things in the trunk. She has so much stuff they pile it in the back seat, too, almost covering Jim.

"Hey," Gloria says, "younz can't leave me alone like this."

"Isn't that what you wanted?" Otto asks.

"Shut up," she says, "this ain't your business. Brandy, I'm your mother, remember?"

"I'll try not to," Brandy says. She turns and walks down the hill. I know she is headed for Otto's house, although she has not been officially invited.

"And Jim," Gloria shouts. "He ain't even in his own mind. If you take him, that's kidnapping."

"How quick some folks are to change their tunes," Otto says. He slides back into the driver's seat and slams the door. I run down the hill after Brandy. Behind me, Gloria insults God and the neighborhood.

Brandy stays with us only one night. Jim stays for two. Otto knows a group home for AIDS patients where there are always vacancies. It is meant for people just like Jim who have no money or family who can look out for them.

It is harder to solve Brandy's problem because Otto doesn't want her to stay with us. Believe me, there is no love lost on Brandy's side either. I feel that if they would just give each other more time, they would find they have much in common. They are both free spirits, are they not? And they are both very fond of me— although maybe Brandy does not yet know it.

None of this matters, because on the second day back from Heaven, my niece disappears. We learn this when the hospital calls to complain that she has missed work.

Otto thinks it is possible she has returned to Gloria's. He drives up the hill to ask. This is very thoughtful of him, but unnecessary. Gloria has been drunk since the night of the fight, and there has been no one in the house except for her. Otto says the house smells so bad even the roaches have deserted it. I don't remember any cockroaches living there, but I get the picture.

On the evening of the fourth day since our return, while we are watching a television show called Survivor, the telephone rings. Otto asks if I wouldn't mind getting it, since he had to miss an important scene because making the popcorn took longer than he expected.

"Hello," I say.

"Damn I'm glad that's you, and not the faggot."

"Brandy!"

"So it's like this, Aggie. You and I kinda traded places."

"Brandy, where are you?"

"That's what I'm trying ta tell ya. I'm in Heaven. And before ya jump to conclusions, I ain't dead or anything. I'm in your Heaven."

Even the slowest turtle can cross the highway as long as a vehicle doesn't hit it. "Are you at Daat's?"

"Don't be silly Aggie, he ain't got no phone. Ya know that."

"But then where—"

"I'm at the Cracker Barrel. That's where I work, see. Can't talk long because I'm only on a break, and I had ta borrow a friend's calling card. Anyway, thought ya would like to know."

"Where are you staying?"

"That's the thing. I'm at the White Deer Motel, but only a queen can afford to stay there. I was gonna ask Grosspop if I could stay with him— Hey," she shouts at someone else, "I told ya I'd only be a minute. Aggie, where was I?"

"You were going to ask my father if you could stay

on the farm."

"Yeah, well then I remembered he didn't have TV or nothing, but that don't matter now. Jennine—she's the girl whose card I'm using—she says I can share her apartment. Just as long as I don't smoke. She don't have a phone yet, but when she does, I'll let ya know."

"I'd like that. Brandy, what do you plan to do in Heaven?"

"Geeze Louise, Aggie, what do ya think? I'm gonna see my grandparents again, that's what. Do a little thinking. Try ta make a little sense outta my life. Who knows, maybe someday I'll even be Amish." She laughs long and hard, while valuable seconds tick by.

"That's a good idea, Brandy." I'm not sure she hears me.

"Say Aggie, how's Jim doing?"

"About the same. He can't seem to get enough sleep—that's all he does. I did speak to him this morning though. He says he misses you."

"Tell him I miss him, too."

"Brandy, about all your stuff—"

"Sorry Aggie gotta go." She hangs up.

Brandy waits three weeks before she calls again. This time Otto answers. I am in the kitchen painting, and he has a long conversation with her before bringing the phone to me.

"She sounds like a different person," he says.

"Brandy?"

"Hey Aggie—I mean Anna—"

"Aggie is okay with me," I say.

"Yeah? Look, I just wanted you to know that I'm all right."

"I'm glad to hear that, Brandy."

"Otto says Jim's doing okay in that group home. That true?"

"I saw him this morning, Brandy. He was feeling good enough to take a short walk."

There is a pause. She knows the lie is white, but wishes to believe.

"He ask about me?"

"Of course." It does not hurt to tell a white lie sometimes. This is one of the important English lessons. Besides, I'm sure Jim meant to ask about Brandy. He usually does.

"So watcha doing?"

"Painting. I have one more painting for the show, and this is it."

"Yeah?" Brandy pretends interest, which is the same as a lie if you ask me.

"Yes. It's called *The Tourists*. It's got an Amish girl selling quilts to a car full of tourists. If you look close you're supposed to be able to tell that the driver of the car is Otto. You, I, and Jim are the other three tourists."

"Cool." Now she is interested. "So when is the show?"

"This Thursday through Saturday. It's going to be at the parish hall of St. Thomas Memorial Church."

"A church?"

"I have to make a donation, of course. And I can't hang anything on the walls. But that doesn't matter. It was Otto's idea to put everything on easels, and Dog Boy and Justin are making them for me. They're actually pretty good at it."

"Yeah, I bet."

"Anyway, Mr. Bonsavage and the photographer from the *Times* are flying in Wednesday night. Otto and I are going to put the men up in a motel in Harmarville. Hobson is off then so he's going to pick them up at the airport."

Brandy doesn't miss a beat, as Otto would say. "Who the hell is Hobson?"

I smile to myself. "He's the fire inspector who investigated—"

"Yeah, yeah, so is it serious?"

"Not yet, Brandy, but things are looking up."

"Yeah," she says, "definitely looking up."

EPILOGUE

It has been three years since the art show at St. Thomas Episcopal Church. The show was a "smashing success," to quote Otto. Mr. Bonsavage, the *New York Times* critic, published a wonderful article that had Otto's phone ringing off the hook for days. Some of the calls were from television talk shows which wanted to book me for guest appearances, but most of them were offers to buy paintings.

One painting, which I titled *Return of the Prodigal Daughter*, sold for the astounding sum of one hundred thousand dollars! It was the last painting I did in the series, and by far the most personal. It depicts a young woman, in modern attire, standing at the end of a lane, looking up a hill at an Amish farm. Her face cannot be seen, but her shoulders tell the rest of the story; you really can't go home again. At least not for her—not for me.

Mamm died only a few weeks after the show. I felt like she waited until then, so as not to interfere with my success. It was stupid to feel that way, I know, but it served a need at the time. At any rate, Jim was too weak to attend the funeral—he died less than a month later—but Otto and I drove out, and spent several days at the White Deer Motel.

Daat was glad I came. As usual, he didn't express this to me, but he treated Otto like an old friend, and it didn't take much to read between the lines. I was pleased to see that Brandy and her "Grosspop" shared what already seemed to be a strong bond.

There is no need to worry about Brandy "turning

Amish." Shortly after Maam's passing, Daat went to live with my surviving brother, Elam. The farm was sold to a cousin. Brandy visits Daat regularly at Elam's farm, but she doesn't get along well with her uncle and aunt. Besides, she has made a new life for herself in Heaven. She quit working at the Cracker Barrel—I think she was fired—after about a year, and is now the manager of Miller's Laundromat. She's dating a man who treats her well, and I think marriage is in their future.

As for Otto and me, we now live in New York City. The move, like most good things in my life, was Otto's idea. He said I needed to be where the action is. He was right. My career as an artist has already far exceeded my expectations—perhaps a hundred fold. I own my own gallery—Anna's Place—in Manhattan, which Otto runs. We share an apartment in the same building as the gallery. We also share many new friends. I think Otto is happier here; he does not stand out as someone unusual, like he did back in Verona.

Hobson and I are no longer involved. We saw each other several times after the move, but things were not the same. I'm sure we would have broken up anyway. Hobson told one of his friends, who told me, that a woman shouldn't make more money than the man in her life.

I go on dates occasionally, but I am very cautious— as if Otto doesn't worry enough for both of us! It is hard to get over such a bad track record, as Otto puts it. It still shames me to think that I let Brandon, a married man, kiss me on the same day my friend Lucia died. Then there is Mickey. Boy, what a loser he was. Tracy called me recently to say that Mickey was caught in Florida, doing another insurance scam, and faces at least five years in prison.

Tracy is planning to visit us over the Christmas holidays. She'll be staying with Otto and me. And this is the big surprise—she's bringing Dog Boy and Justin with her. They'll be staying with us as well. That, too, was Otto's idea. Otto says that when you're rolling in moola, you can afford to be generous.

Moola? This reminds me of the riddles he used to ask. At least once a day I ask myself a riddle of my own. Was it all worth it? I have developed the talent God gave me, but at what price? I will never again experience the closeness of the Amish community. But now I have a new community, one of my own choosing. Is this enough? I still don't know the answer to that.

Sometimes I attend services at an interdenominational church not far from our building. Sometimes even Otto goes with me. I still believe in God, but I wonder if my faith would be stronger if I had stayed in the Amish church—if I had not seen the dark side of Heaven. But life is a journey, yah? Who knows what tomorrow will bring.

ABOUT THE AUTHOR

Although the author of twenty-five nationally bestselling novels, Tamar Myers, like her protagonist, Anna Hostetler, counts drawing and painting as her first love. Tamar began college as an art major, but and switched to English after just one class—during which the professor ridiculed her assignment. Tamar reasoned (falsely) that writers receive less criticism.

Tamar counts America's first Amish settlers among her ancestors. Her mother was a Yoder, her grandmother a Hostetler, and both of her mother's parents are direct descendants of the patriarch, Jacob Hochstetler. There are several Amish bishops in her family tree.

She now lives in South Carolina with her husband, plus a Basenji dog named Pagan and a Balinese cat called Mr. Cheng. She plans to take up painting again when she retires.